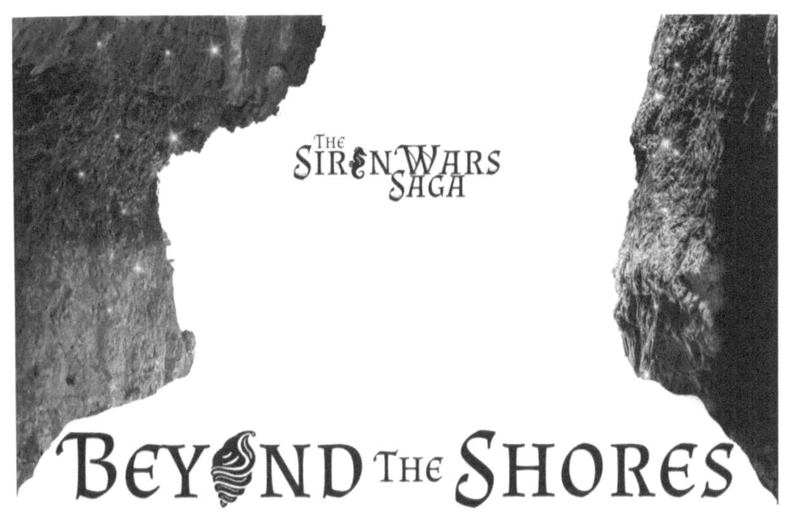

BEYOND THE SHORES

by

K.M. Robinson

BEYOND THE SHORES: Book Three of The Siren Wars Saga.
Copyright © 2018 by K.M. Robinson.

Published by Crescent Sea Publishing.
www.crescentseapublishing.com

Cover designed by Reading Transforms.
Image copyright © K.M. Robinson Photography.

This is a work of fiction. Names, characters, brands, trademarks, places, and incidents either are the product of the author's imagination or are used fictitiously. Any resemblance to actual events, locales, organizations, or

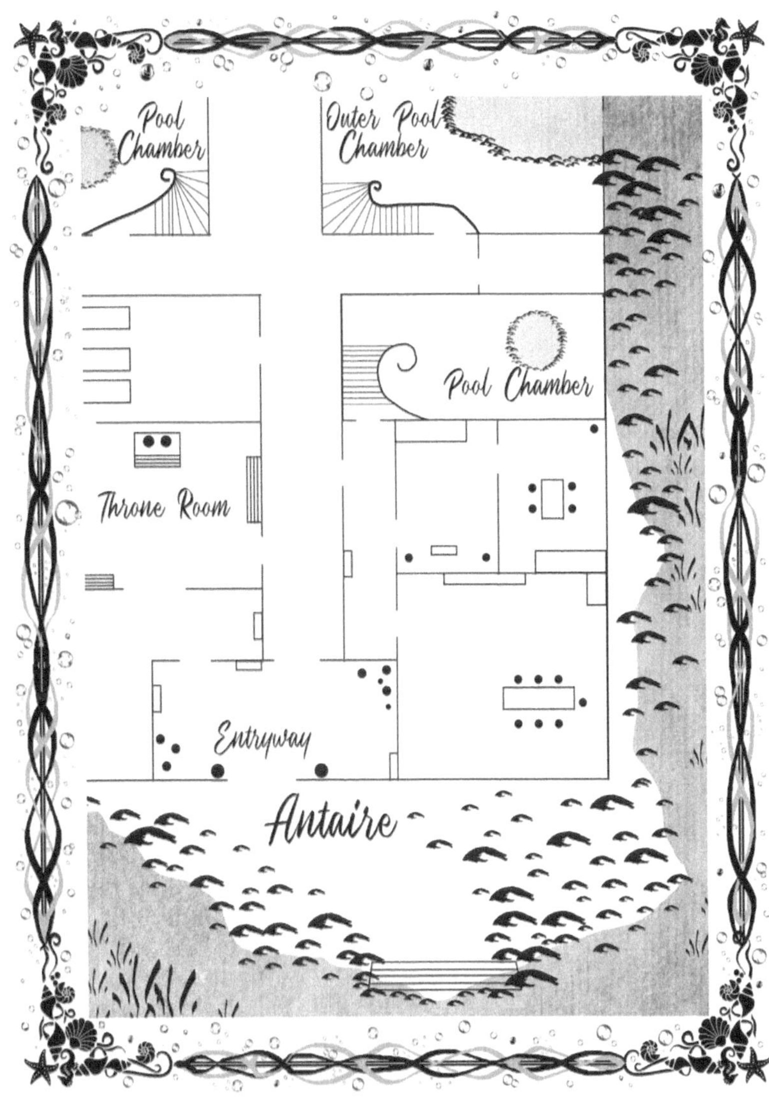

Pool Chamber
Outer Pool Chamber
Pool Chamber
Throne Room
Entryway
Antaire

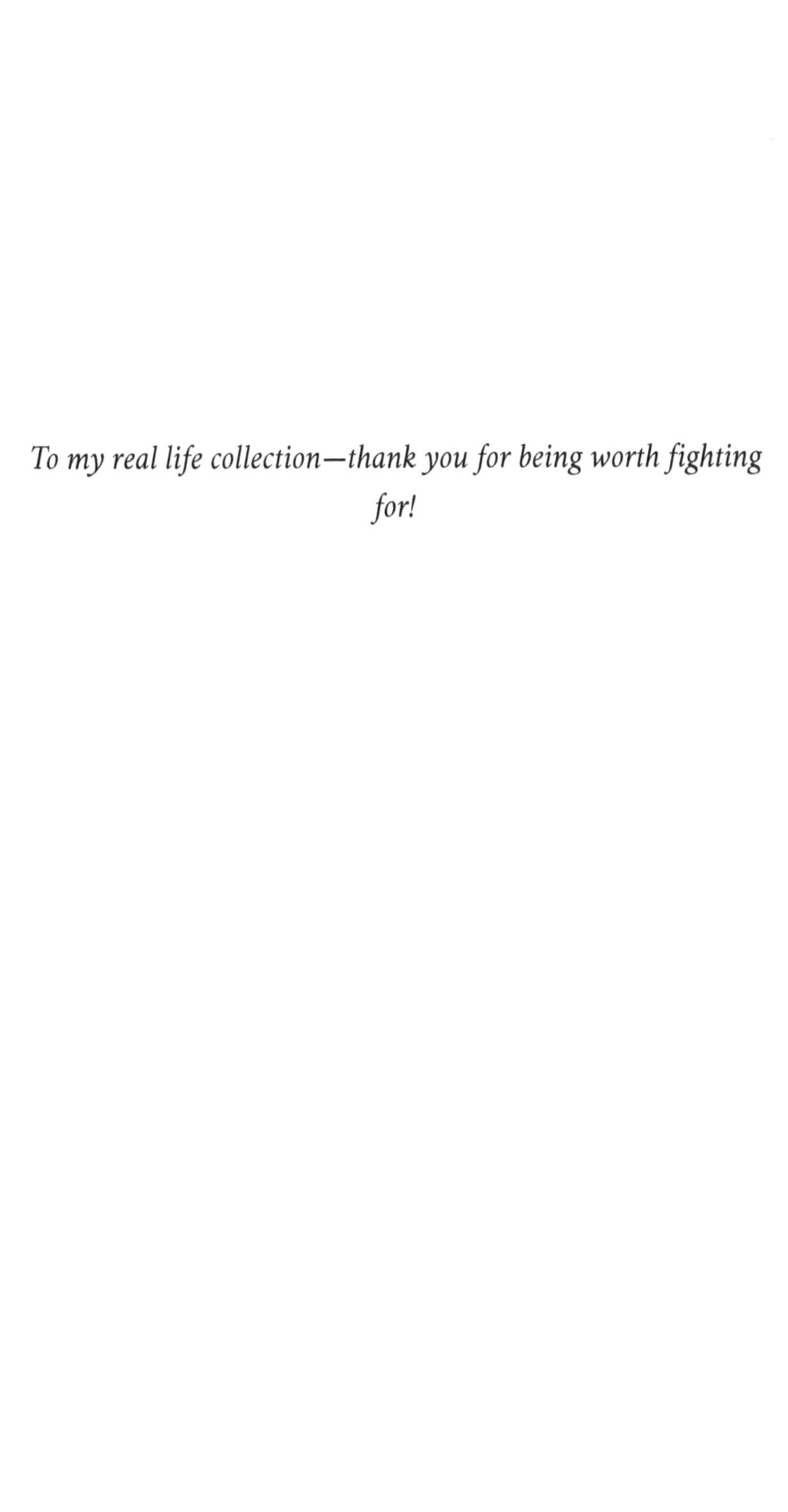

To my real life collection—thank you for being worth fighting for!

CHAPTER 1

IN THE DARKEST HOURS—THOSE WHERE EVERYTHING SEEMS lost and hopeless—we often find our redemption.

This is where I have learned to survive, even as my world falls apart.

Noises are something I've always identified my life by—the sound of my little sister's breathing when she snuck into my bed in the middle of the night as a mer child, the noise a dolphin makes when it glides through the palace hallways, the atmosphere of a kelp forest during a brewing storm—no matter where I am or what I'm doing, when I hear those noises, I'm taken right back to the first time those noises made an impression on me.

The sound of the palace door slamming behind me is one that will haunt me for the rest of my life.

Phorcys starts to stir as the humans carry us through

the halls of the palace. I know better than to speak and upset our captors, but I try *willing* the siren to look at me.

His head lolls back, but he takes in the sights around us, quickly becoming alert. He attempts to sit up, but the humans forbid it. When Phorcys connects with me—upside down as he's pushed back—I shake my head quickly.

Like it or not, the siren is in this with us, and we're going to need to work together to save ourselves.

Merrick wakes but holds deadly still. I've seen him pretend to sleep enough times to know he is alert and listening to everything happening to us. His eyelids twitch, confirming that he knows what's happening and that he's taking advantage of the situation. I let out a quick breath of air from my nose, louder than the rest to assure him that I'm still with him.

The palace glides by me as easily as the ocean does. We slice through the hallways, flipping around corners in the air as the men carry us, doing all the work on our behalf.

Perhaps Nir had it right when he forced his sirens to carry him around the ocean on a makeshift throne. Then again, Nir is dead, so perhaps he's not the best merman to get ideas from at this point.

The hallways are an internal representation of the outside walls, casting an opalescent shine onto the floor as the light bounces off of them. The harsh sunset makes everything glow orange as light streams in through the window.

The chandelier my great-great-grandmother, Aila, had told our family about is even more stunning in person. I look up as we pass under it. Aila had never seen it up close—only through the window from the ocean outside the palace—but I imagine she would have loved this. If I were in the sea, I would swim up and touch the crystals.

I check on Merrick again as he continues to pretend to be knocked out. His breathing is steady, and he doesn't look to be in any more pain than the last time I saw him before the sailors hit him on the head with that oar when they pulled us into the boat, but I'm not entirely sure considering the beatings we've been taking the last few days.

"Let go," Phorcys insists, shattering the quiet. The men threaten him, hoping it will silence his rant. When it doesn't, they move to gag him.

"Phorcys," I say in a hushed voice, trying to still him. If the humans get too close to his face, I'm positive he will try to bite them, and there's no telling what they'll do in retaliation.

He bucks a few times but remains quiet.

Large tapestries fill the halls, dangling from the roof nearly to the floor in shades of gold. Fine, white sand appears to be covering each of them, though it looks like some of it has been swiped away by someone brushing against it, revealing a more brilliant shade of whatever gold it is made out of—perhaps threads of spun gold from the books I once read.

We walk by a throne room, and I peek inside as we brush past the door. The thrones are covered in jewels that sparkle as the sunlight glints off of them, entering through a high window positioned perfectly to bathe them in light. We rush by so quickly that I can't see anything else in the room.

We wind down a set of stairs, and for the first time ever in my life, the stairs I'm encountering are actually *needed*. It's uncomfortable as the men bump down the stairs, jostling me with each step.

"Over there." A man with a sharp nose points down a hallway. "Take her over there."

He points to the right, scribbling on a piece of paper in his hand.

He's separating us.

"Merrick!" I react without thinking it through.

His eyes fly open as he tries to sit up. Merrick reaches for me, his blue hair flopping in his eyes. It's amazing how quickly his hair dried, while *mine* is still mercilessly dripping down my sting-covered back.

"Don't take her," he begs, stretching as far as he can. The men cling to him, refusing to let him reach me.

"Merrick!" I lean toward him, trying to grab his hand.

"Celena!" He struggles against them.

"Please, just let us stay together," I try to negotiate with them. "We'll do as you ask, just let us stay together."

The guards pull us apart. Merrick and I shout to each other as he and Phorcys are taken down the opposite hallway.

"Shut up!" one of the guards orders, lifting a hand as though he might strike me.

I cower, letting them think I'm more scared than I am —much like Tarni spent her entire life doing until her cousin became king and she came out of hiding. The humans don't need to know I'm capable of killing them *before I actually do it.*

Little things stick out of their ears, blocking the sound of my siren song—not that I'm attempting to siren them right now. It looks like maybe they used pieces of rolled up fabric to block me out, but I can't be sure.

I'm close enough that I could reach up and pull whatever it is out of two of the guards' ears. I could siren them quickly enough to disrupt their plan, but at least two would be impervious to my song, and retribution would be swift.

They carry me down another set of steps and around a wall that doesn't reach the ceiling of the room. When we round the corner, an oval-shaped wall sits in the middle of the room with water in it.

I'm dropped into water that's barely big enough for

me to do a flip in. I could sit on the bottom and be fully submerged, but this contraption is designed to keep me where they can get to me. If a human were to crawl in, they could stand and their heads would easily be above the surface.

The water is still—I've never seen the surface of any water so calm in my life. It ripples when I move or when the men tap on it to get my attention. They leer at me as I assess my situation.

"Like your new home, pretty?" one of them asks.

"Do not taunt the siren, you fool," a man who has clearly worked for the king his whole life addresses the grubby sailor. His voice is more proper than the sailor's, as is his ensemble.

I look at him, pleading with my face, afraid that if I open my mouth, he'll take it as an attack and hurt me.

He wrinkles his nose in disgust and backs away. Motioning for the others to follow, they leave the room. I'm alone.

I try to climb over the wall, but there's nowhere for me to go. The floor is massive. By the time I crawl to the stairs where the men brought me in, I'll be discovered— or dead from the exhaustion of dragging myself across the stone. Even if I made it to the stairs, I'd have to climb up them.

There is no escape from this room.

I dart around the water, checking every angle and

side. When I find nothing useful above the water, I lower myself under—*unable to dive*—and search the walls for an escape, hidden message, or anything that can help me. Finding nothing, I return to the surface.

This room is different than the others. The walls are a bright white color but hold no opalescent shine to them. The floor looks like smooth rocks have been positioned to create intricate designs, though the entire floor is a solid white, sculpted only by the shape of the flat stones. It swirls around the room.

A window sits high above me, nearly reaching the ceiling. I can see bits of the pink sky as it fades into night, but the ocean is out of my sight. Soon the stars will be out—I might even be able to catch a glimpse of the moon one last time before my death.

The water bounces off the walls of my prison as I swim around in circles, trying to learn my limited surroundings. I grow to hate that sound.

The color fades from the sky, pulling all references to its hue from the room as it goes. The room grows dark until the moon appears, casting a pale glow through the opening. The light from the window bounces off the water of my prison and reflects on the ceiling and walls. It dances in eerie lines, shattering and moving as it consistently changes.

I breathe out, trying to slow my heart rate. Leaning against the wall, I wait for one of my captors to come fish me out of this place. Every so often, I dip under the water, cooling my skin and hair. I refuse to stay under long though—I don't want them sneaking up on me.

The toll of the last few days weighs heavily on me. I still haven't recovered from most of the trauma I've been through—the jellyfish stings, the beatings, the fights, even the brine pool—but as I'm forced to be still in the water, it all comes crashing down on me. My muscles scream, and I feel like bending in on myself to try to stop the agony. The welts on my back from the stings burn, even though they shouldn't at this point. My cuts pierce into my skin, a constant reminder of the war I was just ripped out of against my will.

I hurt, and I can't help myself to feel better.

Spreading my arms out over the top of the wall, I try to keep myself upright out of the water as I face the steps. I watch, waiting for them.

Eventually, exhaustion wins out, and I slip beneath the surface and curl up on the floor of the mini ocean as the moonlight dances over me.

I wake with a start. My eyes dart around the tiny space, checking the walls and surface above me before I lift myself out of the water. The room is still empty, but the moon is gone, replaced by the very first rays of morning.

The sun is still too low in the sky to be seen, but its pale reach graces the room. Not too much longer and the sunrise should appear, and I imagine, the room will be cast into many colors again.

"Well, well, look who is up."

I start at the voice, whipping around to face the steps as a figure rounds the corner. Last night I could hear men walking on the steps, but I was so focused on the window that I let my guard down, and he snuck up on me.

A second man follows the prince, much like he did yesterday on the boat. His ears are blocked once again, prepared to rescue the prince if he needs it. He scowls at me over the prince's shoulder.

I stay on the far side of the water—if he wants to reach me, he'll have to jump into the water or walk around to the other side, giving me time to change my location. I stay quiet as I watch him.

"If you try to siren me or any of my men, I will have them separate you from your tail, and no questions will be asked." He levels a cool gaze at me. "I haven't talked to your friends yet, but they're next, so don't make me angry."

He walks around the length of the wall, examining me. His servant follows along behind him. The prince pauses back where he started, leaning forward to rest his arms on the wall at an awkward angle as he leans toward the water.

"Who are you?"

"I am Celena, great-great-granddaughter of Princess Aila, daughter of King Gaspar."

"You're royalty?"

"Distantly, yes."

"So you don't rule the ocean?" One finger taps on the side of the wall as he tries to glean information.

"No, my cousins do."

"Why were you sirening my people?" He blinks through his sandy brown hair, dark eyes snapping at me.

"There is a war under the sea between sirens and mer—"

"You're all sirens," he snaps.

"What?" I ask after a moment, taken back by his outburst.

"There is no difference."

"We all have the ability to siren, yes, but some choose not to use it unless we have to—that's why we had the treaty."

"You broke the treaty."

The light shifts in the room as the sun starts to come up, tingeing everything yellow. The prince doesn't seem to notice.

"The treaty was broken." I nod my head in agreement. "But not by my grandmother. She tried to prevent that from happening."

"The mermaids tried to kill my great-great-grandfather."

"*Not* Aila. She and Jarek were friends," I insist.

"Do *not* speak the king's name," the prince growls at me.

"The royals from both of our kingdoms were once united in friendship. The king and my grandmother were friends, and when her cousin tried to hurt him, she saved him. She told us all about him—"

"What did she tell you?"

He looks angry, so it puzzles me that he's still talking to me. The prince watches me like I might leap across the water at any moment and attack him, but also like I'm a riddle to figure out.

"She told our family many stories that have been passed through the generations about how she, Persephone, and your grandfather used to sit on the steps outside and watch the waves together. He would pet their hair, and they'd tell him about life under the sea.

"Aila told us about the chandelier in the palace window that she always longed to see. She told us about Prince Jar—about the prince's mother, and how she was always looking out for him.

"She also told us *in great detail* about the destruction of the treaty, and what Persephone and her mother, Chantay, did to ensure there was a division between us."

He purses his lips, taking in the information, but doesn't look convinced.

"Aila said after she discovered that Persephone and the prince were together, she found them in a cave where Persephone was attempting to siren the prince. She convinced him to dive into the water, and Aila saved him from drowning.

"Your Highness," I begin. "After the human-mer treaty was dissolved, the mer split as well. Those that wanted to hurt you were banished, and the rest of us tried to avoid the humans' wrath. We moved far away from our home and never left our borders until now."

"And just why did you leave, *mermaid?*"

"The sirens—those that wanted to hurt you—also wanted to hurt us because of Chantay's banishment and Persephone's imprisonment. They've waited a century for revenge, and this was their last opportunity."

"Why is that?" The prince leans back, standing on his own.

The prince is looking for information, and I'll gladly give it to him. If I can be helpful, perhaps he will listen. If nothing else, I need to position myself to not seem like a threat to him and his people.

"The last of Chantay's line died without a female heir. Her son and husband were fulfilling her wishes to make both the humans and mer pay."

"That explains why *they* were here. Why were *you* here?"

This prince is nothing like what Aila told us Jarek was like in her stories. That boy was weak and passive—a dreamer. The prince before me looks like he will kill first and ask questions later.

His face has some similarities to Jarek's, but his hair and eyes are different. The prince's chin, cheekbones, and nose are close enough that I feel comfortable believing this is one of Jarek's descendants.

"They attacked us first," I explain, brushing back my hair as it floats in the water in front of me. "They tried to take over our palace and lost. They kidnapped my sister, and when I tried to save her, they took me too. My collection came after us to save us, but when we arrived, the rest of the siren collection was on their way, intent on using us to hurt the humans."

"I thought you said you didn't siren." His eyes narrow at me like I'm lying.

"The mer collection doesn't, but we still have the ability to. Most of our collection has lost it because it hasn't been used in a century, but those of royal blood have more powerful voices."

"And their royals are dead, so they wanted *yours*..." he murmurs.

He turns, starting to walk away, his servant rushing to keep up.

"Wait!" I call. Realizing I shouldn't have, I sink back against the wall, waiting to suffer for it.

The prince flinches but slowly turns.

"You're leaving?" I ask in a small voice, hoping to convince him that I'm not a threat.

He raises an eyebrow, turning again to walk out.

"What's going to happen to us?" I call, braver.

"Answer my questions and we'll see," he calls over his shoulder. His words echo around the room, setting my teeth on edge. The only time I've ever heard an echo was on the surface, and I don't like it. Even so, I can't let him walk away yet.

"Where are my friends?"

"They're in their own little pools," the prince answers.

My prison has a name.

"I need to know they're okay," I call. "Please!"

"They're fine…for now. We'll see how they cooperate." He turns to glance at me as he mounts the stairs. "If you behave, you'll live—for now. If you don't, we can make things very difficult here until we get the information we need and then we'll split you in half. Remember that, Celena."

"*Princess,*" I snap.

"What was that?" He takes a step back off the stairs.

"*Princess* Celena," I correct him.

He appraises me, considering my words.

"Very well, *Princess* Celena."

The prince nods before ascending the stairs once more.

"We'll see how long you last."

Their footsteps fall heavy as they finish climbing the long stairs, turning once they reach the landing, and exit the room as an overwhelming feeling of dread washes over my body. I sink back into the water, waiting.

CHAPTER 2

AN HOUR PASSES, AND STILL NO ONE RETURNS TO THE room. The sunlight changes again, making the room bright. The light bounces off every surface—I'm sure by noon, I'll be blind.

Swimming in the tiny pool is infuriating. All I can do is move in small circles. Eventually, I duck under the water and swim laps back and forth, touching one side, then the other, as I try to think of something I can tell the prince to gain his trust.

Merrick and Phorcys are somewhere in this palace, but I have no way of reaching them. If I can convince the prince to put us together, at least maybe we can help each other cope—though I doubt we'll all fit in one of these tiny pools.

By the time the light starts to fade, I've devolved into thinking about my collection out in the sea. I don't know if my father survived being struck in the face by that sailor. I'm sure Caspian got Coralie to safety, but that still doesn't account for where my mother is. I know Casp and Llyr saw us being taken away—I'm sure they're working on a plan now—but who knows which of the mer survived and which didn't.

At least I'll never have to see Tarni, Murdoch, or Cassidia again.

The pool is decidedly empty, and I wish there were some seahorses swimming around or clinging to seaweed. My stomach makes a noise, reminding me I haven't eaten since early the day before. I wonder if they plan on feeding us here or if we'll wither away from starvation and the stress of whatever questioning they put us through.

"You're a lucky mermaid," the prince says, waltzing into the room behind the wall, feet tapping against the stairs. "Your lover sent you dinner."

He rounds the corner, coming into view. His servant carries a small tray. Once they reach the pool, he hands it off to the prince who looks like he's deciding between throwing it at me or setting it on the side of the wall.

Cautiously, he places it down on the side of the pool and steps back so I can swim over. The silver tray holds three oysters. Next to it sits a dull piece of metal that I suppose I'm meant to use to open the shellfish with.

I reach out cautiously, taking one in my hand. It's difficult to open it, but I don't stop trying.

"He refused to eat them—he sent them to you instead."

I look up at the prince, registering his words—Merrick sent me his meal, which means he hasn't eaten either today.

"Take them back to him," I reply. "He needs to eat."

"He won't take them back." He tips his head, studying me.

"Take one of them back," I respond. "I'll eat the other two. Just don't let him starve."

I hurry to open one of the oysters—a sign of good faith. Inside sits a small pearl, and I can feel the tears burning behind my eyes. I drop it quickly into the water, covering my movement, and eat the oyster.

The prince and his servant watch me as I eat, making faces at my lack of human social graces. I don't have the time—or desire—to care.

"Take this last one back to him."

"We can try again tomorrow with him, but if you don't eat this, *Princess* Celena, it will be thrown back into the sea—your friend had his chance."

I purse my lips, but open up the oyster—it's better for me not to waste an opportunity to gain a little extra strength, than to have both of us suffer for not eating it. I'll lecture Merrick later—if I ever get the chance.

"Now, I suppose we should talk." He tips his head at me again. I've never seen anyone do that so much. "If you're not the princess in charge, then where is she?"

"In the sea somewhere." I blink as I reply. "I would guess they're on their way back to our home kingdom or traveling far beyond that."

"They're not waiting for you?" One side of his lips tick up as he unconsciously snarls—it's not aggressive, but more like he's disgusted.

"They know better than that."

"Oh?"

"Her job is to keep the collection safe—they aren't safe here."

"Do you know how many mermaid bodies we dragged to shore?" He pauses, waiting for me to answer. When I don't, he continues. "We easily dragged fifty corpses out of the ocean on our boats—even more sank, I assume. How do you feel about your group's survival now?"

We lost well over two hundred, but I don't tell him that. All those lives just to save Coralie and me—it wasn't worth it. Coralie's, perhaps, but not mine.

"I think it's wise for them to leave," I reply, waiting for him to lash out.

"I doubt that's going to matter." He sounds almost sad.

"Why is that?"

My tail twitches in the water—I hate being so closed-in. I bump into the side of the pool and have to remind myself not to cringe.

"It doesn't matter." He shakes his head. "Tell me more about the princess."

"I still don't know your name," I say in an attempt to throw him off.

"My name isn't important," he counters.

"Oh? I thought you were a prince. Aren't you important by nature?"

He perks up, my sarcasm catching his interest.

"Tell me about your princess, and I'll consider it."

"Do you want to know about the princess or the queen?"

The prince's eyebrow shoots up, and he squints slightly.

"You have a queen?"

"When your father dies, will you remain a prince or will you become king?" I point out. "Of course we have a queen."

"Fine, tell me about the queen."

"She's lovely. She takes very good care of us. She's protected us for many years."

"What is your queen's name?"

"Almeta," I lie, giving him my mother's name. I won't have him searching out Marilla and my mother has trained me well.

For a moment, I panic, wondering if Merrick was

asked the same question. If he gave them Marilla's name, any advantage I have will be taken away. Merrick is smart though—smarter than anyone I know—and he would have thought ahead to what I would have said. I trust he gave my mother's name too.

"Your turn," I add.

"I am Prince Edmund." He tips his head as if he's bowing slightly to me. "I am the prince of Antaire and the surrounding kingdoms."

"Nice to meet you, Prince Edmund." I brush back my long hair, revealing more of my face. "When can I leave?"

"You're not leaving, Princess Celena."

"So you're just going hold a royal hostage?" I snip at him, moving back in the water slightly.

"What do you expect us to do, trade you?" He puts his hands on his hips, stepping forward. "We can't exactly negotiate with people that aren't here."

People...because that's *another name for mer.*

"You could always let us go," I suggest, waving my hand in the air. Water drips off the back of my knuckles into the pool.

"That's not an—"

"Edmund," a voice echoes in the room, loud enough to make everyone duck. The king's head appears over the top of the wall protecting the stairs from the rest of the room. He stomps down the steps, rounding the corner as he approaches his son with his servant trailing behind him. "I thought I'd find you in here."

The king stops a few feet away from the prince. His dark hair is a stark contrast to the light room, despite the fading sun from outside. He appraises me as I float in the tank, his gaze making me uncomfortable.

"She is a beauty, isn't she?" he murmurs to his son.

"She's fine," Edmund replies, pursing his lips.

"Have you ever seen such vibrant hair?" The king tips his head like his son does, staring at my mane.

He's obviously never met Dylana—*her* hair is vibrant. Come to think of it, so are Merrick and Llyr's hair colors.

"No, father."

The king looks like he wants to examine me closer, but is afraid to change his proximity to me. I wonder what would happen if I swam forward quickly right now —his servant might accidentally crush his head in from trying to slam whatever those things are into his ears to protect the king from me.

"She might be worth something when this is all over."

I try to keep my face still as he speaks, but horror washes over me like the waves I create in the tiny pool every time I try to swim.

"We're not going to decapitate her, father, don't scare the princess." Edmund gives his father a look.

The king looks to his son for a moment before turning back to me.

"I apologize, I didn't mean to frighten you. We won't hurt you unless you give us a reason to do so."

"And I won't hurt *you* unless *you* give me a reason to," I reply, full of bravado. He cringes slightly at my words. The king's lips tug up in a closed-mouth snarl.

"Come, son. We have things to do."

"But I wasn't finished—"

"Let's go," his father interrupts.

Edmund glances back at me once before following the king toward the stairs. His servant quickly rushes up to the pool, snatching away the tray—good thing, because I would have used it against them had they left it unsupervised.

The group hustles toward the stairs, ducking behind the wall. I hear them murmuring as they leave, but with all of them muttering at once, I can't make out most of what the men say.

I consider dragging myself out of the pool once again, but as with before, I find no merit in the idea. The fall would likely be painful anyway.

Moving to the bottom of the pool, I search for the pearl I dropped into the water. It takes a moment to locate it because it blends into the bottom, but I retrieve it and sink against the wall to examine it.

With everyone gone, the place is quiet...but the water also helps with that.

The pearl has a slight pink tint to it. I'm sure Merrick

didn't know it was inside the oysters he sent to me, but it's a nice gift from him all the same. I open up the backside of one of the metal shells on my necklace and pop the pearl inside to keep safe until later when I can show Merrick.

I finally give up and sleep on the bottom of the pool.

"It *is* you," a feminine voice scares me to death when I surface the next morning. I clutch a hand to my chest as I whip around to face the girl—the princess. "My brother said you were here."

She looks at me expectantly.

I stare back at her, but she doesn't say anything as she hovers near the side of the pool. I look around, trying to determine if this is some kind of trap.

"Princess," I regard her quietly.

"I'm Analia," she announces, tossing her dark curls.

I look at her cautiously from the middle of the pool.

"Why are you here?"

"To meet you, of course." She shakes her head as if I'm being foolish. "You're the one that rescued me when those awful men threw me into the sea."

"Okay…" I trail off as if it's a question.

"Your hair is pink." She changes the subject, moving closer.

"Yes," I reply, still leery of her.

"Why is it pink?"

"I've always had pink hair." I blink.

"You were born with pink hair? Do all mermaids have pink hair?" The princess tips her head, but not in the same way her father and brother do.

She's likely only ever seen Dylana and me, and since we both have shades of pink hair, I can understand why she might reach that conclusion.

"No, we have different hair colors. Some have hair like yours."

"Oh." She frowns. "Well, I like your hair."

"Thank you—" My words are cut off as the prince runs down the stairs.

"Analia, get back!" Edmund shouts. He races over to his sister and drags her away, his servant chasing after him as he chastises the young princess. "Do not go near her without one of the servants."

"She won't hurt me, Edmund. She saved me."

"You don't know that, Analia." His voice grows quieter as he tries to be gentler with her. "She's trapped in here, we don't know what she'll do at this point."

"You separated her from her friends, of course she's going to be upset, Edmund." The princess pouts.

I swim to the edge of the pool, resting the edges of my fingers against the wall as I watch the two interact. It's not unlike Caspian and Coralie when she was younger.

"Go back to your room," he instructs. "Father has been looking for you, and you don't want him to catch you down here."

She grumbles before stalking over to the steps and disappearing behind the wall. The prince turns on me.

"If you *ever* touch her—"

"I wouldn't ever hurt her," I cut him off. "She's a child. I didn't even know she was here until I surfaced and she surprised me."

The prince seethes a few lengths away, glaring at me. His face is an odd shade of red, but after a moment, it starts to fade as his shoulders sink back down to their normal height.

"You stay away from her," he threatens again.

"I can't exactly go anywhere." I motion to the walls around me.

"And it's going to stay that way."

"I'm sure," I bite back.

He looks unamused at my willingness to take him on.

"I'm going to protect my sister, no matter what the cost is, *mermaid*. I'm sure you wouldn't understand—"

"How do you think I ended up here?" I snap, crossing my arms. "I have loved ones to protect too. Aren't you lucky I took the time to protect *yours* as well?"

Edmund deflates as I make my point. He takes a deep breath before speaking.

"Thank you for saving my sister," he grumbles.

"You're welcome." I look away as I speak.

"I suppose it's not entirely fair to treat you like this after you saved Analia." He takes a step toward me. "Is there anything I can do to make you more comfortable?"

"Take me to my friend," I reply instantly.

"Is there anything *else* I can do?" he refuses.

"I want to see Merrick."

He sighs, locking his jaw.

"I'll try." His words surprise me. "What can I do in the meantime? Are you hungry?"

"Yes, but I'd rather you make sure Merrick has food."

"He will be seen to." He examines me again—not even Tarni and her sirens watched me this closely. "Do you need a pillow or something to make sleeping more comfortable?"

"I'm fine." I frown, trying to think of something small he can do for me—if I can start by getting him to do little things, it will be easier to convince him to do harder things for me later. "I would like a new net and some seaweed for my *iluse*, please."

"Your what?" His eyes narrow in a question.

"My *iluse*," I respond. "My covering."

"Oh. *Oh.*" He glances down at my chest, noticing how bad my *iluse* looks after all it's been through. "Certainly. I'll have someone bring them to you at once.

"I'll need something to cut it with," I tell him, cringing.

"You can have it back as soon as I'm done fixing it though."

"I can't give you a weapon," he looks at me skeptically.

"I can use a broken shell if I can't have a knife. I'll throw it out when I'm done, and you can collect it."

"What if you don't?"

"Then your men will descend on me with spears and harpoons, I would assume," I offer. "I just need to fix my *iluse,* that's all."

He purses his lips but finally nods.

"Fine. I'll get you your things."

"Thank you." I smile softly to show I'm not trying to be a threat. "And I need to know that Merrick has eaten."

"And what exactly should I tell him to get him to do that?" The prince tips his head in annoyance, toppling his bangs over one eye.

"Tell him…" I think for a moment, glancing around the water. "Tell him that it's his turn to swim backward."

Edmund's face scrunches up in confusion.

"What?"

"It doesn't matter, just tell him," I command, waving my hand.

"Fine."

"Thank you. Please tell me once he's eaten." I turn to swim away and dip back under the water, dismissing him and ending the conversation.

"What's wrong with your back?"

"How do you know anything is wrong with it?" I ask coyly. "Perhaps all mer are like this."

"I've seen more than enough of you to know that isn't normal. Besides, my great-great-grandfather painted enough pictures of you mer to know that's not something passed down through the royal line either."

"Jellyfish," I reply.

He assesses me as I lift the hair off my back.

"Jellyfish did that to you?"

"They had overtaken a community, and I was sent in to retrieve the siren king's mother's necklace. I couldn't escape the creatures, so I had to endure the stings."

"Sounds painful," he muses.

"It was." I turn back to him. "It's starting to heal though—it's not as bad as it was."

"It must have been *awful*." He walks toward me again. I swim back to the wall, leaning my elbows against it.

"It was," I smirk. "Not too long ago, the siren king attacked us in the palace in the old kingdom, and my collection dropped a net full of jellyfish over his head—you should have seen his face after that. I'm sure my back is *nothing* compared to the welts that covered his top half."

Edmund's eyebrows quirk up in surprise as his lips twist into a smile.

"Sounds interesting. What did he do to deserve that?"

"He nearly killed me." I shrug. "Seems that's harder to

do than I thought. Good news though—he's dead now, and the sirens have disbanded, so at least you won't have to worry about them coming after you now—you might run into a small individual group now and then, but the collection as a whole is gone."

"Good to know, Princess Celena." He nods. "I'll also remember not to get on your bad side—or at least, not to get on your bad side when you have access to jellyfish—I hear those things are awful."

He turns to walk away, smirking.

"Have you really never been in the ocean?" This time, I'm the one who tips their head. Edmund swings back around to face me.

"The only times I've been on the water were when I rescued Analia, and then again when I fished you out. It's not safe—especially for royals."

"Shame. The water is lovely." I splash just enough to make the waves rock against the side of the pool, slapping into the side of it.

"All the same, I think I'll leave that to you." He grins, eyes sparkling as he turns to leave again. "I'll be back when your boyfriend has been fed."

I watch him go, sauntering back to the steps, his servant scampering behind him.

"I'll send in stuff for your...*covering*," he calls over the wall.

I grin smugly, knowing he forgot the word I used.

It seems I've made a little progress anyway. I should have asked for some seaweed or kelp to hide under though—I didn't think that through well.

After a while, a group of men steps into the room, each carrying something in their outstretched arms. They look wary at they step up to the side of the pool and deposit their offerings on the wall before quickly stepping back.

"You are to throw this on the floor immediately upon finishing. We will be watching from over there," one of the men yells, over-compensating for his inability to hear around whatever is blocking his ears. I nod to let him know I understand.

I swim to the side of the pool, frightening them all. They quickly dart back as I reach out and pull everything toward myself, dropping it in the water.

I duck under the surface, ready to make myself a new *iluse*. I use the broken shell to cut apart the netting the men brought me. Pulling the old netting off, I tuck the new ropes around my chest.

Thinking things through a little better this time, I secure it on so that it shouldn't fall off if I find myself in a fight with the humans. I carefully weave the shells back into place and break off part of the large shell to hide inside my *iluse*—I'll smash it later to cover up that I stole part of it.

I work quickly, knowing I won't be given much time.

When I finish, I have an entirely new look—it surprises the men when I surface to return the broken shell.

The net is woven tightly around my chest, with a removable piece wrapped around my neck like a halter. I attempt to look as regal as possible, even fashioning a crown out of several of the shells that had been woven into my hair.

My hair flows free, released from the braid it has been in, framing my face. I tucked the rest of the shells into the design on my *iluse* covering it so much that it nearly looks like one of my pearl bodices from a distance.

On the surface, I hold the large shell used for cutting the net up in my hand, careful to cover most of it so they can't see a piece is missing. The men watch in silent fear, slowly stepping back with unease. I turn, nodding to the ground near the wall, far from where the men stand. Looking back, I toss the shell, aiming for the wall. It hits, shattering as it falls.

Motioning with my hand, I invite the men to pick it up. They poke at each other, volunteering anyone but themselves to walk toward me.

"You won't be harmed," I promise.

They finally force three of the men forward, cowering as they watch near the steps. The men tremble as they approach me.

"Princess Aila didn't hurt Prince Jarek, and I don't intend on hurting you," I murmur as they approach like timid seahorses. They glance up at me as they attempt to scoop up the shell pieces, inadvertently leaving several small shards of shell on the ground before rushing back to their friends.

"I didn't hurt you," I call as the men dart away. I roll my eyes as they scamper off.

Sinking into the water, I fall back into my routine of swimming from end to end of the pool, waiting for the prince to return.

A few hours later, a slap against the water nearly startles me as I move in my limited loop. Edmund pulls his hand out of the water, grinning playfully at me.

I swim to the surface, acting annoyed. Exiting the water with my arms crossed, I raise one eyebrow.

His eyes grow wide when he sees my new ensemble. He roams over me with his gaze, looking at my temporary crown, long, flowing hair, and my fixed up *iluse*. I'm sure the shoulder armor has the same effect it's always had, but my new accessories highlight just how fierce the armor really looks.

"How did you do that?" he gapes.

I smile politely, reaching up to brush back my hair regally.

"We're all skilled at this. We tend to create our own outfits for our festivals," I inform him. "You should see what I could have done if you had given me pearls and a week to work."

Batting my eyelashes seems to wake him up from the trance he's in, and he stands straighter. He opens his mouth to speak and closes it twice before getting any words out.

"Yes, right, well…" he sputters. "Your boyfriend ate."

"He did?" I perk up, swimming to the edge.

"Yes," Edmund confirms. "I brought you food too."

He waves to a man standing by the stairs. He rushes over when beckoned, handing a tray to the prince.

Edmund turns, venturing closer to me.

"You didn't kill my men before, so I brought you more oysters."

That's a lovely thought.

He sets the tray down for me, this time only taking a step back. Instead of a handful, I find the tray well stocked with the shellfish. Surprised, I look up at him.

He says nothing, and after a moment, I reach out for the food. Breaking it open, I eat my breakfast. I suppose at some point I should inquire about Phorcys, but not just yet.

"Would you like one, Price Edmund?" I ask, holding an opened oyster out to him.

He grimaces, panic lighting up his eyes—they're brighter than I thought. The prince shakes his head slightly.

"No, thanks."

I pull the oyster back toward myself, unsure of how to proceed.

"They're for you," he tries to recover. "And we don't really eat them raw up here."

"What do you do to them?" My eyes are wider than I intend for them to be.

"We steam them or roast them first."

"Roast?" That's a new term to me.

"Cook them over a fire," he explains.

"That sounds…awful," I reply before I can stop myself. Nothing I've read about fire sounds like it's a good thing.

"It's better than it sounds," he smirks. "Finish eating."

"Prince Edmund?"

"Yes, Princess Celena?" he repeats after me.

"Where is Phorcys?"

"Oh. You mean the one who *doesn't* care." He gives me a look. "I'm assuming he's one of the sirens you've been talking about? He doesn't seem to care about the two of you very much."

"He has no reason to—we killed his king."

"*You* killed him?"

"We were defending ourselves—we didn't mean to—but yes."

I set an oyster shell down on the tray and pick up another as the conversation continues.

"I suppose you're also the one who gave him that nasty wound—or was that us?"

"Most of it was us, some of it was you. Are you sure you don't want to try one of these?"

"I'm positive." He gives me a curt smile and nods. "Why do you ask about him?"

"I'd like to know that you haven't cut him into bits or ripped any of his scales off."

"Why? Is that *your* job?" He looks at me with all the seriousness in the world.

"I've never hurt another mer or siren for any reason other than self-defense. Prying off scales is hardly something I'd tolerate."

"Looks like *you're* missing a few," the prince comments, waving to the water hiding my tail.

"The siren king and princess might have taken a few for fun," I answer, setting the next oyster shell down harder than I mean to.

"Sounds like living under the sea isn't as easy as one would think."

"Not in the least," I agree.

"I have a question," the prince steps dangerously close to me, upsetting his servant.

"Okay." I set the next oyster down before I can struggle to pry it open, waiting to see what the human prince has to say.

"Do mermaids really have the power to let humans breathe under water?

"You're asking if Persephone lied to Jarek." I pause for

a moment. "No, as far as I know, there's no way for humans to breathe underwater. We all believe Persephone really was in love with Jarek, and at first, she believed her love could allow him to join her in the sea.

"After her mother, Chantay, got involved, it became more about revenge for how Jarek's mother shackled Persephone. Chantay instigated the war, not necessarily *Persephone*, though she certainly had a hand in it. I don't believe she intentionally lied to him, I just think she made a stupid choice."

Edmund nods, considering my words.

"I have to go. I'll be back. Perhaps pay attention this time." He throws a look over his shoulder as he strides across the room.

I have a feeling I'm not going to like whatever happens when the prince returns.

CHAPTER 3

When I wake the next morning, I find Analia sitting on the steps, a servant standing behind her. The princess has her head propped in her hands, elbows resting on her legs hidden under a long dress. The bottom of her gown cascades around her ankles, flipping out to the sides.

Her dark hair is still curled—something we don't see under the ocean—and it mesmerizes me even from afar. Her face brightens when she notices me over the pool wall.

"You're awake," she yelps, rushing to her feet so quickly, I'm not sure how she doesn't topple over.

The princess looks back at the man standing behind her. He gives her a reluctant nod, and she rushes toward me. If anyone else had run at me like she is, I'd be terrified, but somehow her exuberance is reassuring.

"Good morning, Princess."

"You can call me Analia." She stops short in front of me, reminding me of a dark version of Coralie. "What's your name?"

"I'm Celena."

She eyes me, narrowing her features momentarily.

"Edmund says you're a princess. Is that true?"

"I am." I nod as she notices my crown and change in appearance.

"Where did you get that? You didn't have it yesterday."

"Your brother gave me some supplies to fix my *iluse* with." I point to my covering so that I don't have to endure any more questions on it. "I made it."

"You made a crown?" she asks skeptically. I nod in reply. "I can't even make myself breakfast, much less anything to wear."

She crosses her arms, turning to spin slightly as she sulks.

"Making a crown isn't hard," I inform her, reaching up to take mine off. "Here, look."

I point out what I did to string the shells together, weaving the extra netting into a tieback with bits of seaweed. If I had access to more from the sea, the crown would have been magnificent—but simple, elegant beauty will have to suffice for now.

"If I get my own, would you show me how?" she asks, pointing to my crown.

"If you wish." I smile at her.

"What's all this?" Edmund strolls into the room, arms fastened behind his back. He smiles at his sister. "I believe I told you not to come in here."

"She's not going to hurt me, Edmund." She grins back at him.

"She'd best not," he replies. "Now run along, Ana. I have things to attend to, and you don't need to be here for them."

That thought frightens me. I feel safer when the princess is here—I suspect her father and brother won't harm me in her presence.

"Analia?" the king questions as he walks into the room.

"She was just leaving, Father," Edmund quickly says. He gently pushes his sister into motion. She stumbles toward the stairs, barely missing her father as she hurries.

"Sorry," she mumbles.

"Run along now, Analia." He smiles carefully at her as she passes him. The king turns back toward me once he's sure his daughter is gone.

"Hello." I'm not sure what to make of his greeting.

"Your Highness," I acknowledge him.

"My son says you've been cooperative."

The water around me suddenly feels cooler. My instincts tell me to dive deep under the surface, but with barely a length and a half between the surface and the floor, I have nowhere to hide.

"I'm willing to try something if you're willing to continue to cooperate," the king continues. "If you *don't* behave, you'll regret it."

"What is it that you want to try?" I ask cautiously. My fingers quietly move toward my *iluse* in case I need one of the broken shell pieces.

"We'll get back to that. First, I have a few questions." He holds back from approaching the side of the pool, hands clasped behind his back. The king stretches his feet apart, locking his knees in place. "What do you know about the human world?"

"Only what Princess Aila and King Gaspar passed down, and now what I've learned since being dragged into your palace."

"Surely your collection has learned a thing or two over the years," he muses, releasing a hand to gesture. The strange way he emphasizes the word *collection* leads me to believe that he's been studying us enough to know our terminology. It seems as though Jarek passed on quite a bit of information about us over the years—from drawings to terminology.

"My collection left Metten a century ago. We live far away now and only ended up back here because of the sirens. The mer haven't had any contact with the humans since the queen decided to end the treaty with King Gaspar. Even the books I've found from shipwrecks haven't told me anything that Aila's generation didn't pass down."

He looks skeptically at me, frowning slightly.

"Where did your collection move to?"

"Deeper into the ocean," I respond, unwilling to give him a location.

"Yes, but where?"

"Come now, your highness, you don't honestly believe I would put my collection at risk, do you? They're far, far away from here where you'll never find them, and they won't bother you. That's all you need to know." I tip my head, mimicking the humans. "I'd happily tell you where the *sirens* are at this point, but most of them are dead, and the rest decided to flee before you dragged me up here."

"Are you uncomfortable here?" the king questions.

"Of course. If I confined you to a tiny cell with locked doors, wouldn't you be uncomfortable?"

"You have water, what more do you need?"

"Even Persephone was given more space than this when King Gaspar locked her in a cell to wither away." I tip my chin up in defiance.

"The king locked up Persephone?" Edmund sounds shocked.

"After we left Metten, Persephone was captured when she tried to murder Aila for ruining her plans. Chantay escaped and formed the sirens, which is why we've been having all of these problems."

"They locked up Persephone?" Edmund mutters again.

"I admit, I didn't think they would have done that," the king responds in a hushed tone, turning toward his son as if I couldn't hear them.

"Persephone was given her chance. She listened to her mother instead of my great-great-grandmother, Aila. She paid the price."

"How long was she held captive?" the king continues to question.

"She didn't last long—a few years. She died very early—some say of a broken heart over losing Prince Jarek, some say it was being separated from her mother. I think she just gave up trying to escape and withered away in that cell—Aila never told us about Persephone's time in the cells though, so it's all speculation. Only the immediate royal family was allowed to see her after she was locked up."

"What did they do when she died?"

I don't like answering the king's questions, but I need to figure out how to get along with these people in hopes that they'll be reasonable about letting me go.

The light shifts, dancing on the ground near the king and prince. Bits of dust sparkle in the air much like the debris floating in the water of the kelp forests in the ocean—it's a familiar—yet wholly new—sight.

"They buried her with the rest of the royals in the crypts—she was still a princess, after all."

"And who are *you* to the royal family?"

"I'm of Aila's blood. My cousin is the reigning queen of...the sea." I almost slipped and said Scylla. "I'm regarded as royal, but I do not live in the palace. We would have to work our way down a very long list of mer before I even came *close* to being in power."

"But you have negotiating power?"

Edmund flinches slightly at his father's words—so little so, that I barely notice. It takes me a moment to register what I saw. He turns to watch his father, covering up the movement.

"I suppose. Are you looking to negotiate something?" I respond.

"Not yet," he replies coolly. "I see you've changed your ensemble..."

"Yes. Your men have been very gracious."

I swim to the wall, placing my hands on the sides to show I mean them no harm—yet. It's almost a shame that I can't siren them over quickly and cut off a finger or two just for good measure.

"Is there anything else you require, princess?"

Both the king and prince have displayed a level of decorum I didn't expect from the humans, especially after how they've been treating me. Despite being a hostage, they seem to acknowledge that I'm a princess—I wonder if they're treating Merrick and Phorcys the same way.

"I would like to speak to my mermen," I inform him.

"And just how do you expect me to make that happen?"

"Bring me to them…or bring them to me. I don't care, just make it happen."

"What about a conch shell, father?" Edmund asks. My eyes dart over to him. "We could listen to her speak and then deliver it—that way, we'd know what was being said, but she'd still have the assurance that her friends are alive."

Friend, singular. Phorcys is *not* my friend.

"I can accept that," I quickly say before the king can argue.

Unable to argue in front of me, he sighs.

"I'll consider it." He takes a step away from the pool. "I have things to see to. I'll be back."

Once he's gone, Edmund turns back to me, his servant still hovering behind him—it's a different man today—this one looks a little braver and closer to the prince's age.

"Just remember who did that for you when the time comes," Edmund says, brushing back his hair.

"Let's see if it actually happens," I remind him.

He smirks at me. His entire face lights up like the mid-afternoon sun beaming down through the ocean waves, illuminating the entire ocean floor in rays of dancing light.

"That's a good point—he didn't actually promise anything. But *I* did, and I always keep my word."

"You'd go against your father's wishes?"

He takes a step toward me.

"Unless it was dangerous, I don't see the harm in keeping promises, even if they're a little inconvenient."

"Interesting," I murmur, watching him move closer.

"What is?" he asks, stepping forward again—his servant looks nervous.

"I thought humans always had to follow the rules."

His expression changes slightly, sensing my challenge.

"Isn't keeping promises part of the rules?"

We stare each other down for a moment, waiting to see who will bring up broken promises first.

"Well, I suppose neither of us is very good at following the rules then, are we?" I flip my hair over my shoulder casually as one side of his lips quirk up.

"And just how do you break the rules, Celena?" I noticed that he didn't use my title.

"If I had followed the rules, Edmund, do you really think I'd be in this position?" I tease. Perhaps I could persuade him to be friends.

"Well," he replies. "I know if *I* had followed the rules, you wouldn't be."

My face goes slack before I can stop it.

"What do you mean?"

"I wasn't supposed to go in the water after all of you, but I did it anyway. I thought if I could stop you from singing, I could end the bloodshed. Father ordered me not to, but I got in the boat anyway, and here we are."

"Did you intend on capturing me?" I ask after a tense moment.

"Truthfully?" Edmund hedges for a moment. "No. I had planned on killing you, but to be fair, I didn't know it was you. When I recognized you, I watched to see what you would do, and then I pulled you up."

Great, so murdering mermaids isn't a scruple for him.

"Don't look at me like that, *Princess*," he adds. "You would have killed me too to protect your family."

He makes a valid point.

"In fact, I believe I witnessed some of that," he reminds me, shrugging.

"Perhaps if we stopped killing each other, we could work out another treaty," I suggest.

"I doubt we'll ever trust your kind again, Celena... It's a nice idea though." He turns as footsteps approach. "Analia!"

"I saw Father leave. I just wanted to see Celena," she

chatters, rushing across the floor. She grins at me as she approaches.

"How old are you, Analia?" I ask. The prince frowns.

"I'm eleven," she replies, tossing her curls again.

"That's a good age." I smile back at her. "I have a sister not much older than you."

"So *that's* who that was," Edmund mumbles to himself, realizing the only reason I killed that sailor a few days ago was to save Coralie.

"Tell me what the ocean is like," Analia begs, twisting her dress around in her hands.

"What do you want to know?" I ask, hoping that if I befriend the girl, her brother will consider working with me.

"Everything." She looks at me as if I'm the most amazing thing in the world. I chuckle.

"Maybe you could be a little more specific, and then we can work up to *everything*."

"What is it like to swim?"

"You've never been swimming before?" I shouldn't be as shocked as I am considering the humans haven't been in the ocean for a century, but I had assumed they had access to smaller bodies of water that didn't connect to the sea.

She shakes her head.

"Yes, you have," Edmund corrects her, rolling his eyes.

"You just haven't been in the *ocean*—aside from being thrown in, and that hardly counts."

"That doesn't count," I agree. "The ocean is magnificent. Everything is alive and full of color. There are currents and different temperatures. The sea creatures are amazing."

"What sea creatures?" Her eyes sparkle as she asks.

"Starfish and seahorses. There are stingrays too—my cousin feeds them every morning and evening. The dolphins are brilliant."

"You've seen the dolphins?" she gasps.

"Seen them? Why, they're some of my very best friends. They give me rides all the time when I need to get somewhere quickly." I try to capture her imagination with my words and create an image for her.

"They're so beautiful. I've only seen them in books and *once* since we arrived at the palace, but I want one as a pet."

"Oh, I don't think you'd have anywhere to keep one in the palace." I wink at her. "But if you wave to them from your window, they might chatter back at you."

"Will you teach me how to make a crown?" she asks suddenly, changing the direction of the conversation as quickly as Llyr does backflips in the water.

"Yes, of course."

"Edmund, could you go get me some shells and whatever else that is?"

"Not now, Analia." He pats her on the head, unwilling to leave her alone with me.

"Here," I say, swimming back from the edge of the wall.

I reach below my *iluse* where I have the extra netting hanging and quickly cut off a strip below the wall where they can't see me—I hope they believe I ripped it. I untangle three small shells from my covering and then set them and the netting on the edge of the wall.

Edmund reaches around his sister, putting a hand on her elbow in case he needs to protect her. The prince studies my offering for a moment before reaching out to take it off the wall.

Deciding it's safe, he passes it off to his sister. She tries to suppress her grin when he hands it to her, but she can't.

I quietly explain what she needs to do in order to fashion it into a makeshift crown. Once she has it twisted properly, she tries to work the shells in, but her fingers can't manage to get them balanced properly, and they topple out each time she tries to put it on her head.

"Here's an idea," I interrupt her frustration. She glances up at me. "Hand the shells to your brother."

I wait as she reluctantly gives them over to Edmund. He holds his hand out gently as she places the broken shells in his palm.

"Now, tie the net around your head with the tie in the

back—just be careful not to catch your hair in it —that hurts."

The girl fumbles with the ties, flinching as she catches her locks in the net. I wince with her each time, knowing the pain of tying my hair into a tieback knot.

Edmund eventually sighs, setting the shells on the side of the pool and spins his sister around to face away from him. Taking the tieback from her, he grapples with it as he attempts to tie it for her. It takes a bit, but he manages to fasten it around her head securely enough that it stays in place.

"Now, just tuck the shells in," I direct as the girl turns to face her brother.

Edmund reaches over to the wall of the pool and picks up one of the broken shells. He's careful to face the sharp side away from her skin as he tucks the shell between the net and her forehead. When he's finished, the crown doesn't look terrible.

"Just like a mermaid." I smile at her, and she beams.

"Will you sketch me like this, Edmund?"

His face dips down, but he nods.

"We can't let Father find out."

She nods furiously, nearly knocking a shell out of her crown. Edmund tries not to smirk.

"You should take that off before he comes in here and finds you like that, Analia."

The young princess sighs, reaching up to remove her

new toy. She cradles it tenderly in her hands, folding it in on itself to conceal it. Miraculously, Edmund tucked the shells in enough that they didn't fall out when she removed it.

"Why don't you take that up to your room?" Edmund teases, waving his hand toward the stairs.

She considers his words, finally giving in to his wishes in order to protect her new plaything. Analia turns back to wave goodbye before ascending the stairs. Edmund waits until she's gone before speaking.

"She was terrified of you until we brought you in here. Now, you're some magical creature she can't get enough of."

"I'm hardly magical," I reply, though I wish I were—I'd use it to escape.

"I appreciate you playing along with her."

"She seems sweet." I offer him a small smile. "She reminds me of *my* sister."

I emphasize the thought again, hoping to reinforce the idea that he shouldn't harm me because I have a family too. I see the spark in his eyes as he catches on to what I'm doing, but I don't have time to react.

Loud footsteps fall on the stairs, crashing into the room hurriedly. The guards rush around the corner, coming quickly toward the pool.

"What's happening?" I ask Edmund as I quickly swim back.

The men close in on me, a few holding weapons, others holding a net.

"Edmund?" My voice is high-pitched and terrified as the guards run at me.

"I don't know," he replies as the men cut him off from me.

"Edmund!" I shriek, knowing either he will save me, or I'll have to fight the men off myself without being able to siren them—their ears are covered.

The large net covers the top of the pool, closing me in. The ends are tied to spears that they shove in the water, and the men drag the net under me, scooping me out of the pool viciously as I scream.

CHAPTER 4

I STRUGGLE AGAINST THE NET AS IT DRAGS ALONG THE bottom of the pool. The spears against the rough rock create a horrific noise in the water, though I don't have time to focus on it as I thrash in the water, trying to free myself.

In truth, it doesn't matter if I struggle—they have complete control of the situation. My reaction is merely an instinct—the very core of me fighting to survive against that which I know is wrong. I will fail in every way, and this struggle is simply so I can console myself with the fact that I tried later on when it's all over.

"Enough!" Edmund shouts, trying to quiet the men as they attempt to haul me out of the water. I restrain myself from whimpering as they crunch my body into itself.

"Sorry, sire," one of the guards addresses him when he

finally catches their attention. "You'll have to see your father about this."

Edmund storms off, face red. His hands are balled into fists at his side as he stomps through the room.

"Come on now, girly," the guard snaps once the prince is gone.

The men start off toward the stairs, carrying me between them as if they're afraid I have a disease that they'll catch if they touch me—they probably assume I'll kill them if I can reach them. I glance down at the shells on my *iluse* and consider it.

It's less jarring going back up the steps to exit the room as I swing from inside the net. Logically, I suppose it makes sense that it would be more bumpy when I was riding on the arms of men standing on different levels of steps than it is now as I'm balanced in a swinging net.

The guards carry me out of the room, and a tightness creeps into my chest—I don't think I'll be seeing this room again. The light dances through the window for me one last time, sparkling against the crisp white walls and floor.

The hallway is much cooler than the poolroom where I had been kept. The tapestries appear to have been cleaned off since my arrival.

We travel through several halls, turning around several corners until we step through a doorway. I try to study my surroundings like my mother trained me to do, but it won't ever help me—there's no way I'll be able to drag myself this far, even if I do escape from wherever they are taking me.

This new room is different than the rest of the palace. The noise echoes different, twisting and turning off the sides of the room. When we walk around the giant wall, I discover it's a larger version of the room I just left, though this one isn't as spotless. The white walls have been replaced with rock walls, though flat and not like the inside of a cave. Their tan color reminds me of the ocean floor in crystal light.

A huge pool sits in the middle of the room, taking up the majority of the floor. The water laps quietly against the edge of the slightly-raised wall.

The men weave their way around a set of shorter walls, designed to be like the grooves of brain coral—a maze. Walking up to the water, the men fidget as they attempt to change my positioning.

Without any ceremony, they lift the spears from their shoulders where they were supporting me and throw the net toward the water. I tumble away from them, crashing hard into the surface of the water.

Splashing around, I try to free myself from the netting that miraculously slid off the spears without dragging the weapons into the water with me, which is a shame—I would have liked to have used them.

When I finally free myself and surface to see where

the guards are, I find them backing away quickly from the pool. They stumble over the walls on the floor, tripping into each other as they hurry to leave the room.

Silence washes over me as the men escape, leaving me with waves of fear pulsing against the inside of my chest just like the water against the side of the pool.

It wouldn't be hard for me to climb out, though, by the time I navigate the maze, I'm sure I would be caught. The floor appears to be raised at different levels, almost like seats or long benches that people could sit on—perhaps they mean for people to stare at me in the pool.

I need to know what I'm facing, so I dive under the water. Miraculously, the pool is deep enough that I can do so. Under the surface, I discover that the pool is luxuriously deep compared to the tiny pool I was just in. The walls below are like those of a cave, the rock jutting out sharply before pulling back in.

In the bottom corner, a light glows. No, not a light—an opening.

Swimming to the bottom as quickly as I can, I realize I'm in a pool attached to the sea, and that bright spot is an exit. I dart toward it, desperate to find help on the outside of the palace.

The palace itself sits on a rocky cliff, only the steps at the bottom of the cliff extending into the water actually touch the ocean. If I'm able to see the exit in the distance, this must be an underground tunnel that leads to the sea.

The bioluminescent glow on the walls of the tunnel assures me that I'm correct in my assessment. The bars covering the exit promise what I should have known all along—they'll never let me escape.

My fingers close around the metal bars as I test my prison. I imagine this is how Persephone must have felt like once King Gaspar locked her away inside the palace at Scylla.

I can see the outside world, glowing blue in the waters in front of me. The tunnel isn't long—I can see where it opens up into the ocean beyond it—but it's empty, void of mer. A starfish crawls along the seafloor, walking toward me.

At least I'll have a friend, assuming it manages to come all the way into the pool. Fish swim in the tunnel, though most avoid the pool. I stretch my hands out, hoping to entice the creatures to come to me.

In the opening of the tunnel, a stingray glides into the water, changing course almost immediately as it swims back out. I sigh, watching it go. I'm jealous, though I can't begrudge the little creature its freedom.

A slap on the water above gets my attention. I look up and find what appears to be an oar lifting out of the water. It drips onto the surface, leaving little marks like the rain does when it storms out at sea.

"I trust you find this more comfortable." The king

offers a restrained smile as I surface a few feet in front of him.

"What is this?"

"This was something King Jarek was having built for your ancestors to visit the palace. Apparently, Princess Aila and that sea witch, Persephone, had wanted to see the palace, and Jarek was working on a surprise for them. Obviously, it was updated immediately once they found out about the sireny." He motions toward the tunnel entrance I just left. "I thought perhaps this would be more accommodating for you, Princess."

"That was thoughtful of you." My words are restrained. I'm still reeling from the way I was just carried in.

"Of course there will have to be a few rules," he adds, waving his hand in the air. "You may swim where you like, but if I call you, you must surface immediately. You will stay in the pool at all times—do not try to leave this room—I have men posted outside the door.

"Oh, and don't get any ideas about trying to pull any nonsense in here. If you go against my wishes, or actively work to hurt any one of my people, I'll skewer you, and won't think twice about it."

He turns on his heels and walks away through the maze of tiny walls no higher than his knees, hands clasped behind his back.

"I have some matters to attend to. You may explore

your new home, but I'll be back to speak with you later. If you're lucky, you'll make yourself useful here, and this might be your home for a very long time."

If I don't, he'll kill me. Grand.

Once I'm sure he's gone, I dive back under the water. The bars are too close together to allow me to slide between them—something I'm sure Jarek's mother ordered knowing how tiny Aila and Persephone were. I can fit my arm up to my shoulder through, but my bone structure is to wide to allow me any further, and I know enough not to try to fit my head through the bars.

A tiny octopus rests on the ocean floor, tentacles wrapped around the bars. I pick it up and set it on my wrist, allowing him to wrap around me.

Companionship—even for a few moments—is my saving grace.

The creature sits on my arm, content to let me swim around with him on my wrist. I explore the rest of my prison. Two hours pass as I run my hands over every inch of the walls, looking for hidden doors or anything that might help me.

When I find nothing, I sink to the sand and pick at the shells that have washed in. Discovering a few that might work as weapons, I hide them in the corner where I can easily reach them if I need to.

A slap on the water indicates that my presence is being requested. I set my new friend on a small ledge on the wall of the pool and return to the surface, making sure my hair is angled so that I won't look *as* ridiculous when I leave the water.

Instead of finding the king staring back at me, I'm greeted by the prince. His expression is timid, as if he doesn't quite know what to say.

"Do you like it better here?"

"I *don't* like how I was *brought* here," I inform him. He cringes.

"I apologize."

"Tell that to the scales I lost." I blink. I'm not sure when I decided to be so bold with the prince, but now that I've started, it won't do me any good to back down.

"At least you have more space here. You can swim around." Edmund shrugs at me.

He moves around to sit on the edge of the wall. All I would have to do is reach up and wrap an arm around him to drag him into the water and drown him—*why is he sitting here?* His servant looks horrified, but then, so do I.

The prince twists around to face me, one knee raised so that his foot dangles as he balances himself on the far side of the wall.

"What are you doing?" I ask, nose wrinkled.

"You're not stupid enough to try to hurt me here, and even if you were, the guards would all follow wherever you take me. They're willing to sacrifice themselves for me, and you're no match for the number of men who would enter this pool and destroy you. I'm safe here, and it's easier for us to talk."

He smiles at his servant, trying to make him more comfortable.

"Sir," the servant shouts, unsure of his own volume with cloth in his hears. "Your father would not be pleased—"

"My father needs information. He doesn't care how I get it." Edmund waves the servant off.

"What does he want?"

The prince turns back to me, looking me over.

"He wants information on your collection. More than that, he wants information on how you siren humans—we need to be able to defend ourselves, and if we can understand how you do it, we can protect ourselves and our people."

"You've already figured out how to block our voices." I nod toward his servant. "Why does anything else matter?"

"We can't always cover our ears, Celena—that's ridiculous. We have to know how to prevent this from happening again." He pauses for a moment, drumming his fingers on his knee. "The alternative is killing every mer in the sea, and I don't think you want that."

As far as I know, there are no secrets to this, but hope makes us believe all sorts of things...and so does fear. They're desperate for answers so they won't stop looking for them, even if they don't exist. No mer would ever be so illogical.

"You and I can either work together on this, or we can do it on our own, and I'm positive that will be far more deadly for your kind." He shrugs. "All I need to know is how this works."

"I have no idea, Edmund. I sing, and you listen, that's all I know."

"But *why?*"

I shake my head, sighing.

"Fine, but we'll have to figure this out soon," he says, not giving up. "One way or the other, we'll figure out how this works and stop it."

I honestly don't know if it's something that can *be stopped.*

This close, I realize how slender his fingers are as they tap against his knee. He has a long nose like Jarek's portrait has. His dark eyes catch the light beautifully as it bounces off the surface of the water.

"I've answered all of your questions. I think it's time you answer some of mine." I wait to gauge his reaction.

"You really think you're in a position to negotiate?" he asks, amused.

"I think your father sent you on a mission, and if you want to return to him with answers, you're going to have to cooperate with me." I hope my bravado works in my favor.

"What do you want to know?" Edmund asks, leaning back slightly.

"You know what happened to the mer since the treaty was broken. What happened to the humans?"

"We left." He rocks forward again, leaning slightly on his knees toward me. "As soon as King Gaspar refused to hand over Persephone, we knew it was war. Jarek was moved inland to a different palace. A generation later, we moved to one of the other castles, and it wasn't until my grandfather took power that we moved closer to the ocean so he could oversee the export business better.

"Our major export is still what we harvest from the sea, and we were having trouble with pirates—and sirens —so we needed to be here to defend our exports. My father was here dealing with the mer, and you know the rest."

I dislike how he still groups us in with the sirens, but I don't correct him this time. I tentatively place the tips of my fingers on the wall far enough away that I couldn't touch him even if I reached out.

"There's not much else to tell. We left, now we're back."

"Do you intend on staying?"

"*I should think not*," he replies, appalled. "We just need to handle this, and then we'll return inland."

"I haven't eaten today," I remind him, abruptly changing the subject.

"I'm aware," he waves a man over from his place by the stairs.

This particular servant seems to look less stressed about being in my presence, but his eyes roam over me longer than I like. I'm sure he's thinking about how much he could get for selling my scales to siren-collecting humans who want a piece of the myth.

Once he steps back, Edmund waits for me to open my food. Instead, I reach around the large pile and scoop it into the water in front of me. The shells hit my tail on the way down—stinging— but I don't let him see that.

He looks shocked at my actions, eyes wide as he shakes his head back and forth a little.

"Why did you do that? Didn't you want them?"

"I'm saving them for later. I thought it was more important to talk."

The last of the bubbles I created subside around my stomach, popping gently against my skin as I lean back on the wall. Crossing my arms, I lower my head, looking up at him like Aila used to look up at Jarek from the palace steps—though *she* was a free mermaid. I want him to feel like he has the power in the situation.

"I would have waited." He almost looks comical as he pouts, though he's very serious.

"Perhaps next time you'll bring your own meal and join me."

"Perhaps," he murmurs in return. "You're an unusual princess, Celena."

"And you're an unusual prince, Edmund," I retort. "I doubt many princes would sit on the wall of a pool next to their enemy without a second thought."

"I told you, you're not going to hurt me."

"You're awfully trusting of that, though you're correct —I don't want to hurt you."

"I noticed you didn't say that you *wouldn't* hurt me." He quirks an eye brow up, giving me a cocky look.

"I noticed you still have me locked up and separated from my friend and the rest of my collection. I *also* noticed the way I was brought in here."

"You've mentioned that," he reminds me.

A starfish crawls on the ocean floor beneath me, catching my eye, but I force my gaze to stay on the prince —something that was easier to do in the tiny pool a few rooms away where there were no distractions.

"I thought you needed to be reminded of it again." I smile, batting my eyelashes. "You realize this entire thing is ridiculous, don't you?"

"If you're going to suggest a treaty again, the answer is still no. We're not going down that path again. We just want our waters clear, and to never see the mer again."

"What if I take them far away? We can go farther than we were. None of them would fight me on it—they want to be away from you far more than you want to be away from us. *We're* not the ones hunting humans as trophies."

To be fair though, the sirens *did* build part of their kingdoms out of the skulls of their enemies, but I don't need to remind him of that.

I'd be more than willing to guide the collection beyond Scylla. I'd even be willing to travel north to Keldori, though I'd genuinely prefer the warmth of Dariah over the cold temperatures of our mer to the north. Ambra came to our aid during the battle with the sirens—I'm sure they'd be willing to take us in until we could rebuild somewhere else.

Based on what I'd seen as Tarni and Phorcys dragged us across the ocean, it might even be easy to find an old siren settlement and transform it into a new kingdom for our collection. We'd have to find one that *hasn't* been taken over by jellyfish though.

"You're very optimistic, Celena."

"That's not what they usually say about me," I joke.

"No? What *do* they say?"

"Nothing nice, I'm sure," I reply, making him laugh at me.

"I've heard some rather unpleasant things about myself too, Princess. I suppose not everyone is going to like us."

"Did you feed Merrick today?"

"I told you I would take care of him, and I did. I promise."

"Edmund!"

We both turn as the princess rushes into the room. She flies around the maze as if she's spent her entire life navigating it. Coming to a halt in front of us, she barely refrains from flinging herself at us. Instead, she gracefully sits on the wall next to her brother, moving her dress as she sits to spread it out.

"Father says she can stay with us," she grins at the prince before turning to me. "You get to stay with us forever, Celena. You can live here forever and be my mermaid."

"She's not a *pet*, Analia—" Edmund gapes at her.

"You keep saying that." She shakes her head. "Do you like your new home? I can decorate it and make it prettier if you want. I might have them put a bed down here so we can spend the night together sometimes, so you don't get lonely—"

"Analia!" Edmund shouts indignantly.

"I don't want her to feel alone, Edmund!" Analia shouts back. "You can stay with us too if you want, but I'm staying with her for the first few nights."

"You will do no such thing," he argues back, putting his hands on his hips. He winces as he moves as if his shoulder hurts.

"I'm not staying here," I announce, making Analia swing toward me.

"Yes, you are. Father said you can be my mermaid. No one else has one. I'm sure my friends will love you."

"You're not showing her off, Analia, and your friends aren't even here," Edmund replies, standing to his feet. "And Father isn't showing her off either. She's a captive, not a show pony. She's here to provide us intelligence, not to be your plaything."

"But she's my friend—she saved me. I want to spend time with her."

"You can, but stop calling her *your mermaid*—she doesn't belong to you. She has her own life. You wouldn't like it if I said you *belonged* to me simply because you're my little sister, would you?"

"No," she grumbles. "But I don't want her to be all alone down here."

"She won't be—it will be fine."

It doesn't surprise me that the king wants to show me off as a status symbol. A dead mermaid is a prize to be shown off, but a living one is a miracle, I'm sure. Sailors don't do well with keeping us alive once their bloodlust kicks in.

"But she *is* alone when we're not here, and Father won't let us stay down here all the time."

"She won't be alone, Analia. It's fine." He looks down at her from where he towers over her.

"How?" the little girl demands.

As if on cue, people enter the room, rushing around the wall. They struggle with someone, but I can't see around the front of the group. The noise is nearly as loud as when we were locked in battle outside the palace walls.

Several people trip, falling over themselves as they struggle against their captive. The king's head appears over the top of the group, still walking down the stairs. He follows behind him as the shouting intensifies.

Elbows and hands fly, mixed with threats and shouts of fear. They fight against each other, unable to work together to accomplish their goal—whatever that may be.

Another guard trips over one of the short walls, revealing their captive.

Everything jolts in pain as I launch myself forward, feeling like I'm being stung with a thousand jellyfish all over again.

"Merrick!" I scream when I see him.

CHAPTER 5

MERRICK TWISTS AROUND VIOLENTLY, TRYING TO SEE ME AS he fights against the humans.

"Celena!" he yells back, trying to get to me. He flinches in pain as the movements hurt him.

"Stop fighting," I shout, trying to calm him—he's safe now—or at least as safe as we *can be* in this palace.

They're bringing him to me, and we'll be okay now.

He slows, locking eyes with me, and I realize just how damaged he is as he hangs upside down from the men's arms.

"Merrick," I gasp quietly as I take in the sight from inside the pool. Edmund twitches next to me but says nothing.

The men drop his battered body in the water, and I rush to him, letting him sink into my arms as I seethe at the prince. My teeth are gnashing so hard that I have to force myself to stop so I don't break them.

Traitor, my eyes glare at him.

He swallows—apparently, he wasn't ready to tell me they had been torturing Merrick.

"He wasn't supposed to be brought in yet." He turns on his father.

"We have things to do, and it doesn't matter."

"He's in no condition to be moved, Father."

I cradle Merrick in my arms, pulling him back in the water until I reach the far wall—thankfully, the humans can't reach us unless they enter the pool, and I fully intend on drowning anyone that tries.

"Then he shouldn't have made things so difficult—none of this was necessary."

"Is *this* what you meant when you said she wouldn't be lonely?" Analia turns on her brother, stomping her foot. Her hands on her hips make her look slightly older than her eleven years. "You knew they were going to bring him in here."

She wrinkles her nose, glaring at Merrick. I can feel my nostrils flare as I take in her expression—like I'm some kind of possession to her, and Merrick is here to take me away. It makes me nervous.

"Relax, daughter. They'll be good for each other." Her father puts his hand on Analia's shoulder, guiding her away. "Maybe they'll mate, and you'll have even more mermaids to show your friends."

Edmund looks as though he's been struck. He glances at me quickly before following his father.

"And if *he* doesn't, I'm sure the other one will. Either way, it won't be too terribly long before you have more to impress your friends with," the king adds as he leaves.

Edmund turns back to me and shakes his head once before hurrying after his family. Not caring what he meant, I drag Merrick under the water to protect him.

Swimming to the bottom, I tuck us away in the front corner where they can't see us. Tears well up in my eyes, slipping into the water as I settle us on the ocean floor.

"Merrick," I murmur, pulling him against me.

Brushing his hair, I wait for him to look up at me. His eyes sparkle as he grins at me. Reaching up, he buries his hand in my hair, cupping my chin as he leans in to kiss me.

"What happened?" I whisper, unable to speak any louder.

"I didn't do what they asked, and they took a few scales."

"And beat you," I correct.

"That too," he acquiesces. "Can't exactly get away in those tiny pools. Have you been in here the whole time?"

"No, I was in a tiny pool too. They just moved me here a few hours ago."

Merrick's hand traces over my arm, checking me for injuries. His eye looks swollen, and there's a small cut in front of his ear.

"Are you hurt?" he asks quietly.

"I'm okay. There's an exit over there, but it's blocked." I wave to the tunnel. "It leads to the ocean, but maybe we can find a way out. Did you see anything when they transferred you?"

"Just the hallways—nothing we can use."

"You did a number on a few of those guards." I smirk at him. He winces as he tries to return my look. "Oh, Merrick. You couldn't have just kept your mouth shut? You had to antagonize them?"

"How do you know I *didn't*?"

I tip my head down, giving him the most withering look I can manage. He chuckles at me.

"Fine, I gave them a hard time—I think I deserved a little fun after everything we've been through."

"We may need to have a conversation about your definition of *fun*," I tease him. "Are you hungry? I have food."

"I could eat," he says, releasing me.

I swim over to the oysters I dropped in the water earlier and scoop them up. When I return, I drop them next to Merrick and swim up to the ledge I left the octopus on to wait. He's still sitting there, and I return him to my wrist before taking a seat next to my boyfriend.

"Who is this?" Merrick asks in surprise.

"He's cute, isn't he?" I hold up my wrist for him to see.

"Not cuter than me though, right?" He grins at me, looking out from under his long, blue bangs.

"Eat your food." I hand him an open oyster so he doesn't have to open it himself. "How are we supposed to get through this?"

"I don't know, but at least we're together now." He raises the oyster to his lips, and I suddenly remember the pearl he accidentally sent me. "And at least we can swim around again."

"Speaking of which, thanks for the pearl."

"What?" His brow furrows.

"When you refused to eat and sent me your oysters, I found *this* in one of them." I dig the pearl out of my necklace and show him. He smiles softly.

"Yeah, well, I guess I'll always find a way to get you little presents."

"So I see," I agree. "But if you *ever* do that again, Merrick, I'll make all *this* look like it's nothing."

I wave my hand at his injuries as I emphasize my point.

"Are you threatening me?" He jokes.

"I am. Do *not* put yourself at risk for me again, Merrick. Never refuse food for me again. I need you to stay strong for the both of us."

"I hear you," he says quietly, informing me that I've made my point.

He leans forward, setting the oyster shell down between us. His sigh makes me close my eyes, drinking in the sound of it.

When Merrick kisses me, everything else quiets. The edges of my fins lift off the sand, fluttering every time his lips come into contact with mine.

Floating up off the ocean floor, I move to cross my tail over his, drawing closer to him. He darts forward kissing me as he wraps his arms around my waist, pulling me against his chest.

My hand roams up his forearm making him latch onto my hip harder, dragging me closer to him. Over and over again our lips meet, eager to make up for the time we were apart.

"Merrick, I—"

He kisses me, cutting me off.

"I know," he mumbles against my skin. "I—"

"Mhmm," I mumble back, returning the favor as I kiss him.

We lack the array of fish we had the first time, but the light from the tunnel adds a beautiful glow to the other side of my closed eyelids. I clutch his shoulders in my hands.

Reaching up, I tangle my hands in his hair, running my fingers through his tresses. He moans quietly as my fingers work their way through his blue strands. I pull back on his short hair near the base of his neck, tipping his head up slightly. Darting forward, I kiss the tip of his chin as he grins, watching me.

"You're certainly good at this. Have you been practicing while I wasn't looking?" he teases. The tips of his lips edge up slightly as he gives me a smoldering look.

"Hmm, and here I thought I needed a little more practice." I shrug playfully as he tips me off of his lap, depositing me next to him.

Merrick shifts to face me, covering me with his arm as he wraps around me. I lean against the wall, making sure that I don't move and accidentally hurt him. When he finds a comfortable position, he brushes my hair back, tucking it behind my ear.

"What's with the outfit change?" he asks, taking notice.

"I think I'm starting to get through to Edmund."

"Who?"

"The prince. He seems to think that because I'm a royal, I'll work with him. I've been trying to befriend him in hopes that I can be the *Aila* to his *Jarek*, and maybe fix all of this."

"It's not a bad plan, but do you really think we can trust him even if he *does* seem to be playing along?"

"I'm not sure, but I think it's our best shot for now. I think we need to get him to see that we're not trying to hurt them—I keep telling them that we're not sirens, but I didn't exactly help our case when they saw me kill that sailor to save Coralie."

"I'm sure she's fine," he murmurs gently, closing his eyes as he leans his forehead to mine. He's so sweet when he's trying to take care of me. "Casp took her to safety, and I heard him calling when they dragged us out. He never would have left her if she wasn't safe, so she has to be safe."

"What about the rest of our families though? Did you even *see* yours at any point?"

"I didn't," he confesses. "I just have to believe they're okay for now. Everyone would have protected Marilla and Dylana, so I'm sure they're getting the collection to safety right now."

"I heard Llyr with Caspian before they brought us in, so I'm sure they're working together on this," I echo his list of certainties. "Maybe we'll get lucky and find a conch shell to send out to them so they can find us. They might have better luck getting us out from the other side of the bars."

"That's a good idea. I haven't seen any conch shells yet, but there are starfish and stingrays—"

"And your little friend there." He nods to the octopus I peeled off before we kissed moments ago. It sits not too far away in the sand.

"And him," I agree. "I'm sure other things will make

their way in, and it seems like the current is bringing objects in as well."

"So we'll keep a close eye out for one. Maybe if we wish on that starfish over there, it will work out."

I humor him, closing my eyes to wish on the starfish. When I open them back up, Merrick hovers so close that we're practically touching.

"Now, we should probably get back to eating," he taunts me. "Feel like opening a few more of those oysters up?"

I sigh happily, reaching for our food. If I could spend all of my time with Merrick, I would be a very happy mermaid.

Opening the oysters, I hand one to him before indulging in one myself. We save several of them for later in case the king decides to withhold food from us, though with the way things are washing through the tunnel, I'm sure we'll find additional food sources at some point.

We talk about what we experienced in our separate pools. Merrick's room was similar to mine—bright white walls with a sparkling floor. His treatment was rougher, as evident by his injuries. The king spoke to him a few times, but mostly it was the guards.

Edmund visited a few times, but it appears that the majority of his time was spent with me. Analia, on the other hand, only came to see me, though whether it was her own decision or her father and brother's, I'm not sure.

"Do you know what happened to Phorcys?" I ask.

"I haven't seen or heard him since they separated us. You?"

"I haven't heard anything from him either. I wonder if he's cooperating with them."

"I wouldn't put it past him—he has to survive *somehow*. His siren collection is gone now, which means he's basically alone. If he thought he could leverage *us* to get something out of it for *himself*, he probably gave them whatever they wanted."

Truthfully, I was afraid he might do just that. I don't trust Phorcys or any of the sirens, and if it comes to saving his own scales, I wouldn't put it past him to put the blame on Merrick—he could even be the reason they were so brutal to Merrick to begin with.

I need to stop thinking like this—I don't know what he has or hasn't done yet. It's all conjecture, and guessing games like that could get me in a world of trouble.

"You're wondering if he blamed me too, huh?"

"How did you—?"

"Because I know you, Len. Always have, always will."

Merrick has always been an incredible partner—we've worked well together from the start. We know what the other is thinking, what we'll say, and how we'll move. He and I trust each other implicitly.

"Eat your food, Merrick," I pretend to chide him.

While he finishes his meal, I create an area for us to store food in for later use. I pull some of the seaweed in that's wrapped around the bars of the tunnel entrance and create a little basket to store small items in on the sand.

When I'm finished, I use the extra to create a *sarasa* for Merrick. If he's going to be trapped here, he should look the part of a royal mer. So far, they've treated me with more respect because of it.

I loop it around his neck and shoulder, settling it on his opposite hip as he moves his upper body to assist me. Adjusting it to sit properly across his chest, he smiles at me.

"This is great, thanks, Len."

"You're as much a prince as I am a princess, Merrick. Don't forget that."

He understands that I'm not talking about birth lines and doesn't fight me on it. Instead, he lifts his arm for me to join him in the corner. I nestle against him, falling asleep in his arms as I promise to show him around our new dwelling in the morning.

"Celena," a voice whispers. I take a deep breath, coming out of my sleep. I smile, remembering that I'm safely wrapped in Merrick's muscular arms. I nestle closer to him, keeping my eyes closed as I enjoy the moment.

When the voice shouts, it frightens me awake fully. I bolt upright, launching Merrick into action. Before I can even assess the situation, he's swimming in front of me, broken shell in hand, ready to defend us from whoever is yelling at me.

"Knock it off, Merrick," Caspian calls from the tunnel exit.

"Casp?" I dart around Merrick, shocked to see my twin.

His hand rests on the bars separating us, and he reaches through for me with the other. I swim to him quickly, taking his hand in mine as he pulls me close to the bars for a difficult hug. The metal presses into my body uncomfortably, but I don't care—my brother is here.

"How did you find us?"

"Accident. We've been checking every cave we could find near the palace. We've even taunted the humans to come out in hopes of sirening them, but no luck. We were here not long after you were taken, but we decided to double back this morning."

"Hey, brother," Llyr smiles, reaching through the bars to clasp Merrick's outstretched hand. He eyes Merrick's bruised face. "Looks like you've had an interesting time."

"What happened to you—are you safe?" Caspian asks,

not caring about the conversation Llyr and his best friend are having right next to us.

"They put us in tiny pools—like a rounded wall that contains water so small we could barely swim at all in it —and we were separated until last night."

"Why did they put you together?" Llyr interrupts. Noticing our change in attire, he adds, "And where did you get the *iluse*, crown, and *sarasa* from?"

"Prince Edmund is trying to give me a little more freedom so I will cooperate more with them."

"What does he want?" Caspian gives me a worried look, not giving me a chance to explain our wardrobe change.

"I'm not positive what the king wants, but Edmund wants to learn how sireny works so he can prevent us from using it against humans."

"And he wants to destroy us all," Merrick adds. "He told me their goal is to rid the waters of mer so their sailors can do their jobs without fearing for their lives."

Caspian's grip on my fingers tightens as he pulls my hand toward him. I can feel the worry in his fingers as they nervously twitch against my hand. For a moment, he looks deeply into my eyes, and we have an entire conversation without the others in that one look.

"We need to get you out of here," Casp whispers.

"I know. We need to get through these bars somehow,

and I have a feeling broken clam shells won't get the job done," I joke, trying to lighten the mood.

"At least you know where we are now," Merrick reminds us. "Where is the rest of the collection?"

"We have a group of them here," Llyr replies. "Dylana is with Keone and Natale. Thirty of us stayed behind to try to help—or to stop the humans if they come after us again."

"I sent Mom and Dad with Coralie," Caspian says quickly. "They're all okay…mostly."

I breathe a sigh of relief—I've been so worried about my father. Caspian is quickly explaining his injuries when a slap sounds on the water above us. I look up.

"They're signaling me—I have to go, or they'll hurt us."

"I'm coming too," Merrick says, following me.

"We'll wait here," Caspian calls as I dart away.

I surface before Merrick does—he's not able to move as fast as I can yet. When I rise out of the water, I discover Edmund is waiting for me, mercifully without his father or sister.

His lips pull back in a grimace when Merrick joins us.

"Not you," Edmund says.

I look over my shoulder to Merrick as something passes between the two. When I turn back to Edmund, he's pointing at the water.

"I just need to speak to Celena. You may go."

Edmund's voice is clear and strong as he waits for Merrick to leave.

"I'm not leaving her," Merrick challenges. "I don't trust you."

"I've been with her alone for the last four days, *mer*," Edmund counters angrily.

"That's four too many," Merrick growls back, placing his hand on my back.

"It's fine," I say softly, trying to diffuse the situation. "Merrick, I'll be fine."

I turn back to him, blocking my face from Edmund with my hair. I drop my eyes down, telling Merrick to go back to Caspian and Llyr. Reluctantly he follows my orders, dipping down slowly into the water so only the tips of his shoulders and his face remain.

"I'm right here if you need me," he says pointedly to me.

Once he's submerged under the water, I turn back to Edmund, waiting to see what he wants. Merrick's hand glides down my tail, letting me know once he's actually left my side.

"What did you need?" I ask coolly.

"I wanted to come check on you," the prince replies.

"*And?*" I know better than that.

"*And* I wanted to apologize for yesterday and let you know that we're not going to force you into anything."

"I see." I cross my arms. "Though it seems like you're forcing me into quite a bit here already."

"We won't make you do...*that*," he corrects, reminding me of what the king said to his daughter before they left. "I know my father and Analia want to show you off—no one else in the kingdom has a mermaid—but I doubt you want a bunch of people in here poking and prodding at you."

"Where is Phorcys?" I demand. "What are you doing to him? Are you beating him like you beat Merrick?"

"Merrick didn't cooperate—I couldn't help that."

"You ripped his scales off," I insist on placing the blame on him. "Do you know how long it takes those to grow back?"

"I had nothing to do with that. I wasn't there when that happened, I was with you."

If he hadn't wasted so much time with me, maybe he could have prevented Merrick's injuries. I internally growl at myself for trying to keep the prince with me for so long to convince him to help us—instead I only made it worse for us inside the palace walls.

"You could have stopped it."

"Yes, I could have," he confirms. "But I still don't trust you, Celena. You're restricted here, and under our control, but if you find an opportunity to get the upper hand, I don't know what you'll do."

"I told you, my only goal is to get out of this palace

and return to my collection so I can take them far, far away."

"And now you know what will happen if you try something you shouldn't." He waves at the water where Merrick disappeared. "The guards might have wanted to hurt him because he is a merman, but I don't relish in causing people pain. He brought it on himself when he fought against my men, so like it or not, Celena, he did this to himself."

I open my mouth, about to protest.

"No, you don't get to be righteous about this, Celena. He went after my men, and you yourself delivered retribution against *my* men when they went after your sister. If he had cooperated like you did, he would still have his scales. The other merman is cooperating—mostly—so he's in better shape than your friend.

"You *should* know though," he quiets his voice, telling me something he doesn't like admitting. "Most of it was him fighting to get to you. The entire time, he just wanted to know about you. I think they frightened him a little in hopes that it would get him to cooperate, but it just made him fight harder."

"What do you mean *they frightened him?*"

"I spent most of my time with *you,* but one time I heard them tell your merman that they were hurting you, and it would be worse if he didn't cooperate. I'm pretty sure he made it out of the pool and across the floor once before they found him."

I'll have to ask Merrick about that as soon as I escape this conversation. I don't like the idea of him being hurt for me, and if he threw himself outside of the pool and dragged his tail across the floor, I might have to lecture him.

"And you didn't think this would encourage me to *not* help you?" I say incredulously. My hands float to my hips under the water. He frowns.

"We can still hurt you both, Celena. Try not to forget that."

He turns on his heels, walking away. Edmund doesn't turn around as he mounts the stairs—he's annoyed with me.

His footsteps fade as he quickly stomps away. I duck under the water, racing back to the boys.

CHAPTER 6

"WHAT DID HE WANT?" MERRICK DEMANDS BEFORE I CAN reach him. I slow as I approach the bars.

"Why did he flinch when he saw you?" I ask suspiciously.

"I might have hit him at one point."

"Excuse me?" My eyebrows shoot up. It figures that neither of them would readily admit to that.

"We really don't have time for this," Caspian interrupts, raking his hand through his hair.

"It wasn't intentional." Merrick refrains from rolling his eyes, but I can tell he wants to. "He got in the way during a struggle."

"Is that why he's favoring his arm?" I gasp, realizing what I had been seeing.

"Probably," Merrick grumbles.

"Where is Llyr?" I snap, suddenly realizing he isn't with us.

"We sent him to find Keone and the girls," Caspian replies. "We're working on a plan—it would be great if you could get your head in the game."

"We need a way through the bars, that's as simple as it gets." I shrug as I place my hands on the metal near my brother's.

"The humans have ways to cut through metal." Casp frowns. "Too bad we can't get around easily in the palace to find something."

"Do you think we could trick them into bringing something close enough to us that we can take it from them and get out before they catch us?" Merrick asks, already knowing the answer.

"They're not that stupid. Although," I pause, "If I can get them to trust me, and they leave the princess alone with me, I can probably convince her to unwittingly help us."

"Good, try anything," Caspian says as he lurches back in the water, trying to pull on the bars.

"You've been trying that since I left, haven't you?"

"Do you have a better idea?" Caspian growls, pulling on the bars again.

"Enough, Casp." Merrick puts his hand out. "That's not going to work."

"We need to be logical. We're not getting out of here

today," I direct the conversation. "We need to think longer term. We'll play their game *up there*, and *down here*, we'll work on escaping.

"The bars go into the sand," I point out. "Maybe we can tunnel out under it."

"I'm pretty sure there's rock under the sand," Caspian replies, looking grim. I notice an area that's dug out a bit —he must have checked.

"We're going to need supplies," I continue, ignoring his comment. "You can bring us food—they aren't feeding us much in here."

Caspian floats up in the water, straightening his neck up. He looks ready to break through the bars and murder the king.

"They aren't feeding you?" He blinks at me, jaw tight as he jerks a shoulder back in annoyance.

"Some, just not enough. Go find us some food before they come back. We'll be fine here."

He looks like he wants to argue, but he glances down at my stomach once before flipping around and careening out of the tunnel.

"That will keep him busy for a few minutes," Merrick smirks. "How much trouble am I in?"

"Edmund told me you crawled across the floor?" I cross my arms angrily. "You could have been killed."

"I wasn't. I had to get to you." He reaches out, offering me his hands. "They told me they were torturing you. I had to get to you, and if I couldn't do that, at least I could keep their focus on *me* so that they'd leave you alone."

"You're an idiot."

"Probably." He shrugs.

"No, definitely," I correct, taking his hands. "That was not a bright thing to do."

"I got that." Merrick gives me a patronizing look. "I'd do it again if I had to."

"Of course you would." I sigh as he pulls me closer.

"I have a feeling we won't be left alone again for a while, so if you want to kiss me, now is the time."

I glance up quickly, surprised by his words. He's right, of course—our collection won't leave us alone now that they've found us.

Merrick pins me against the wall a length away from the entrance to the tunnel where Caspian and the others will have a hard time seeing us if they return. I wrap my arms around his neck, playing with the ends of his hair as he crushes his body against mine.

His fingers work their way into my hair, magically making me forget all of my stress. I laugh, enjoying myself as he kisses me, making him chuckle against me. Each slow kiss reminds me of how lucky I am to be in this merman's presence, *let alone* how lucky I am to be kissing him.

Merrick's hand moves slowly down my side, close enough to my back to make me shiver, but just far enough to the side to make sure he doesn't hit the welts from the jellyfish while still avoiding the knick on my side. I shudder as he reaches my tail. He grins.

In retaliation, I slowly drag my hand off his shoulder, onto his chest. By the time I reach his abdomen, only one finger is touching him, but it's enough to make him cringe forward and gasp, eyes alive with sparks.

"Len," he whispers as I walk my fingers around his hip to his back. I drag them up his spinal chord, and he clutches at me, locking eyes with me.

His lips hang open in amazement just enough that I can't help but do something about it. I press my lips against him, spurring him into a passionate kiss as he lifts me up in the water, both arms wrapped around my waist.

Merrick moves his lips along my neck, brushing my hair back with his nose before kissing my skin again. I whimper as he hits a spot that tickles, and I cringe into him only to catch his chin with my finger and move his mouth back to mine.

My tail moves around him. I perch on his hip as he rests me back against the wall, slowing our pace once again. His shoulders are tight under my grasp, and I tip my head to the side more to accommodate his lips.

We pull back to catch our breath—and stare at each other—for a moment before a loud splash sounds overhead.

A body tumbles into the water, creating a cloud of

bubbles so thick that we can't see who it is. Merrick whips around, holding me behind his back against the rocks, allowing me the advantage of preparing a weapon where the intruder can't see.

I quickly reach for my *iluse*, pulling a shell out and placing it in Merrick's hand. He holds it in front of him, ready to strike out at the humans while I untangle my own weapon from my covering.

Even for all the beatings Merrick took, he's still able to move remarkably well when needed. He's never been one to let things hold him back…though occasionally he pushes himself too far for the sake of a mission.

Orange fills the water as the bubbles clear, mixed with a flash of sandy yellow—Phorcys.

He dips down backward in the water, trying to get away from the surface.

"What do we do?" I glance at the tunnel entrance.

It's doubtful that we can trust Phorcys at this point, but there's no way to hide Caspian and the others from him.

"Emphasize what's in it for *him*," Merrick murmurs.

"Phorcys!" I yell just as he flips around. His eyes grow wide when he sees me, but immediately narrow when he catches sight of our weapons.

"We're less likely to hurt you than they are," I warn him as he starts to swim back up pitifully. He seems to have healed some in the last few days, but he's still clearly suffering from the wounds I gave him during our fight.

He appraises us as he slides down in the water. I almost dart forward to help him sit, but then I remember that I don't actually care about his comfort.

"What is this?" he asks.

"It's the ocean," I reply curtly. "We just can't escape the bars."

I motion to the tunnel, and his eyes grow wide.

"We have to get through them," he says anxiously.

"We tried, we can't break out," Merrick informs him. He holds his hand up, cutting Phorcys off as he tries to speak. "But we have another plan."

Phorcys raises his eyebrows, waiting for more information.

"Part of our collection is here," Merrick addresses him. "They're going to help us escape."

"Where are they?" Phorcys demands, sitting up.

"They went to get the others, and to find us more food." I tuck my shell back into my *iluse* and cross my arms.

"Food?" My words catch his attention.

"They haven't been feeding you?" I ask.

"Not much," he admits, though I'm not sure if it's an act or not.

I swim over to where we have the rest of the oysters

from last night and pull them out. I carefully hand them to Phorcys, allowing him to eat.

"Caspian will be back with more anyway," I murmur as I join Merrick across the pool.

"How many of them are here?" Phorcys asks without looking up.

"Enough," Merrick answers, intentionally being vague. Our enemy doesn't need to know how many of us stayed behind. "What did they say to you up there?"

"They asked a bunch of questions," Phorcys says before taking a mouthful of food.

"Such as?"

A school of fish swims into the pool, circling the area as they flash their bright red color. I nearly reach out to touch one, but then I think better of it and keep my focus.

"They wanted to know about sireny and where the mermaids were located." He rolls his eyes, chewing a bite of food. "Obviously I have no idea where they are now."

"Did you tell Edmund about sireny?" I ask.

"What is there to tell?" he snips back. "We sing, they listen. I don't know how that works."

Strangely enough, I believe him.

"What in the seven seas is *he* doing here?" Caspian calls from the tunnel exit.

Phorcys snarls at him, not bothering to get up.

"They dropped him in here a few minutes ago,"

Merrick replies, running his hand through his bangs that I had been playing with not too long ago.

"This is the last crab's leg," Caspian mumbles angrily. "We're getting you out of here."

He drops a pile of oysters on our side of the bars and starts pulling on the metal again. Casp motions for Merrick to join him.

"Celena!" Dylana's voice travels through the tunnel, and I race toward it.

We collide against the bars at the same time, gathering each other's hands in our own. Her hand bumps the cut on mine, and I try not to flinch. She and I speak so quickly that the boys just blink at us, but we understand every word. When we calm down, she eyes Phorcys.

"We can't get rid of him," I inform her before she can ask.

She tilts her body, looking around me.

"I see she left quite the scar," she shouts over to Phorcys.

"Jealous?" he retorts, setting down the final oyster shell.

With great effort, he gets up and swims over to us, resting a hand on the bar. I have a feeling he's making his injuries look worse than they really are.

"Back off," Llyr orders him as Phorcys lurks closer to Dylana.

"No, let him get closer," Natale sings. "I'll slice his hand off while he's busy staring at her."

She grins sarcastically at him for a moment before settling into a rather unpleasant look—if she could treat him like an oyster, she would tear him apart. My cousin glowers at the siren, but he doesn't back down.

"My mother is dead because of you," she finally adds. "You're going to want to be very careful when you make it out of here."

"I had nothing to do with that," he remarks casually.

"You and your sirens lured us out here to fight your war with the humans—*all* of this is your fault." I wouldn't want to be Phorcys when Natale gets unrestricted access to him.

At the back of my collection, another merman floats up in the water, trying to see over everyone. It's hard to see his features in the backlit water, but it's even harder to recognize him because I don't *actually* know him—I recognize his voice though.

"What exactly is the plan here?" Quilo asks, his Ambraian accent evident.

"We need to find a way to get them out. Any ideas?" Llyr asks.

"Why would we have ideas?" Quilo retorts, tipping his head like Edmund does.

"I thought maybe you did things differently in Ambra," Llyr replies, shrugging. "We haven't exactly come up with the best ideas for this yet, so I thought maybe you could help."

"We'll help, we just don't know *how*," the Ambraian mermaid—Larina, I think—responds, pushing her way through the collection. "Looks like you got yourself into quite the mess here, huh?"

She eyes me as she runs her hand along the bars, trying to get an idea for what we're up against. Larina busies herself assessing the situation. It looks like a few others from their collection stayed to help us as well, but it's hard to see from my vantage point.

Larina notices Phorcys in the distance and smiles softly, waving around me. I turn back to look as the siren nods to the Ambrian mermaid, and I realize *they* must have been the friends Phorcys mentioned before we were captured. I *knew* someone had to have helped him after we left him for dead—the Ambrian's just didn't know any better.

"He's a siren," I whisper quietly so Natale doesn't hear. Larina's face falls as she realizes their mistake. I cut her off before she can apologize. "It's okay, just don't let him out of your sight when we get out of here."

She nods.

"I'll make sure the others know."

Merrick places a hand on the small of my back—we're floating so close together that no one can see his movement, but I'm grateful he's next to me, supporting me through this. Natale calms down as we wait, tossing around every idea that we can come up with—none of them seem like they'd cause anything but a whirlpool of trouble.

"If only we had something to pull it with," Llyr mumbles. "We could use it as leverage to bend the bars."

"But what?" Merrick asks. "We don't have access to anything, and it's not like the humans will just give us chains so you can all pull on it at the same time."

The idea hits me as fast as a jolt from a jellyfish. I jerk up in the water, frightening Merrick as his hand moves on my back.

"We *do* have access though." I grin as a plan formulates in my head. "Casp, do you remember The Ropes?"

He gives me a look indicating that I might be insane, but Phorcys lurches forward in the water as he realizes my idea. Merrick turns to me, catching on at the same time my brother does.

"You have to be careful," I say sharply before he can speak.

"We'll be fine," Caspian promises.

"*Casp*," Merrick growls, warning him not to be foolish. "Do *not* die for this."

"Whoa, wait, what?" Larina gasps. "Who's dying?"

"The Ropes is a place where dangerous things were dumped in the middle of the ocean floor—anchors and chains, ropes, and other dangerous things mer could get tangled in," I explain. "Phorcys showed it to us once."

I glance at him sideways, glaring for just a second before turning back to the collection.

"If you get caught in there, you might not come back out," I warn. "You don't have to help with this—"

"We're helping," Quilo cuts me off. His collection nods.

"Okay, but you all have to be careful. Just get things we can use from the outside perimeter, and for the love of coral, *don't* go inside to get chains and tools."

"We'll get what we need, Celena, but we'll be careful," Caspian promises, taking my hand. "It's going to take some time, can you stall until then?"

I nod.

"Good, stay alive until we get back. We'll leave a few of the guards here with you in case you need anything," he adds.

"Dylana and Natale will stay," Llyr interjects. The girls vehemently protest, but he shouts above them. "They will stay because they can siren the humans better than the rest of us, and if you need help, you're going to need them around."

"Not that they can do us much good from *that* side of the bars," Phorcys grumbles loud enough to be heard.

"They can surface if they need to. The guards will be here to back them up. Between the three of you *inside* and the two of them *outside*, maybe you'll stand a chance," Llyr snips, turning to swim away. "We need to move."

Caspian hugs me quickly through the bars before darting after Llyr. The collection rushes out of the tunnel, leaving it feeling empty with only my cousins on the ocean's side.

"Phorcys, go away," I demand, waving him back. "We need to talk."

"What, I'm not part of the team now?" he scoffs.

"You've *never* been part of the team," I correct him. I consider grabbing one of the fish that swims past me and throwing it toward him, but that would be cruel to the fish to have to get too close to the siren.

"Not even when you curled into my neck as I carried you back to your baby sister?" Phorcys leers at me, prompting Merrick to dart toward him a bit in the water, clearly struggling to restrain himself as the siren hisses. "*Jealous?*"

"You will *not* touch her again." Merrick's fists are balled at his sides. Dylana looks shocked as she places a hand on the bars, but Natale watches quietly.

"That's up to *her*." Phorcys smirks. He risks a look at me around Merrick.

When Merrick turns back to face me, his face is surprisingly calm, but his eyes spark fiercely. Phorcys swims to the back corner, taking a handful of the new oysters with him—I have no idea when he picked them up.

"I've got him," Natale mumbles, watching over my shoulder as I turn my back on the siren. "I *really* don't like that guy."

"Nope," Dylana agrees. "So what do we know about the king?"

My cousin eyes Merrick's injuries, reaching out to touch his arm above a cut. She pauses us for a moment as she swims to the end of the tunnel to instruct a guard to find a few supplies for her to take care of our wounds. When she returns, I inform her of everything I've learned about the king—Merrick adds in his own details about the guards.

"Miss me yet?" Phorcys sings, interrupting our conversation from across the pool.

"Nope," I call over my shoulder, not bothering to turn around. Natale snarls at whatever face Phorcys just made, but I still refuse to look.

A piece of Dylana's hair floats toward me as the current drags more water into the pool. She reaches up and tucks her pink locks back just as one of the guards arrives with her supplies.

"Can we trust him?" Natale murmurs, still spying on Phorcys over my shoulder.

Dylana quietly examines Merrick's injuries, patching

him up as best as she can. He winces as she hits a tender spot on his arm.

"I doubt it, but we don't have much choice at the moment," I mutter. "He could turn us in if he doesn't like what we do."

"He knows he'll die if he does that—there's no way the humans will let him live."

"I don't know...he might risk it. We just have to be careful," I reply, making eye contact with Natale.

"I can tell that you're talking about me," Phorcys calls over.

"We're talking about dying, so I suppose that's the same thing," I viciously call over my shoulder, earning a smirk from Dylana. Natale's eyes glitter, and she barely manages to hold a straight face. A second later, she glares over my shoulder.

Phorcys swims over to us, joining us near the bars. He settles on the sand, back against the wall as he stares into the pool area.

A slap sounds against the water overhead.

"What's that?" Dylana asks, looking up.

"I'm being summoned." I sigh as I swim back.

"Shouldn't you *all* go?" Dylana looks concerned when the boys don't move.

"They're afraid of the boys." I frown, continuing to swim up. "They're only negotiating with me because I'm a princess, and I saved *their* princess."

"*You* definitely don't want to go up there, Dylana. They're very anxious to meet you." Merrick's voice fades away as I reach the surface.

I expect to find the king waiting for me, not Edmund after the way he stormed off. When the prince pats the wall next to him, indicating that I should pull myself out of the water and sit next to him, everything inside me screams that I should swim away.

CHAPTER 7

I FORCE MYSELF NOT TO TREMBLE AS I SLOWLY SWIM toward the side of the pool. The prince smiles at me, but I can't return the look. Tentatively, I stretch my hand out on top of the wall, preparing to balance myself so I can leap out of the water to join him.

Fifteen guards stand in a semi-circle around the edge of the pool, far enough back that they can't hear our conversations—even if they didn't have their ears blocked —but close enough that they can skewer me if I attempt to drag their prince into the water.

With both hands on the wall, I flip my tail as hard as I can and propel myself out of the pool. I land sharply on the ledge, the edge biting into my scales as I misjudge the distance.

"Are you okay?" Edmund smirks as I grunt in pain. Glaring, I quickly remind myself not to and soften my gaze.

"Why am I here?" I demand to know what he wants.

"I apologize for getting upset before. I thought we could talk. I brought food." He waves a guard over, and I realize he has been holding a tray—not a weapon. The man sets the food between us.

"What is that?" I ask, wrinkling my nose.

"A slice of an apple," he replies, picking it up. It crunches when he bites it. "Go on, try it."

It looks like a perfectly smooth inside of an oyster shell, free from blemishes, in the purest off-white color I've ever seen. A rim of red covers its contour. The food is cool to the touch and smells tangy.

"It's fruit, just try it," Edmund encourages, pushing the plate toward me.

When I bite into it, my mouth explodes with the new taste. It travels up into my ears, making me shiver—it's strange but good. I take a second bite, this time not reacting nearly as badly. Edmund grins at me.

"I thought you might like that. You should try the cheese too." He motions to a yellow thing on the tray.

Instead, I reach for the oysters he as also provided on the other half of the tray. I'm starting to get sick of only eating oysters at this point, but I'll have Natale find us some other food once I return to the water to make sure we have a balanced diet so we don't get sick.

"Tell me about your sister." Edmund picks up a piece of the cheese and pops it into his mouth.

I see his game now—he's trying to connect with me so he can manipulate me easier. I can play that game, especially because it *could* work in my favor if I convince him to connect with me for real. If nothing else, perhaps I can learn valuable information about his family to use against him.

"She's young, but she's lovely."

"I saw," he agrees, reaching for another apple slice as I pry open an oyster.

"I meant as a mermaid, but she's beautiful too."

"Her tail is a nice color," he offers, and I nod.

"Blue and green is a good color for her, especially with her hair. She would be very intrigued by these apples of yours." I reach for another piece of it.

"Analia likes apples too. She's been very anxious to come see you—we haven't told her we put the other merman in here yet—I don't think she'll be pleased."

"She wants to keep me all to herself?" I ask, saying the words he won't. "I appreciate you not treating me like a possession, Edmund. Tell me more about Analia—perhaps if I can talk to her, she'll stop thinking of me like a toy."

Sitting on the wall of the pool up in the open air is a strange sensation—much worse than sitting on the deck of the ship when the humans attacked us outside of

Scylla. I feel exposed as I hunch over onto myself, trying to get comfortable. The breeze in the room is discomforting as it kisses my skin, and I'm grateful my hair is covering my back, though, I think because I'm wet from being in the water, it's making me chilled.

"She's a very energetic little girl when we're alone. She's rather quiet and sullen in public, but that's how she was raised to be—her actions reflect on us, so she must be regal and refined."

I understand that—Dylana and I were raised the same way—our actions reflected on our mothers, though we were raised to be *fierce* rather than meek.

"What does she like to do when she isn't in front of the world?"

"She likes spending time with her horse." I perk up at his words, jostling my dripping hair as it sticks against my skin. He looks amused, one eyebrow raised. "You like horses I take it?"

"I've never seen one," I admit. "Aila passed down stories of the horses and creatures she would see when she visited the palace steps though. They sound lovely."

"Perhaps I'll show you one day," he murmurs, reaching for an apple slice. "You'd like the summer palace."

He's taking me to the summer palace?

My world stops. I can't leave the ocean—he can't just transport me wherever he likes. I have to stay in the water. I'm not his pet that he can just take around from palace to palace. Isn't this exactly what he told his sister she couldn't do?

If he takes me away, I know for certain that I will never come back. I'll die before I let him remove me from this palace and take me to another.

He notices me cringing, and I realize that I'm starting to dry out—I need to get back in the water.

I look at the water, glancing away from him. Panicked, he holds his hand out.

"Please don't go," he begs, catching my wrist. "I'm not planning on moving you, I was just talking. Don't run away."

"I need to get in the water." I can hear the tremor in my voice. "I'm drying out—I need to get in the water."

"But you'll stay here?" he whimpers. He knows he's messed up his plan—I can't let his folly destroy my chance at winning him over.

I nod, preparing to move to slide into the pool.

"I just need to be back in the water." At his nod, I slide off the wall, thankful to put some space between us. At least when Aila was sitting on the steps near the palace, she could stay partially in the water.

The pool feels cool around me. For as cold as I had been sitting on the wall with my dripping hair, I realize my skin had been rather warm, and it feels like it's sizzling as I sink back into the water.

Dipping down under the gentle waves, I douse my

hair. I come up feeling refreshed, despite being nervous. I smile, trying to assure him that I'm being cooperative.

"So, Analia likes horses. Do you?"

"I enjoy horseback riding. I haven't been in a while though. I've been too busy."

"Doing what?" I ask impertinently.

"Well, most recently, handling the war here. But before that, I was working with my father on kingdom business. We had a few things to take care of, and my father asked me to oversee them."

"It doesn't sound like you were too happy about it."

"Some of it was fine." He sighs. "Some of it I wasn't pleased with."

"Such as?" He casts a withering look at me as I speak. "*You* wanted to be honest."

"I may be searching for a bride," he grimaces.

"Oh." I'm taken back by his admission. "That sounds awful. Aren't you a little young for that?"

I can't imagine being forced to marry at our age—the prince can't be more than a year or two older than me.

"Aren't you a little young to be sirening men to their deaths?" he counters. "I'm trying to put it off a little, but there are alliances to be made with the other kingdoms. It's my job to see which one is the right fit."

"Girl or kingdom?"

"Kingdom." He smirks sadly. "My wife is just what comes along with it."

"Have you met her yet?"

"I think so, but my Father still has to decide if it's the right fit."

"Do you like her?" It's strange how normal this conversation is—it's almost like I'm talking to Dylana back in the Palace in Scylla—without all of the gushing, of course.

"I honestly don't know. She seems nice, I suppose—but then, I suppose they all do."

"She's not the one you would have picked?"

I twirl a piece of hair around my finger, waiting for his answer. This is much deeper than I had anticipated.

Something moves in the water below me against the wall of the pool—the water waves against me. An oyster —or what I *assume* is an oyster—gently collides with my tail before falling down in the water. Merrick wants to know if I'm okay, but he can't risk being seen by the prince. He must be hiding against the wall.

I casually swim closer to the wall, resting an elbow on it while dropping my other hand into the water to wave him off. The water pulses against me again, letting me know he's left.

"I don't know which of them I would have picked. It's my duty to marry as my father tells me to—Jarek kind of ruined that for us."

I give him a quizzical look, and he sighs, dipping his hand into the water to create ripples.

"Jarek fell for Persephone—or was lured in by her—or both. After that, we weren't trusted to make our own choices. The reigning kings and queens decided whom the royal children would marry."

What a stroke backward! *For coral's sake*, if they tried that under the ocean, the *entire collection* would have been beside themselves. We've always been allowed to choose our own mates. Dylana, of course, has certain responsibilities, and with that, limitations, but she still has a say.

"I take it that's not a problem where you come from?" He sounds discouraged. I shake my head. "Tell me about your merman—the blue haired one."

"His name is Merrick," I inform him, knowing that he already knows. "He was my partner—we work together."

"Doing what?" His fingers continue to dance in the water, sending little ripples to wave against the skin on my arm that's still mostly under the water.

"Whatever the queen needs us to do. We help the royals," I reply, avoiding details.

"Your cousin."

"Yes." A moment later, Edmund nearly falls in the water, jumping up from his seat, but not entirely leaving the wall as he jerks his hand out of the water. "Oh!"

I turn to follow his gaze as he blinks at the water, and discover a small stingray brushing against the top of the water.

"Careful!" he cries.

I reach out to pet the velvety creature. He swims up to me, tickling my hand, but I have nothing to feed him.

"What is that?" Edmund demands, cradling his hand next to him as if he had been bitten.

"It's a stingray." I reach out with both hands, practically scooping the creature up into my arms like I did to Coralie when she was a baby.

"It has wings." His voice still sounds too high, but he edges toward the wall again.

"Kind of." I frown at him, continuing to pet the stingray. "You can touch him if you want—he won't hurt you."

Edmund blinks a few times before cautiously readjusting his seat on the side of the wall. He decides to watch me before making up his mind about offering up his hand to the vicious beast in my arms.

The stingray flaps, begging for a treat.

"Sorry, little guy, I don't have anything for you," I murmur.

"Why is it doing that?" the prince asks. He looks like he's flinching as he reaches his fingers out and pulls them back.

"He's hungry—he thinks I'll feed him. Last chance…" I offer the stingray to him again, holding it toward the prince so that he can pet it.

Just when I think he won't, Edmund reaches out,

dipping his finger just below the surface of the water. He gasps when he touches it, not expecting the texture—to be fair, they feel a lot different than one might imagine them to.

Edmund smiles, petting the stingray. He laughs when it flaps in the water, splashing quietly. After a few moments, the stingrays gives up and dips back under the water in search of food elsewhere.

I wonder if one of my friends let the stingray in on purpose.

"I've never seen one of those before," he murmurs, trying to see the stingray as it swims away.

"Is it as lovely as a horse?" I ask, giggling. He turns to look at me, grinning as he contemplates his answer.

"Maybe." He nods. "You were telling me about your friends."

"Yes," I reply, moving back to lean on the wall. "Merrick is amazing. He takes such good care of everyone—me, his family, the royals—*everyone*."

"Ha," he scoffs. "I did *not* see that side of him."

"Of course you did, you saw how he tried to get to me—to protect me from you. He crawled out of a pool and across a floor, and endured beatings to protect me."

He looks as though I've struck him.

"I suppose that's true. Perhaps I misjudged him."

I leap out of the pool, sitting next to him on the other side of the tray again. His head pulls back slightly, once again surprised by me. He lifts a hand, holding off the guards.

"Tell me about the other one," he encourages. I take a deep breath.

"Phorcys. He's *horrible*." I turn to face him, looking out at him from under my lashes.

Edmund chuckles, leaning back to support his weight on his hand, straightening his shoulder.

"He seemed pretty eager to learn about you, from what I heard. I didn't spend much time with him. Sounds like he hates your merman though."

"He *should*, we messed him up pretty badly."

"I think there's some jealousy in there too, am I correct?" Edmund teases, a sparkle in his eye.

"I really have no idea," I protest.

"Oh, come now… *you know*."

"Fine, maybe. Phorcys and the siren princess captured my sister and dragged us out into the open sea—to *here*. Along the way, he might have come up with some weird reason to like me, but I honestly don't know if it's that, or he's just being rude."

"And what would have given him that idea?" Edmund prods. He glances down when I flick my tail in the water.

"When they sent me into the jellyfish, I was hurt badly enough that I could barely swim. Phorcys had to carry me back, so I assume it was connected to that."

"He thinks he saved you? It sounds like it's straight out of a book," Edmund comments.

"*Merrick* is the fairytale knight. Phorcys is more like the dragon." I pause. "Are there dragons around here?"

Edmund laughs, lighting up the room. His smile makes me smile back.

"First, there are no such thing as dragons—they're made up. Second, how do you know about knights and fairytales?" He continues to smile at me as he waits for an answer.

"From the books you humans drop in the ocean." I feel a little embarrassed about not knowing that dragons were mythical, but Edmund doesn't seem to mind.

"I'll have to make a note to stop doing that—if we're going to educate you, the *least* we could do is to do it properly. No more dragon books." He laughs again, quieting after a minute.

"I'm sorry you have to marry a girl you don't know," I say softly, leaning forward to touch the wall with my hand. If it were any of my friends, I'd cover their hand with mine, but Edmund is human, and we're not close.

"I'm sorry you have a creepy merman chasing you around." He offers me a half-hearted smile as he sobers, laughter dying away.

Footsteps sound, echoing off the walls of the room. Edmund's eyes grow wide and his gaze darts to the pool.

I jump off the wall, splashing as quietly as possible into the water just before his father rounds the corner.

Edmund is on his feet, not giving his father any reason to find grievances with his son. The king frowns at us, raising an eyebrow, but given the distance between his son and me, he can't say anything.

I watch him warily, waiting to see what he wants. He nods for his son to leave, taking a place in front of me. He widens his stance, placing his feet so far apart that they match the distance between his shoulders—it's so strange to think of having feet that separate instead of one tail.

Edmund slowly leaves, watching over the wall as long as he can. I listen to the footsteps as they go, but I don't think he makes it all the way out—I think he's paused to listen. His father doesn't notice.

"So, Princess Celena. I need some answers from you. So far, we have not been successful in gaining any insight from you or your friends. We've tried convincing each of you individually, but now I think it's time to switch our tactics."

He looks down at me. The king's hands are clasped behind his back—something that appears to be trained into the royal males. He looks remarkably like a stern version of Jarek, the softness of his features fading away as he studies me with a harsh gaze. It's as unnerving as it is captivating.

"I want to know how sireny works. My son will

continue to speak with you in his own way, but if you don't tell *him*, you'll have to tell me." He pulls his hands in front of him, crossing his arms across his chest. Bending his arm at the elbow, he lifts one hand to his face to stroke his chin. "I'm not unreasonable, but this *is* your last chance. If you don't tell us by tomorrow, I'll take matters into my own hands.

"Perhaps your friends won't talk when we torture them but based on what I've seen of you, *you* will speak to me if I hurt *them*. You're strong when it comes to handling things yourselves, *mermaid*, but your weakness is your collection and has been since Gaspar's time... And I know better than to hurt a princess when I have other available options.

"Tomorrow, you will give us an answer, or I'll start ripping your mermen to pieces in front of you, starting with the blue-haired one. Do you really want to be left alone with the other?" His eyes spark as he speaks. "Think about it, Princess. Their lives depend on your answers. Cooperate, and the three of you can live your days out here. We'll take care of you here, but those are your only two options. Choose wisely."

He tosses something at me. It slaps against my chest before falling into the water. A dark blue scale sinks back and forth in the water until I reach out and snatch it in my hand—Merrick's scale.

He nods sharply to me once before sauntering away.

"By tomorrow."

I swallow, waiting until he and the guards have all filed out of the room before I sink back down into the water. I can hear the king and his son arguing over the wall once he reaches the entrance where Edmund has been waiting for him. Their voices fade quickly.

Tears prick at my eyes—I have no doubt the king's threats are serious, but I don't have the answers he's looking for, which means I only have until morning to get us out of here or he's going to go after Merrick again.

I know he and his son won't hurt me anytime soon—they think I have answers—but I can't survive watching them pick Merrick apart piece by piece.

"Well?" Merrick says when I return. My tail curls under me as fear creeps into my body.

"Merrick, we have to get out—*tonight*."

CHAPTER 8

"WHAT HAPPENED?" MERRICK GAPES AT ME, LOOKING LIKE he wants to rush to my side. Instead, he lets me swim to him.

"They've given us a deadline. I have to tell them what makes our sireny work or they're going to start the torture again."

"We've been through this before—"

"No, you don't understand," I cut him off. "They're not torturing *us*. They're torturing *you* in front of me so that I'll talk—they already know we won't talk to save *ourselves*."

"They won't be back tonight," Dylana shakes her head.

"I can take it," Merrick announces. "It will be fine, we'll just survive it until that point. Caspian and Llyr will come back and break us out, and we'll escape."

"And what if you die before that point?" I snap.

"Then you two will escape," Merrick says matter-of-factly. "Celena, let's not be ridiculous here. This is going to happen—we just have to be prepared for it. It will all work out."

"*That's* not being ridiculous?" Dylana chides. "You're just going to *swim into this?*"

"No, I'm going to go up there and fight them, but if it means Celena gets out, then I'm fine with it."

"You understand," Dylana says calmly before I can, "that *she's* better at this game than you are—*miraculous, I know*, but she is—and Celena will find a way to take it *for* you, don't you?"

Her hands are on her hips when Merrick turns around to face her. She's right, of course, but he doesn't like it. He keeps his frustration checked—as he's been trained to do.

"I'm sending the guards to find Keone and the others." Natale sounds upset—something I rarely see from her when she's not pretending to be meek. Even before she revealed her training to us, I rarely saw her as anything but even-tempered. She darts down the tunnel.

"We don't have long until it gets dark," Dylana takes charge. "If we can get you out while it's still dark, that's probably our best bet."

She squints when she notices I'm holding something in my hand. I open it to reveal the scale. Her face goes pale when she recognizes what it is, then immediately swings to Merrick as he realizes it came from his tail.

"Oh, Merrick," she breathes.

"I'm fine, Dylana, really," he insists. I hand the scale to him, and he examines it before dropping it, shrugging. Dylana catches my frown and nods slightly, indicating that she'll pick it up when he isn't looking as it twists in the water through the bars, resting gently to the side. It's strange, but it seems wrong to just let the scale float away.

We spend the next hour strategizing our escape.

Through the window in the ceiling, the moon looks orange, not too far off of the same color of the starfish that crawled into the pool earlier today. The creature is resting in the corner of the pool now, basking in the glow of the moon, high in the sky.

Clouds move across the sky—dark black like the night itself—covering the moon as if it were one of the bars blocking us from the outside world. They shift in the sky, blowing with the wind as they cover and reveal our light source. It glitters through the rippling water on the surface.

I dive back down, assured that there are no humans in the room above watching us. They have no reason to think we may be escaping in the middle of the night—as long as we remain quiet and under the water, they shouldn't catch us.

We all took turns sleeping early in the evening to make sure we were ready for our escape. I didn't sleep much, but knowing my friends were watching out for me, I rested on the ocean floor long enough to feel a little better.

"It's still clear," I inform everyone as I join them again.

"I think this is attached properly," Keone mumbles. He had returned before the others with two of the guards carrying chains from The Ropes—the others were still digging out supplies when they left, but the three mermen raced back to start setting up once Natale's charges found them and told them to hurry.

He tugs on the chains to see if they'll hold. Dylana and Natale swim over quickly, helping him test it.

"Don't pull yet," Merrick warns. "We don't want you to get strained before the others arrive to help—we only get one shot at this."

"They should be here soon—they weren't that far behind," Keone adds. "Now, we just have to hope this thing works."

Our goal is to bend one of the bars far enough that we can squeeze through. I'll go through first because I'm smaller than the mermen, and help pull once I'm on the other side. Merrick and Phorcys are about the same size, so they both should be able to make it through once we bend it far enough.

The tunnel glows a deep blue color, casting everything in a layer of bioluminescent glow that's much deeper than it is during the day when light filters down from the surface. It's comforting, but at the same time makes it a bit harder to see what we're doing.

Dylana ditched her crown of shells for a smaller one with fearsome broken pieces much like mine. It was a wise choice, considering what we're swimming into once we make our escape.

"I know everyone left for Scylla, but are they still there or are they moving?" I ask, pushing my floating hair behind me. In the blue light, it barely looks pink.

"They're pausing at Scylla to decide what to do. If they leave, mother will have left signs for us in several locations so we know where to find them," Dylana replies. "If we get separated, just race for Scylla, and we'll all meet up there."

We've always had predetermined meeting spots in case any of our operations ever went sideways, so the group already knows where to check. I'm positive Natale and Keone know where our meeting places are from observing us so closely over the years in secret. Phorcys has no way of knowing, and Dylana doesn't tell him... neither do I. I'm sure the group from Ambra will either stay with one of us or head back to Ambra if we get divided—I'm just grateful they've helped as much as they have.

"Princess," one of the mermen addresses Dylana. She turns as he offers his report. "There are a number of places we can hide in if we need to during the escape. One has a tunnel straight through it that we can use to confuse them."

It's probably the one Merrick, Caspian, and our small team used to get around the sirens on our way here. It's a smart plan.

"They're here!" another merman shouts from the far end of the tunnel. Moving back, he reveals the tiniest hint of light, but it's quickly swallowed up as Caspian and the others rush in.

Chains drag along the ocean floor, but they're also carrying other things too. I can't make out any of the details until they get closer. It looks like some of them are carrying poles, while others have chains and ropes.

"We found this," Casp informs us as he drags part of a large metal rod behind him. Llyr holds the far end, struggling to keep it up. Natale swims over, grabbing the middle in an effort to help support it. "If the chains don't work, we can try to push it with this."

It makes sense—if we push the rod between the bars and push on it, it should make the bar pop out in the middle, bending it in half like that time we found that sunken ship and couldn't get one of the doors open.

When we used part of a railing we found as leverage and pushed against it, the door flung open, and we were able to go inside to explore—we didn't find anything, but at least we knew the room was empty.

They quickly wrap more chains around the bar we've chosen to try to bend. Llyr arranges the group in order, instructing them which chains to hold and where to float in the lineup.

"We're going to count down and all pull at the same time. Merrick will tell us when to stop, so be listening for his instructions. We'll try this several times before stopping to check on our progress at which point, we'll reevaluate what we're doing if we need to in case we need to try another strategy," Llyr continues. "Take a minute and get ready, we're going to start momentarily."

He swims over to us smarmily, a wide half grin on his face.

"So, princess, when this is all over, this makes me your hero, right?" He grins at me before winking at Merrick. "Careful, Merrick, she's going to swim off with me when this is all over."

"Mhmm, I'm sure," Merrick jokes. "Maybe you should save the talk until *after* you get us out of here."

"Yeah, yeah, brother." Llyr waves as he turns away. "Take the lead."

Merrick and Llyr may not be actual brothers, but

they're as close as Caspian and I have ever been. It's sweet to watch…in a sickening way.

The collection picks up the chains all connected to the bars in a similar location. Phorcys and Merrick watch over the chains to ensure none of them slip too high or too low once the collection starts pulling.

We had considered attaching a chain to the bar next to it so that we could pull from the inside, creating a larger gap in a faster time frame, but none of the three of us inside the pool are in any condition to be doing the heavy lifting required to bend a metal bar in half. Still, a chain rests on the sand on the second bar, just in case.

Merrick gives the order, and the collection pulls, straining against the chains. Their tails thrashing in the water create waves that stretch out to me after a moment, pulsing against my body. Several of them grunt as they pull, but the bar doesn't move.

"Stop," Merrick commands, holding out his hand as if they were watching him instead of facing away as they pull.

The group pauses, letting the chains rest in their hands. The pulsing water fades around me as I inspect the bar from two lengths away—it doesn't appear to have dented it at all.

"Ready?" Merrick asks after a moment, indicating that they should prepare themselves to pull again. "Again."

The group pulls, and I wish on the three starfish

inside the pool that it works this time. The moon casts a strange orange glow in the water that mixes with the blue from the tunnel in an unsettling way while my friends fight for my freedom.

This time, the bar starts moving.

It's not enough to escape, but there's a visible bend in the bar, giving us all the hope we need to keep going. I nearly start cheering the collection on when I hear a slap on the water above me.

Merrick quickly stops everyone as we all whip around to listen. The slap sounds again.

"Did they catch us?" Dylana squeaks.

We wait in silence to see if the splash would happen again or if it was a fluke. After a moment, another splash sounds, this one gentler.

"I'll go." I start swimming.

"Celena, no!" everyone gasps behind me.

"One of us has to distract them, or they'll *definitely* know something is wrong. I'll be fine."

'It's the middle of the night—whatever this is, it can't be good," Merrick growls. "I'm going with you."

"No, you need to stay here and help them," I refuse to let him join me. "Just pay attention in case I signal you. If I wave, that means to hurry up. If I place my hand flat, that means to standby, and if I do nothing, then it's okay. Just *watch.*"

Without waiting, I rush to the surface, slowing only

when I can tell who is on the other side of the water. Edmund stands along the side of the pool, waiting for me.

"You *are* up," he murmurs as I surface.

"I wasn't," I pretend to yawn, slipping into an actual yawn. "What did you need?"

"Oh." He frowns. "I'm sorry, I didn't mean to wake you."

'It's fine, what do you need?"

"I couldn't sleep," he admits. "I thought we could talk."

Glancing around, I realize he's alone—there are no guards here.

He either trusts me, or they're hiding somewhere.

"Do you want to sit with me?" He takes a seat and pats the wall next to him.

"I think I'll stay down here," I reply softly. "It's too cool for me to be out right now."

He nods, glancing around as if he's just noticing it's cooler than it was during the day. Edmund turns a bit to get more comfortable.

I move my hand in the water, leaving my palm out flat so that my friends know to wait a moment.

"I've been thinking," Edmund starts, sounding reluctant. He dives forward, "It's different here than I expected. A lot of it is what Jarek used to tell us, but it's so much more than that here.

"The people are incredible, and they work so hard, but

they're also in such danger. The towns are magnificent, and I see how easily this place could be incredible again if we allowed people back into the area—I mean beyond the sailor's families.

"I want to fix this place—I want Antaire to be prestigious once again. I want to restore it to its former glory. We're a kingdom built on exports from the sea, and yet we live nowhere near it—it's shameful. The other kingdoms look down on us for fearing the sea. I don't want that under my rule."

"Why are you telling me all this?"

Maybe I *should* have taken a seat on the wall with him, I could have put a hand on his knee and convinced him to tell me everything, one friend to another. The water separates us too much, creating a wall between us. I swim closer.

"I don't know why, Celena, but I think I actually trust you. I think you're either the best actress in the world, or you genuinely just want to leave and not hurt my people.

"I know my father will never acquiesce to a human-mer treaty again, but I think he's wrong. I think we need it and I think you and I are going to be the only ones that can make that happen." He looks desperately at me as if I control the fate of his entire world and what I say next will cast him as the greatest king Antaire has ever known, or banish him into oblivion.

"How can that happen when your father is in charge?

Even if you and I wanted to form an alliance, we'll both be old enough to have grandchildren by the time you take over as king."

"I don't know, but I think we need to try. I heard stories of more attacks today—I don't want my men to die any longer. If what you say is true, you don't want this war either. We need an agreement in place, and we need our leadership to enforce it with harsh consequences for anyone on either side that disobeys.

"We don't have to be friends, we just have to have rules and boundaries. It doesn't have to be like before."

I'm not sure it ever *could* be like before—humans and mer being friendly with one another. Though, I'd almost like to try with Edmund.

For a moment, I wonder if there's an easy way to murder the king and install Edmund as Antaire's official ruler early. I blink, shaking my head just slightly as I banish that idea from my mind.

I pull my hand up, releasing them from worrying about me.

"So you want the two of us to create a treaty that might not ever go into effect?"

"I do."

"You know I'm not a reigning royal, right? I don't have that kind of power." I swim closer to him, setting a hand on the wall.

"But your cousin is the queen, you have her ear, don't you? Wouldn't she listen to you?"

"She'll listen to me, but I don't know if this will work."

"Can we try? I just want to try." He sounds so sad as he speaks. "I just want this to be over, and this is the only way I see how. Don't you think you and I could get along, Celena? Outside of these walls when you're free, can't we try to be friends?"

"You were rather insistent on offering to torture me until just now…"

"Aila would do this," Edmund retorts, challenging me to make a choice.

My great-great grandmother had risked her life multiple times to save the human-mer treaty. She fought against her own cousin—*someone she adored*—to protect the alliance. Aila did everything in her power to save Prince Jarek and rescue him from her cousin, and it cost her the friendship that she held dearest to her outside her family. Now, a century later, I have the opportunity to restore that alliance.

One way or another, we're escaping tonight, but once we get out, it would be wise to keep Edmund on our side. Perhaps one day the treaty could be real—there's no telling what the future holds.

I take a deep breath and launch myself out of the water to sit on the wall beside him. He looks surprised but attempts to keep his composure as I drip on the wall, the water traveling over to where he sits.

"How do we do this?" I whisper. I'm nervous—I don't know what this means for our future, but I think I trust that he means what he says and that he actually wants a treaty.

"We need to discuss the terms. Then you take it to your queen, and I'll take it to my king."

"How do you expect me to do that?"

"I'll free you, Celena. I'll get you out."

I suck in a breath—he's offering to free me….but is he offering to free us *all*?

"Merrick?"

"I'll try," he murmurs, reaching out to take my hand. "This is bigger than the both of us, Celena. I'll do my best, but we're talking about protecting entire kingdoms here."

"No, we're talking about creating a treaty that may not ever come to fruition—what do you think will happen when your father discovers I'm gone?"

"He won't kill the only mer he has left." He purses his lips.

"Maybe not, but what else will he do to them?"

"He wants to show you off, Celena. If he doesn't have the pretty one, he'll need to keep the other two looking decent."

"Or maybe he'll want to prove how fearsome they are with their scars."

"This is getting us nowhere, Celena." He releases my hand, aggravated.

"Fine, let's work on the treaty," I agree, knowing it won't matter anyway—we're freeing ourselves. "We can talk about how to get us out of here later."

In the orange moonlight, his sandy-colored hair looks almost red. I imagine my pink hair has taken on an orange tone as well, but he doesn't say anything. He holds a hand out, waiting for me to put mine in his as an agreement.

I reach out, touching his hand. It's warm against mine and feels almost as comfortable as holding Llyr's hand when we occasionally have deep conversations together. Humans are less comfortable holding hands than mer, so I know this is important to Edmund.

"I promise, I'll get you out of here, and I'll do everything I can to get your friends out too. I'm not sure how yet, but I will."

"I believe you," I squeeze his hand to let him know I'm on his side—even though I don't need his help to escape.

"I am going to do everything in my power to support the mer and form this alliance. I don't want to live in a world where we're surrounded by unnecessary war. We'll undo what Jarek and Persephone did. We'll work together and fix all of this."

"What is *this*?" the king gasps, a mere length away from us. Edmund and I jump, and I nearly topple off the wall into the water—only his hand on mine keeps me in place. I don't know how the king snuck up on us, but he managed to overhear our conversation.

"You sirened him," the king whispers, accusing me.

"No," I gasp back, pulling my hand from Edmund's.

"No!" Edmund shouts, standing to his feet.

"You sirened my son, you sea witch!" The king's shrieks alert the guards by the stairs and they rush over to assist.

"She didn't, Father," Edmund shouts, hand between the king and me as he tries to block part of his father's wrath. "We want to create a new treaty between the mer and the humans—we want to end this."

"She tricked you into saying these things, son." The king looks aghast. "You don't know what you're talking about because she whispered these thoughts into your mind. This isn't truly how you feel!"

"It *is* though," Edmund argues. I can barely turn to see both of them fight. "Antaire is a glorious kingdom, but we've been exiled from the sea—the source of our wealth and power. We need access to it again! The only way is with a new treaty. It doesn't have to be like the last one, but it needs to exist!"

The guards close in, spears ready. I leap off the wall into the water to protect myself. I hear Edmund call my name before I slam into the water.

Unable to keep myself above the surface, I bob under

the water just long enough to see Dylana watching me with a terrified look on her face as Merrick and Phorcys try to pull the bars open from our side of the divider. The bars are wider now, but still not enough to fit a mer through them.

"Hurry!" I shout to them, rising above the water once more to distract the guards. When I surface, the king is trying to wrestle his son away from the water.

"Get her!" the king shouts, directing the men to capture me. I swim back in the water, putting more distance between us—if they enter the water now, they can still drag us out, but if I can stall and give them more time to open the bars, we have a chance.

"Celena, get down," Edmund calls, trying to get me to dive under the surface where his men can't reach me. He waves his arm furiously as his father turns bright red even under the orange light of the moon.

A loud splash to my left makes me turn. Several more follow—the guards are in the water, spears in hand. They look nervous, but not nearly as frightened as the men who usually show up in this room. Their fear of their king must be great to convince them to jump in after me.

"Celena!" Edmund calls, not understanding why I won't leave.

I start shouting, hoping to draw the men's attention. I back up toward the far wall, knowing I can draw them away, and then dive under the water and swim beneath them faster than they can track my movements.

"Sire!" one of the guards in the water shouts, "The mermen are trying to escape!"

A shadow crosses over Edmund's face for a moment, but he doesn't hold it against me that I'm trying to escape. He nods briefly, telling me that it's okay.

Brilliantly, Edmund flings himself into the water, taking his father with him. In sheer panic, the king releases his son as the guards swim to save their king. The prince makes his way to me, swimming across the surface.

"I want to stay here, Celena, and I want to stay in peace. I want this war over. My father might not think there can ever be a treaty again, but I do. Meet me at the cave. Go!"

He turns his back on me as he pushes me under the water.

I dive for the exit, but it's not open yet.

The tunnel is still blocked, though there's a definite opening in the bars. Caspian and Llyr have forced the metal rod between the bars, seeing the commotion, and as many strong mermen as possible are pushing on it, forcing it apart. It moves with a loud groan every time they throw themselves against it.

"Hurry!" I scream, racing toward them.

As soon as I reach Merrick, he pushes me at the opening, demanding I try to fit through. Unable to fit, I pull back.

"Look out!" Phorcys shouts, pulling Merrick back.

Merrick whips around to face him as a spear lands between us.

Several of the guards drop their spear in the water, and they float down to us. Others intentionally throw their spears, but the water slows their decent, allowing us to easily avoid them.

While Caspian and the others try to break the bars on our prison, we quickly collect the weapons, knowing we'll need them later. I pass the extras through to Dylana and Natale who distribute them on the other side of the bars.

Turning, I hold my spear out, ready to attack. Two of the guards dive under the water, swimming toward us. The king must have ordered his men to attack us because the entire group turns tentatively before taking a gulp of air and diving below the surface. Some have knives in their hands, others rope, though some retained their spears.

I prepare for battle.

Unsurprisingly, the king and Edmund are no longer in the water.

Llyr yells as one final push bends the bar in half behind us. Caspian screams for us to move.

Before I can turn, Merrick grabs my tail and pulls me

backward, much rougher than our usual fighting tactics. I keep my spear up as he drags me through the water, waiting to take out any human that gets too close.

Phorcys pushes his way through behind me and the entire collection floods out of the tunnel. Merrick doesn't let go until we're in the open waters—it surrounds me like a whale swallowing krill.

I've never felt as free as right now, but I don't have time to really experience it—we're swimming for our lives.

CHAPTER 9

THE ORANGE LIGHT OF THE MOON SHIFTS AWAY INTO THE muted colors of early morning. Schools of fish float gracefully by, but their colors nearly blend with the dark waters.

Merrick and Caspian cling to me, both wrapping an arm around my waist as we swim as quickly as we can. Llyr and Keone keep an eye on Phorcys, Dylana and Natale taking a place behind them in case he tries something stupid, and they need to assist the boys to stop him, though I doubt he will.

Once we're a safe distance away, I quietly tell my brother and my boyfriend what happened.

"It doesn't matter, we're leaving," Caspian informs me.

"Edmund told me to meet him in the cave."

"Which cave? He didn't give you any specifics?" Merrick asks, a bit more open-minded.

"I assume he means *the* cave," I reply. "The one where Persephone sirened Jarek."

"And Aila saved him," Caspian adds. "You're still not going. We need to get as far from here as possible.

"This is our only chance at overcoming this, we can't swim away from this opportunity. Edmund helped me escape—I believe he wants this treaty to work. Even if we can't make it happen while the king is alive, someday, Edmund will be in power.

"We don't ever have to go near the humans again, but now even if we stumble upon them, they won't be able to hurt us for fear of punishment from their king."

"And what if they secretly kill us and the prince doesn't find out?" Caspian makes a good point.

"I don't know, but it will at least stop *some* of the murders," I point out.

We duck under a sea turtle that obviously doesn't care that we're in the ocean with it. My hair slaps against its underside as we move to avoid hitting it.

"They're launching boats," one of the mermen from Ambra says, ducking back under the water.

"This is our only chance to go back," I murmur.

I stop in the water, nearly causing some of the mer to collide with each other to avoid swimming into me. I mumble an apology as I drop back to Dylana. Regardless of what the boys say, it's her choice.

Words tumble out of my mouth as I explain, stating my case. After a moment, she slows.

"We go back," she announces to everyone's shock. "We have a chance at a treaty. I can sign it—we can end this war now. We go back."

She looks around the group as they wait for directions.

"You don't have to stay, but Celena and I are."

"We stay," Llyr says, taking the lead to support us.

"We stay," Caspian quickly adds, refusing to leave my side. The rest of the group echoes my brother. Phorcys grinds his teeth but doesn't say anything, nodding briefly when I make eye contact with him.

"Where do we go?" Dylana turns to me, knowing of everyone here, I know the direction of the cave from Aila's stories.

I point, and we all turn to swim back, hovering as low to the ocean floor as possible. We stay as close to the kelp forests and caves as possible, hiding any way that we can.

"I trust her on this," Dylana whispers when Caspian swims up next to us. "If she got through to the prince, we have to try. If there's a treaty in place, it might just save us. You know that if there isn't, the humans won't stop until we're all dead and they control the seas."

We pause inside a cave, letting Llyr ensure there are no ships nearby in the dark colors of the early morning water. After a moment, he waves us forward, and we dart out, swimming to the next momentary shelter.

We continue forward, darting around rocks and broken ship pieces on the ocean floor. Carefully, we avoid the fishing nets the humans had left when the siren attacks started.

Swimming low in a bed of seaweed, we glide over the ocean floor toward the cave. The seaweed tickles my skin, but I don't have time to care. I brush it away from me with my hands as I flick my tail to swim forward.

We don't see the net off to the side, so when one of the mermaids swims into it, her scream terrifies us. She pulls back, attempting to untangle herself, but the humans pull her up quickly.

The abandoned fishing net must have caught on something near the surface for the humans to have so easily found it—there's no way they could have put this in the water without us seeing it as we approached, so it must have already been here. Their ship is so far away, it's barely noticeable on the water, but in the distance, if I look hard, I can see the outline of the boat floating against the waves.

They drag the Ambraian mermaid across the ocean. She claws at the ground as she is forced over it, bumping into the sand over and over as they haul her in. Her fingers scrape at the loose sand, looking for anything to hold onto.

Eventually, she grasps a shell, but the quick motion of the moving net knocks it out of her hand. She yells, desperate as it topples away.

We push as hard as we can, trying to reach the girl in time. With weapons ready, we close in on her, ready to cut her free. She catches a shell in her hand once more, this time holding tight enough to keep it in place. She hacks at the ropes as Llyr and Caspian reach her.

They slice into the net, ripping it open. She forces her way out as the three mer are lifted high into the water. The boys quickly check to make sure she is free of the net and for an instant, I flash back to the start of all this— when a siren mermaid got caught in the human nets outside the reef barrier protecting Scylla, and I met Tarni, Roni, and Tiko for the first time as they mourned their dead friend—how far we've come in a month.

The mermaid rushes into the arms of her collection, and they comfort her, helping her swim with an injured tail. It's not too bad, but she'll be sore for a while. She tucks her blue hair behind her ear as she holds on to Larinia.

Once the humans pull the net up, they'll see what happened and know they've found us—we have to move.

We quickly follow Merrick—he's swimming surprisingly fast for all of his injuries—and dart low to the ground again, this time swimming two at a time to avoid spreading out.

The ocean is a blur as we swim, my mind drifting ahead to the cave, wondering what I'll find. I don't even know if Edmund will be there.

What if he couldn't escape his father? What if the king tortures the meeting location from his son, or worse—he guesses on his own?

I can't let anyone go into the cave with me until I'm sure it's safe. One of the boys can wait at the entrance, but it's illogical to have them swim in with me.

I'm not even sure what the cave looks like. I know Aila said there was a ledge where Jarek stood, and that the cave was deep, but the stories she told were always more about the events than the setting—of course, they could have eroded over time until we just had the main events of the story, but I have a feeling she never described it much to begin with.

We move sideways, swimming in a large arch to reach our destination in an effort to avoid the areas they might think of to check. Dylana and Natale take places by my sides, edging Merrick and Caspian out so we can talk.

"I know you're going to tell me you want to go in alone, but I have to be there to negotiate this treaty," Dylana whispers.

"You two aren't going in there without me," Natale snaps. "We do this together."

"Aila, Kailania, and Ebba back together again?" I smirk, trying to make light of the situation.

"If one of you suggests finding Tarni, I'll give you to the humans myself," Natale sneers, but we know she's joking. I'm still not used to this new version of her.

"She's not really of Chantay's blood—we can skip her on this little adventure," I reply. "But you're still not going in with me."

The two argue with me, insisting on joining me inside the cave with Edmund.

"Merrick will guard the cave—or Caspian or Llyr—and I'll go in alone. If it's safe, *then* you can come in with me." I look at Dylana, purposely avoiding Natale. I'd prefer she stay outside with the others. Neither of her demeanors will be helpful during the negotiations.

"I need your help anyway, Natale," Keone swims up next to us, invading our private conversation. "While the guys are keeping them safe, you and I need to make sure the humans don't find them."

I imagine Natale wouldn't say no to an excuse to get near the humans—if there's an altercation, she could hurt them for what they did to her mother and no one would hold her accountable for striking out at them. She turns to her boyfriend, and they argue quietly. Her body language changes when he brings up that very point, and she changes her mind.

Now the only challenge will be convincing the mermen to let me go in alone. Merrick glances over at me around Dylana. We make eye contact and I know he knows what I'm about to pull on him—he's always been able to read me.

We slow, feeling confident that we're far enough away that the humans won't know where we went. Unfortunately, it also means we have a long way to go to get back to the cave. Turning, we start our path back toward Jarek's cave.

"That's it?" Caspian asks as we stare from inside a seaweed bed. The water is cooler as a cold current moves through the ocean.

"Looks like it," Dylana mutters. "Celena?"

"That's it," I reply, remembering how my great-great-grandmother described the cave. My great-great-grandfather, Troy, had waited outside with her until she discovered that Persephone was sirening the prince over a century ago—I'm staring at the rock where he had hidden himself out of sight.

Aila may have received all of the credit for rescuing Jarek, but Troy was essential in the success of that day. If he hadn't been there for Aila, she never would have been able to save the prince. Troy never took any of the praise though—he always deferred to Aila. From the stories I've heard, they were the couple all mer should aspire to be.

I wonder if my great-great-grandparents would be proud of me as I try to fix the treaty they worked to protect. I like to think they would be.

"You must be in awe," Caspian smirks next to me. "I'm sure Cor will have a fit when she hears about this."

"Probably," I joke with my twin. "Maybe we should skip over this part when we tell her later."

"Talking about how Coralie is going to hold this against you for the rest of your life?" Merrick swims up next to us, putting a hand on the small of my back. It's amazing that he doesn't flinch when he brushes over the raised welts the jellyfish left—I'm sure they don't feel pleasant—it's a good thing those are starting to heal. "I have a feeling Aila wasn't decked out in shoulder armor when she was here though."

He winks flirtatiously at me when I turn to face him.

"You know our sister well." I grin at him. "And maybe I'm more fierce than Aila."

"Aila saved *a nation*—you're saving *several*." Caspian snorts at Merrick's response, but his eyes are serious as he nods his agreement to me quietly.

I take a deep breath, staring at the outside of the cave.

"Let's go," Merrick says before I can ask if he's ready.

Caspian and I traded weapons—he took my spear while I have his trident. I clutch it in my hands as Merrick and I head for the cave. If Edmund is there and brought people with him, I'll have to be prepared to fight. I know better than to swim into this naively. If this is a trap, then it's likely there will be nets or some kind of trap door like the one Morgen used in the palace in Scylla to trap the sirens. I'll have to watch for those as I enter.

We pause outside of the cave entrance. I touch the wall, letting my fingers dance over the bumpy rocks. A slight blue glow filters out, but I only spot it because I already know what to expect inside the cave.

Merrick peeks around the cave entrance, and I take a place just below him in the water, looking around the rock wall as well. When we don't see anything, I covertly turn my head to Merrick, knowing my hair is hiding us, and brush my lips against his. He moans softly, not expecting the display of affection. He grins, opening his eyes as he motions me into the cave, promising he'll be watching.

The inside of the cave is magical. Streaks of light are embedded in the walls, glowing a magnificent blue color. The light from the spores sparkles off of the water and reflect back onto the walls. It's almost as magical as the Scur Caverns Merrick showed me when we were in Metten—also a favorite of the royals from a century ago.

If Edmund doesn't show up anytime soon, I wouldn't be opposed to calling Merrick in for a few moments alone.

I didn't see any nets as I swam in, but I turn to check behind me to ensure there is no trap door waiting to cut me off from the world. When I find nothing, I look to the ledge.

"Prince Edmund?" I call out just above a whisper. Placing a hand on the ledge, I flick my tail just enough to raise myself out of the water a little to get a better view.

Nothing stirs in the cave except the shifting blue glow from the walls. I call out again, slightly louder but don't expect much. As I turn, something shuffles beyond the cavern walls on the far side of the ledge.

A human peeks out from around the wall of a cave and panic seizes my chest. I start to dive into the water, but a man's voice stops me.

"It's her."

"Celena," Edmund calls out from behind the rocks. He quickly appears around his servant, moving toward the ledge. His eyes scan the water, looking for signs of trouble. "I'm here alone."

He turns back to his servant, waving him in. Surprisingly, the servant doesn't have anything blocking his ears from me. The man clasps his hands in front of him and waits for directions—he looks like one of the humans that protected the prince in the palace, but there were so many of them that I can't be sure. He watches me carefully as I swim halfway between where I was and the ledge.

"Did you make it out okay?" Edmund asks. I nod.

"We're all relatively safe. How did you escape?"

"My father has the palace on lockdown, but I've read Grandfather Jarek's journals from after he left the palace —he had maps of everything. We took one of the secret entrances—I doubt he even knows we're gone. To be fair, he's a bit busy hunting you."

"We can't stay long, sire," the servant says.

"I know, Jackson." Edmund never takes his eyes off me.

"I have to get the princess," I blurt out, surprising even myself.

"What?"

"The princess... I have to get her to do this treaty with you."

"I thought *you and I* were creating the treaty," Edmund comments, frowning.

I duck low in the water, preparing to signal for Dylana to join us.

"I'll be here, but she has to be the one to work it out with you."

"She's *here?*" he yelps. "I thought she left."

"Her mother did," I reply. "Dylana stayed to save us."

Edmund looks impressed by her loyalty as I slide under the water. Merrick is watching me, not taking his eyes off of me.

"He's here. Get Dylana."

Merrick refuses to turn until he's sure I'm staying under the water and not returning to the surface. He leans around the edge of the cave entrance, motioning Dylana to join us. She swims quickly from the seaweed bed the rest of the collection is hiding in.

"Edmund is here with one of his servants. They're waiting for us. His father doesn't know he's gone, so we need to be as quick as possible. I'll back up whatever you want, cousin," I mumble quickly. She nods, following me to the surface.

"Wow, this is beautiful," she murmurs before we surface.

Out in the air, Dylana looks radiant as she hovers out of the water. She looks regal with shoulders back, her deep pink hair flowing down her back. Her shoulder armor sparkles under the blue bioluminescent glow of the cave. Edmund and Jackson quietly gasp when they see her.

"Princess," he regards her solemnly.

"Prince Edmund, my cousin tells me you want to make a new alliance with the mer." Dylana sounds remarkably like her mother as she addresses the human prince.

"I do. What should I call you?"

"My name is Dylana. I am the daughter of Marilla,

Queen of Scylla, Metten, and the surrounding kingdoms. I will speak on her behalf today."

"You're sure your mother will be okay with this?" Edmund asks nervously. He twists his hands together, watching us.

"Yes, my mother trusts my judgment, and we both would like for this war to end," Dylana says confidently. She's far more self-assured than Edmund. "What would you like to discuss?"

"Terms for a truce," Edmund explains. "Terms for a future alliance, and rules and consequences should someone break the terms we will set forth to our people…umm, mer. Mer and people."

I quietly will Edmund to calm down—I've never seen him so nervous, even when he first captured me. He glances at me and nods slightly, shifting back on his feet to steady himself. He redirects his gaze to Dylana.

"Terms for the truce first?" Dylana asks. "I say we call for an immediate end to the fight. My collection has already left and does not plan on returning to the area, so that would mean your humans would only be responsible for not seeking us out."

"Agreed, but I should let you know that I don't have my father's blessing for this yet."

"I understand. This is an agreement between you and the mer collection. If your father does not abide by this, we won't hold his actions against you *once* you take power. Until then, if your father attempts to attack the mer, we can not be held to the terms of this agreement if we need to protect ourselves, but we vow not to actively come after the humans."

"I appreciate your deference. I know this isn't an ideal situation, but I promise I'll do my best."

"I've explained the situation to my cousin, Edmund. She knows why you're doing this," I add.

I allow Dylana and Edmund to discuss terms, waiting patiently. On occasion, I make comments, but I spend most of my time focused on the cave itself. I memorize every inch of it—both in case I end up back here *and* in case I never see it again.

Jackson watches me intently, but his attention is divided between Dylana and me. I'm sure it's mesmerizing watching two pink-haired mermaids float in a cave, but his head is bobbing back and forth between us so much that I'm starting to get stressed out—I wish he would hold still.

An hour goes by as they work out details, compromising where they must, arguing over other things. I dip my face in the water once in a while to let Merrick know that things are going well—he watches from the entrance, quietly slipping a little closer each time I check on him.

They still have a long way to go, discussing what locations would be devoted to which group in an effort to avoid each other when shuffling sounds behind the prince and his servant. Panic is written all over Edmund's face as he turns.

He waves his hand to us, indicating that we should hide. Dylana and I duck under the water, swimming to the ledge so we can surface again, hidden by the rocks.

"Prince Edmund, we have orders to return you to the palace," someone addresses him formally. "You are to return immediately at which point you will be remanded to your chambers until you can be escorted back to the Winter Palace tomorrow."

"What?" Edmund sounds shocked. "I'm not going back to the Winter Palace—there's too much to be done here."

"Sire, your father has said you are not to return to the palace here again." The man's voice is hard and unrelenting. Edmund won't be able to convince him of anything. "You are to come with us at once. If you will not come on your own, the king has instructed us to take you back by force."

Dylana looks worried, but I'm furious—we've worked too hard and lost too much for this treaty to be destroyed.

"Jackson, I'm going to need you to trust me," Edmund says somewhere over our heads.

"Yes, sire," the servant replies. I can hear Edmund and

Jackson walking back, closer to the edge. It takes a moment, but then I realize what they're doing.

"We're here," I shout, letting him know that I understand what his plan is. Dylana looks horrified until she realizes what we're doing.

The prince and his servant splash into the water.

CHAPTER 10

"HOLD YOUR BREATH," I INSTRUCT AS I GRAB ONTO Jackson. Dylana wraps her arms around the prince, and we drag them under the water as the guards above shout, preparing to follow us.

Merrick's confusion is evident, but he immediately flips in the water to wave off the rest of the collection. He shouts that we have the humans and need to move.

Jackson's fingers claw into me in terror, bubbles escaping his lips as I drag him further down into the water. I hope Edmund isn't as rough as his servant, but unlike Jackson, Edmund knew what to expect.

Merrick whips back around, holding his trident out to the guards as they jump into the water—they're not nearly as fast as us, even as we carry humans through the water—so they're no real threat at the moment.

Dylana and I dip down through the entrance to the

cave, coming up on the open waters side. We flip our tails as quickly as possible, rushing toward the surface before the humans run out of air. They come up choking in the mid-day air.

"Jackson?" Edmund asks as soon as he can breath.

"I'm here, Edmund," he sputters, still clutching at me. "Are you all right?"

"I'm fine, friend. We have to get out of here." Edmund treads water on his own, spinning to look around at our surroundings. "There. There's a boat—they have to listen to me."

He starts swimming toward the large vessel, expecting us to follow.

"We can't go over there, Edmund," I remind him. "We can't be anywhere near them."

"I'm going to command the ship, and we'll finish this treaty," he replies.

"You think they're just going to listen to you?" Dylana asks, glancing at the ship. "Those guards in the cave didn't listen—why will these men?"

"I'm the prince, Princess Dylana," Edmund retorts as he brushes his sandy-blond hair back with one hand. It drips in his face almost comically. "They don't know I'm not representing my father at this point, so they'll have to listen."

"And once you have this ship of humans, what then? We still can't go near it, it's too dangerous," I remind him.

"We'll think of something, but we can't stay in the water unprotected like this, Celena," he points out. "You stay here and just watch for my signal. I'll move the ship away from the rest, and we'll find a way to talk without the rest of the sailors finding out. Just keep watching Jackson or me, and one of us will direct you to the right place."

My heart stutters as he brings Jackson into this—I don't know him, and I certainly don't know where his alliances lie.

"I trust him," Edmund whispers, leaning closely so only I can hear him as his nose crashes into my hair. "He's loyal to me."

The two start to swim off as Dylana and I shrink back.

"We don't have a choice, do we?" Dylana asks.

"No, we don't. We have to finish putting this treaty into place."

The collection hovers below us in the water—I can feel Merrick's hand on the edge of my fins. Dylana nods, telling me it's okay to duck under the water to update the collection while she watches the humans above.

I stay just under the surface, still at Dylana's side as I inform them of what happened. Caspian and Llyr nod, looking grim.

"We have to follow them—we're so close to having a treaty everyone can agree with. We can't swim away now."

"We'll do what we can," Llyr says, "but we're also not risking your lives for this. The collection is already long gone—they'll be safe, we'll make sure of it—we just need to get back to them. This treaty is a good thing, but not if we have to die for it—we can survive without it."

He glances at Dylana's tail, and I know he's worried about her. Llyr has always been good about hiding his feelings, but I've always been equally as good at fishing for information.

"They're moving," Dylana drops down in the water. "We have to go."

Llyr volunteers to swim above the water before anyone else can, leaving the rest of the collection to trail behind him under the water. He guides us for several minutes until we get too close to other ships. Diving under the water, we risk getting closer to Edmund's boat so we don't lose it, swimming so close that if we sped up, we'd be directly under it.

"That's not right, is it?" Larina asks.

"I don't think so," Quillo answers her, putting a hand on her back.

I tip my head up to see what they're looking at and find a small rowboat moving away from the boat Edmund is commanding. The oars dip into the water, pushing the boat further away from the vessel.

"I'll go," Llyr announces, but Caspian's hand stops him.

"Let me," Casp says. "Your hair is a bit…noticeable in the light right now."

My twin hands me his spear to hold. Carefully, Caspian peeks out of the water, hovering just enough that his eyes are over the surface. He floats above the water for a few moments before sinking back down with us.

"It's the prince."

"We have to follow them," I reply instantly, changing our direction as the humans row away from the boat. I definitely don't mind escaping from that thing.

Edmund dips a hand into the water, wiggling his fingers under the surface—it looks like he can't quite reach into the water all the way. Eventually, he pulls it up, leaving it in the boat with him.

I dart ahead of the others, swimming up to the small rowboat. Intentionally staying on the opposite side as the large boat they just left, I slip carefully above the surface.

"I'm here." I hear both of them jump above me as I startle them. "Sorry."

"Get us out of here, Celena," Edmund requests. "Before they notice we're gone."

"They didn't see you steal a boat?" I can't believe that he could have possibly taken a boat and escaped without someone noticing.

"We might have thrown someone overboard to distract them," Jackson grumbles, obviously upset.

How did we miss a person in the water? Maybe we were too distracted by the rowboat.

"Do you have any rope in there?" I ask, putting my hand on the side of the rowboat.

Edmund looks around at the boat, moving random objects—apparently, the sailors were treating the rowboat as if it were made to be used as storage.

"Oh." He moves something. Edmund holds up a length of rope. "Yes, actually. Why?"

I reach for it, and he hands it to me. Working quickly, I tie a knot at one end and slip it over the front of their boat.

"We'll help pull you—it doesn't look like Jackson is going to last long at those oars." Jackson puffs his chest out, looking annoyed, but the way he's breathing tells me he needs a break. He clearly wasn't made for this kind of labor.

Under the water, I hand the rope off to Keone who takes the first shift pulling the humans across the sea. We swim quickly away from the sailors, hoping they don't take too much notice as the tiny rowboat skims across the surface of the water.

I don't bother surfacing for now—we're faster under the water. I'll check on the prince in a while. Dylana takes a place next to me, and we discuss what else the royals still need to work out.

Eventually, Edmund taps on the water, trying to get our attention.

"I really think we need to find a better way of doing that," I respond, coming out of the water.

"Well, for now, it's what we've got," Edmund doesn't look amused at my attempt at a joke. "Where are we going?"

"Somewhere safe." I grab hold of the boat, catching a ride like I sometimes do with the dolphins.

"Where, Celena?" He refuses to be dragged around without answers.

"We're going to Metten. Your father won't be able to find you there."

The prince pales.

The sun has shifted, leaning more toward late afternoon. It sparkles below the surface, casting long rays of light to sparkle on the ocean floor. I wish I were under the waves to see how the light dances with the colorful fish and sea life, but it's a sight I see every day, so it's more important to speak with Edmund. I've seen enough of Aila's world to keep me happy for now.

"You'll be safe in Metten," I promise. "We'll bring you right back here when we're done."

"We can't breathe underwater, Celena, how do you expect us to go to Metten?"

"We're not taking you to the palace, just to the area. We have borders set up so humans can't access the kingdom easily. If you weren't in this tiny boat, you wouldn't be able to reach the kingdom waters.

"Our plan is to bring you inside the barriers so we can finish the treaty. They won't be able to reach you there."

"Unless they come in on small boats too," Edmund points out.

"Would they really do that? They're pretty scared of the water."

"If my father orders them to, yes. Of course, he's not here and doesn't know what's going on yet, so I suppose we have some time."

"Should we perhaps get the princess up here to start talking this through while we're traveling?" Jackson suggests, clearly still annoyed at me.

I had considered having Dylana talk to the prince, but it's one thing to have *me* strain to stay above the water to have a conversation with the prince, but it's an entirely different thing to have Dylana struggle while also trying to negotiate.

"This isn't exactly easy, you know." I direct my comment at Jackson. "Swimming above the water is a lot of work."

"You're hanging on to the boat," he points out.

"It's still difficult, Jackson," Edmund comments, silencing his friend. "We can discuss the treaty when we arrive in Metten. You're welcome to stay up here and talk with us, Celena, but I won't force you to. If you'd like to sit in the boat with us, we can make room for you for a little while, but I won't hold it against you if you'd like to swim under the water."

Phorcys appears out of the water behind me, latching onto the boat. Edmund makes a face, unable to restrain himself in time. He winces, realizing his mistake but attempts to cover it over with contempt for the merman.

"What do you want?" Edmund asks coolly.

"I came to find out why Celena is still up here." He gives me an icy glare. "Your boyfriend is worried."

He's not—Merrick trusts my choices. It's *Phorcys* who wants to interject himself into the conversation, and that's just his excuse. I'm a bit surprised the mermen let Phorcys surface, but I'm sure they have their reasons.

I give Edmund an apologetic look, nodding for Phorcys to return to the water.

"You know he likes you," Edmund mumbles before I leave. "Careful."

Once under the water, I let the boat drift away as I stop Phorcys. I know at least one of the boys—Merrick, Caspian, or Llyr—has noticed and is keeping an eye on me, so I don't worry about the boat straying too far.

"What do you want, Phorcys?"

He raises an eyebrow at me, crossing his arms to match mine.

"I want to know where I float in all of this." He puts on a brave face, but any mer would be nervous in his situation—his collection is gone, he's swimming with his enemies, and the humans aren't far behind. He has nowhere to go and no one to depend on. If we force him out, what is he supposed to do?

"I don't know, but I'm positive what you choose to do between now and the time we get back to Scylla—or wherever the collection is—will affect the queen's decision on your fate."

"So there's a chance I'll go all this way with you and still have to suffer?"

"Considering how many mer you killed—or had a hand in killing—I'd say you'll be lucky if they don't put you on trial and sentence you to the shark barrier without your disgusting shark skin protection.

"You're also lucky the queen doesn't believe in sending mer out there, no matter what they've done. It's only ever happened in extreme cases."

"And if *you* had to decide what happens to me, what would it be?"

A stingray swims by him, nearly knocking into his arm. It glides over my way, tilting around me.

"I think you'll have better luck getting into the good graces of the princess—she's not allowed to be biased when it comes to deciding on these things."

"Celena, I have a feeling my fate rests more in *your* hands than in anyone else's. I need to know how bad this is going to be—should I leave now?" Phorcys' voice is gruff as he glares at me, fully prepared to push me out of the way to make an escape if he senses that I might be lying to him.

"I have no intention of making that decision, Phorcys. I don't like you, I don't think that's in question, but I'm also not going to force you out. Like I said, your actions here will influence a lot of people's decisions about you, so figure out your life and get things handled.

"But if you plan on swimming off, we'd better never see you again, Phorcys, because we won't hesitate to hurt you if you abandon us now."

I turn, swimming away. He has a choice to make.

Caspian and a few of the guards swim ahead to Metten to make sure we aren't swimming into a trap. When they return, Caspian nearly collides with me, he's swimming so fast.

"The entire collection is in Metten." His smile is bigger than I've seen it since before all this started. "Celena, they're all still here. They didn't leave."

"*They're here?*" Dylana's tail twitches in excitement. She hasn't seen her brother since she left Metten to handle the battle. I'm sure she's worried.

"They're waiting for us. Your mother will meet us when we get there to talk to the prince." He reaches out to take her hand, sharing his excitement. "Then we can drag him back toward land and be free of them forever."

"Did you see Morgen?" Dylana's eyes are pulled back wide as she waits for an answer.

"No, but they said he's doing much better."

Dylana visibly sighs, her entire body lowering in the water. Llyr's eyes sparkle when he notices her relief.

"I didn't have time to tell them much, just that we were bringing Edmund to Metten. They're making preparations."

"Mother tried to force Coralie back to Scylla with the children, but she had as much luck as we did," Caspian informs me as we pick up the pace to Metten.

"That mer child is a *force*," I joke. "Were *we* ever that bad?"

"I mean, we *did* try to sneak pets into the house."

"And *that* worked so well." I laugh, batting at Llyr's tail as he slows in front of me, nearly hitting me with his fins. "Speaking of which, I don't think I told you yet—that's how Coralie and I found you out in the open waters. I found the *sarasa* on the rock, and we played that game we used to play when we tried to sneak things in, and *that's* how we found the rest of your signs."

"Well, at least we did *something* right." Caspian bumps his shoulder into mine. "Cor's handling it all pretty well from what I hear."

"Whom did you talk to?"

"Mom." He offers me a smile. "If you think Marilla doesn't have her overseeing everything, you're crazy."

Caspian's smile drops, and he grows somber, glancing over at Natale.

"She was pretty upset to hear about—" he nods to Natale, not wanting her to overhear us talking about her mother's death.

"I'm sure," I reply quietly.

Ahead, the coral reef looms ahead of us—the barrier.

"I suppose we should tell Edmund—it's been a while since I checked on him anyway."

Caspian nods, releasing me. I swim to the surface, slowly lifting myself out of the water so that I don't frighten them. They both turn to me, looking out of the boat.

"I was wondering where you'd gone off to," Edmund jokes.

"We're at the barrier," I explain, lifting my hand to hold the edge of the boat. "The collection stayed in Metten to wait for us—the queen will be joining us shortly to finish negotiations."

Edmund gulps, looking nervous, but he straightens his shoulder much like Dylana does when she's taking a position of authority over something.

"It will be fine," I insist. "Dylana and I will be there the whole time."

"She's not going to drown me, is she?"

"You came all this way thinking that was a possibility?"

He sighs heavily. Turning, he looks out at the open sea —nothing but water for leagues.

"I guess I was a little focused. I didn't think about all the possibilities."

"I suppose that was your doing?" I turn an accusatory glare at Jackson, wondering if he turned the prince against us. Maybe I shouldn't have left them for so long.

"My job is to protect him. I came on this little journey to make sure he was safe. I flung myself into the ocean with a bunch of mermaids set on killing humans—you don't get to judge me, Celena—I'm here to support my prince."

My entire face falls.

"I'm sorry," I say, only partially remorseful. "You're right. You're doing your job, and I shouldn't criticize you for that.

"Be warned, Celena, I'll kill you first if you're lying to us."

"That's assuming you're alive to do so, Jackson." Fear creeps into his eyes, but he holds his face straight at my threat. "We really don't need *you* to make this treaty happen."

"Enough. We don't need any extra hostility right now. Celena, Jackson and I are practically brothers at this point in our lives. Please treat him accordingly. Jackson, she's foreign royalty, and I will not stand for you being disrespectful, friendship or not."

Jackson nods.

"There they are," I redirect. "That's the queen."

I point behind Edmund, and he turns around on the bench he's sitting on in the rowboat to see. A pod of dolphins swims in the water around the queen—a strategic move in case we need to move her quickly. They stay by her side, cutting us off from Marilla.

Whoever is pulling the boat, slows as we approach. The boat glides through the water. I stop its motion when we get close enough, allowing Marilla to swim up to us. Dylana joins us to make the introductions.

"Hello, Prince Edmund," Marilla greets him. She glitters in a fearsome shell crown. Her *iluse* is covered in shells and sparkling crystals mixed with the pearls that are so celebrated in our collection. She wears royal shoulder armor that glints in the sun. "I'm pleased you've decided to enter into negotiations with us. We would very much like to end this war and separate our groups so that this does not happen again."

"I think that is a wise decision, your majesty," Edmund agrees.

Dylana quickly explains what they've already discussed, pointing out areas they did not speak on or have not reached an agreement on yet. Marilla nods, listening to her daughter.

I linger by the side of the boat as Merrick takes a place beside me. Marilla raises an eyebrow for a moment but allows him to stay by my side.

Merrick's hand slips around my waist as he pins me between him and the boat. I lean against him, but jerk forward suddenly as one of the dolphins bumps me in the back.

I turn around as Merrick snorts, quietly making fun of me. I pet the dolphin for a moment until it swims away—I've missed them. Wrapping myself around Merrick's arm, I focus back in on the conversation as Marilla works out details with Edmund. He glances at me for a moment but looks back to Marilla almost immediately.

"Did you ever think you'd live to see this day?" Merrick whispers in my ear, voice low and intentionally flirtatious.

"I didn't," I reply, refusing to take the bait—we don't have time to flirt right now. The sun is setting, and we need to get Edmund back safely to the shore.

My mother eyes me from her place in the line of mer several lengths away. She raises an eyebrow and smiles just a hint.

Marilla was smart to keep the collection back so that they didn't surround the human prince and his servant— we don't need them to be any more nervous than they already are. It's nice to know that my mother approves of

Merrick—even though I haven't seen her long enough to tell her that we're together yet.

Caspian and the others wait below, hovering underneath the boat part way between the ocean floor and the surface in case we need anything. They're deep enough to be out of the way, but close enough that they can assist us if we signal them. The rest of the collection is preparing to fight off the humans if they find us once we leave Metten.

I rest my head on Merrick's shoulder, and he tips his head on mine. His shoulder armor is uncomfortable, but I don't care. Merrick shifts, sensing that it's slightly painful against my cheek, lowering his shoulder so that I'm not putting as much weight against the side of my face to rest against him.

Through the water, I can see Phorcys grumbling to himself as he stares. Keone and Natale glance at him at the same time, but he just crosses his arms and continues to stare. I'm surprised he bothered staying with us. I had thought Marilla's gaze would have scared him when she saw him before approaching us, but not even *that* turned him away—he must be more nervous about being alone than I thought.

It's a shame we don't know where Cassidia—I doubt Tarni is still alive—is so we could send him off with her. Perhaps if Marilla decides to let Tiko and the others go, he could leave with them and cross the barriers into the open waters. Maybe they could even return to Shadare or Rochay.

The light fades out of the sky, leaving a dark, murky color. Several midwater squid glow in the ocean below us, lingering near our collection. Metten's palace and dwellings can't be seen from the surface, but I'm sure the collection is hiding most of the bioluminescent glow tonight to be safe.

Merrick leaves me, diving into the water. When he returns several minutes later, Caspian is at his side, helping to carry a rock covered in spores that glow. They set it on the side of the boat, allowing Jackson to move it between him and the prince so they can see better until the moon appears.

The two stay next to me, floating in the water. They can sense I'm getting dried out and gently push down on my shoulders until I dip under the water for a moment—Marilla and Dylana have already taken turns to sink under the water momentarily.

It feels cool, but that's only because I've been out in the warm air for so long. I sigh, and Merrick squeezes my shoulder, still holding on to me. Running my fingers through my hair, I shake the dried pieces loose, letting them soak up the water. After a moment, I finally relent and swim back up, leaving the water until my shoulders are exposed once more.

It appears as though Edmund and Marilla are finalizing everything. She swims toward him to shake his hand—something important in both human *and* mer culture. The prince reaches down, stretching his arm so that Marilla doesn't have to do most of the work. Jackson leans back slightly, making sure the boat stays balanced.

"And you're sure you want to go against your father's wishes?" Marilla asks before removing her hand from his. "If you want to change your mind, Prince Edmund, we won't hold it against you. We'll take you back to Antaire safely."

Jackson suddenly gasps, clutching at his chest. When I turn to look at him in the limited moonlight, I notice a long dark line protruding from his chest. His eyes are wide as Edmund screams his name, leaping forward in the rowboat to help his friend.

"Get down!" Marilla shouts, diving under the water.

A spear pierces the surface of the ocean, barely missing me. It's followed by more.

CHAPTER 11

JACKSON'S BODY TOPPLES INTO THE WATER, DRIFTING DOWN as Merrick and I dart away from the boat. I turn, allowing Merrick to pull me as I watch for oncoming spears in the water—one of them hits the servant's leg as his corpse sinks.

"Edmund," I call, realizing we left him to face his fate alone.

The fleet of small rowboats closes in on the prince from one side—they must have determined that they couldn't cross the barrier in their ships and did exactly what we did, skimming over the surface with the small vessel.

I'm shocked any of the humans were brave enough to attack Jackson when they easily could have missed and hit the prince. Edmund's body isn't in the water, so I assume they want him alive.

The entire mer collection races to our aid. We stay closer to the ground than the surface as we loop in a giant arch under the rowboats, positioning ourselves to surface on the far side of the tiny fleet to surprise them.

Marilla attempts to surface with us, but my mother drags her back. Llyr mimics the motion, forcing Dylana down to the ocean floor.

When I surface, the rowboats are surrounding Edmund, bumping into him. He stays in the center of the boat, trying to avoid their reach—he looks terrified. The men shout that the king has offered a reward to whichever sailors brought the prince back.

Several of the sailors try to stand in their boats in an effort to step into the prince's at the center of the crowd. One man rocks violently as the entire boat lurches to the side—a merman bravely knocks another boat, shifting them all in the water in a ripple effect. More of our collection moves under the boats to help, attempting to avoid the spears being thrust into the water between the tightly packed boats.

"How do you want to handle this?" Merrick asks quietly, assessing the situation. "I don't think we can get his boat away from them."

"Isn't it funny that we're up here fighting *for* a human?" Phorcys appears next to us, trident in hand. I'm not sure where he got the weapon from, but as long as he doesn't stab *me* with it, I don't care.

"I suppose you suddenly have an idea of how to help?" I snip at him.

"Other than leaving him here?" Phorcys sneers. "Siren them."

"We're not sirening them. I doubt they can even hear us anyway—they know what they were sailing into."

"Then you have to kill them," Phorcys replies. "What's more important—the prince or *all of them?*"

"If we get him in the water, we can swim him out of here," Merrick comments, ignoring Phorcys. "I just don't know about what we do after that point. We can't swim him all the way back to Anataire without a boat."

"That's a problem for later." I shake my head. "We have to get him now. *Natale!*"

My cousin looks over, poised to stab a human in a boat. She grimaces, moving her arms back to strike. Instead, she hits the side of the boat, toppling it enough that the man falls into the water. Natale rushes to my side.

"We're getting Edmund and swimming away with him. As soon as we have him, and are far enough away, get the collection out of here—we don't need any extra deaths."

She nods, darting under the water to watch us sneak up to Edmund's boat. I lead the way, Merrick and Phorcys trailing behind me.

"What are you doing?" Caspian shouts, noticing our

movements as I count the boats overhead, trying to locate the correct one.

"We need to get Edmund into the water!" I shout. "We're going to take him away."

"And do *what?*" Caspian calls, knowing we don't have another boat to put him in.

"We'll figure that out later," I reply.

"It won't help if he's dead," Phorcys replies darkly.

Caspian swims over to join us, leaving his post.

"Which one?" he asks, looking at the underside of the boats.

"One of those." I point. "That one, I think, but I'm not sure."

"So we tip them all and figure it out after," Caspian replies, working with my line of thinking. Without waiting, he propels himself toward the boats. We follow behind him.

I slam into one of the boats, rocking it. Moving back, I hit it again as it bounces on the waves, this time, tipping it enough to knock the humans out.

Unfortunately, I had miscounted—the men I tip out aren't the prince. Two sailors panic in the water, trying to surface. One glares at me, realizing what happened. He tips his spear toward me and thrusts it at my stomach.

Caspian reaches out, taking the hit with his forearm. He doubles over in pain as blood blooms from his injury.

In our rush to save the prince, I had forgotten that

blood would fill the waters—this time at night. While I doubt there are any sharks in the area at this point, anything is a possibility, and I hope our collection is safe.

I lurch forward to help Caspian, but a waving arm catches my attention. Edmund thrashes in the water. When he finally sees me, his movements halt for just a moment before he struggles to get to the surface for air.

"Go," Caspian commands. He whips his tail out, slamming into a human who turned toward me.

I jerk my arm back, hitting the man in the face with the flat end of my trident. His unconscious body floats in the water, and I realize I just sentenced him to death—he can't save himself from drowning.

I rush to Edmund as he surfaces, gasping for air. I pop out of the water next to him, quickly hissing in his ear for him to take a deep breath and trust me. He does, gulping in the night air before I drag him back down under the sea.

Caspian joins us, cradling his arm as we bypass the boats in the water. Edmund's fingers dig into my arm when he runs out of air. We aren't far enough away yet, but I'm forced to surface to keep the prince alive.

Edmund coughs when we reach the night air, and he slams his hand against his chest, fighting to keep control. He drags in several ragged breaths before nodding to me, telling me it's okay to take him back under the water.

Merrick and Phorcys appear, looking a little worse

for the wear, but my boyfriend slips his hand around Edmund's upper arm and helps me propel him through the dark water.

We stay near the surface, just far enough below the waves that we can't be seen, but high enough that we can easily give Edmund access to the air he needs to survive on short notice. He attempts to hold his breath for as long as possible for us, but each new dive is shorter than the last as his lungs start to rebel.

"There's nothing but open water, where do we take him?" Casp asks. Thankfully the bleeding on his arm has stopped, but I convince Merrick to dive below and find something to wrap my brother's arm in.

Phorcys takes Merrick's place, helping me move the prince through the water. Once I can no longer see the boats, we take Edmund to the surface to swim, allowing him to breathe.

Swimming in the waves isn't easy, but we drag Edmund along, allowing him to hold on to our upper arms as we swim for him. He weakly kicks his feet along with us, but holding his breath for so long has worn him out to the point of being practically useless.

He stays quiet for a long time as we move through the water. Merrick returns, wrapping Caspian's arm in seaweed to protect it. He allows Phorcys to continue to assist me, instead of taking a place at my side.

"You have a plan yet?" Merrick mumbles just loud

enough for me to hear. The back of his hand brushes against my hip as he pulls ahead of me slightly in the water. Warmth shoots through my body, tingling in my scales.

"I've been trying to think about the maps of Metten," I reply. "I know there was an area where the ocean floor was closer to the surface. There was something about it that made ships unable to go there—well, certain places anyway—and the rest of the area was hard to navigate."

"I remember reading about that during my studies—" Edmund's words are cut off by a small wave slamming into his face. He sputters before continuing. "It's a rocky area that most ships can't get through. The mer navigated certain boats through it at certain times of the year because the harvest was so good, but ordinarily, it's not something we could make it through on our own."

"We could go there until we have a better plan," I suggest.

"I've seen drawings of it," Edmund continues. "There are rocks stretching out of the water."

"At least you'd have somewhere to sit."

"Okay, we'll go there for now. Which direction?" Merrick asks.

"I'll go leave a trail," Caspian sighs, ducking under the water to leave a marked path for the rest of the collection to follow behind us.

I dip below the water, watching him go as I wet my

hair. Someday soon I'll be able to stay under the water, and when that day comes, I may never surface again.

"Feel better?" Edmund jokes when I bring my head back up out of the water. "I've noticed you do that a lot."

"As fun as it is being up here…" I trail off, rolling my eyes as the prince smirks. I have a feeling that Merrick wouldn't be so calm about my interactions with Edmund if he were a merman.

"Want me to take over?" Merrick asks, relieving me. I nod, and Edmund releases my arm.

Scooting over, I take the opportunity to dive under the water, twirling around a few times to work the kinks out of my muscles. I stay under the water for a minute, needing a moment alone. I like being around my collection as much as the next mermaid, but I haven't had a minute to myself since we escaped the palace.

If the area we're taking Edmund to is hard to navigate, that *should* mean that the king will have trouble following us.

The water rushes over my hands as I race ahead, suddenly eager to pick up the pace. The moonlight sparkles down from above, now high in the nighttime sky.

Despite my exhaustion, I feel alive as I spiral through the water. My instincts tell me to leap from the water like a dolphin, surprising the others, but I know how ridiculous that would be. Instead, I surface, swimming ahead of everyone.

"Slow down, Len," Merrick calls playfully. "Not all of us can keep up."

Edmund mumbles an apology, but Merrick brushes it off good-naturedly. The prince looks relieved when I glance back, but he also seems to be getting a little of his strength back after being carried for so long.

Caspian swims below us, leaving a trail of signs for our collection. I wave down to him when he glances up, and he smiles. It's hard to see through the dark water, but the light is just strong enough to make out some of his features.

I wonder if Edmund has thought this through yet. His father has to know Edmund went against his wishes, so what does that mean for Edmund's return? Will his father lock him away like Jarek's mother did to him a century ago? Will the crown be taken away from him and instead passed on to Analia—and what will happen if *she's* in charge?

The moon shifts in the sky as we swim. The colors start to change when we finally swim into the area where the ocean floor rises closer to the surface, and Caspian joins us to avoid the vicious rocks resting on the ocean floor.

A few minutes later, we see the first of the rocks

protruding out of the water. It's small—small enough to miss, especially from the deck of a ship—but it's there.

We're all quiet as we linger through the rocks. We take our time moving around them to avoid accidentally scraping our scales against the rough edges hiding below the surface. Edmund stops kicking his feet, allowing the boys to guide his path through the water.

When I spot a cavern entrance looming ahead, complete with a massive set of rocks piercing through the water, I point us in that direction. Edmund climbs up onto a green-covered rock. He slips at first but manages to take a seat.

He glances around from his new throne in the sea, admiring his temporary kingdom. The walls of the cavern glow with bioluminescent spores, though not nearly as brilliantly as the other caves we've been in recently. Fish swim in the water as day breaks, leaving the area in a mint colored glow that would make even Llyr's hair jealous.

I take a seat on a rock near the prince that hasn't bothered leaving the comfort of the sea. Merrick leans against the rock next to my tail, resting his shoulder against my hip. Phorcys sulks a few lengths away while Caspian unwraps his arm to check it.

"Here." I reach out to him, beckoning him over so I can look at his injuries. I wince when I see it, but it's not life-threatening. "Maybe next time don't take a spear for me, okay?"

"I will take a spear for you *every single time*, Celena," he grins up at me, emphasizing his words. "You and Coralie…*Merrick*, not so much."

'Thanks, buddy."

"You're welcome, brother," Caspian replies before cringing as he realizes that it has new meaning now that I'm dating Merrick. He glances between us.

"It'll be okay," Merrick jokes.

"So this is your…brother?" Edmund asks, looking directly at me.

"Edmund, meet my brother, Caspian. Casp, this is Prince Edmund."

"I hear you threatened my sister and tortured my friend." Caspian's voice is dark as he pretends to threaten the prince. Edmund's eyes grow wide.

"He's joking, Edmund. Casp, stop scaring him." I roll my eyes. Caspian drops the scary act and offers the prince a smile.

"If you ever try anything like that again though—"

"I know, you'll drown me," Edmund interrupts. "I get it. I get *all* of it."

Merrick and I chuckle, knowing he's been threatened so many times already that it no longer affects him. Merrick takes my hand, running his fingers over the back of it.

"I'm sorry about Jackson," I address the prince. He sighs deeply, casting his eyes down to look at the water.

"He helped me escape—he was a traitor. I should have realized that earlier. I never should have brought him along."

"You don't know what would have happened if he had stayed," I offer. "He could have just as easily been held accountable back in that cave."

Several colorful fish swim over to me, darting around my tail to investigate who I am. Once they're satisfied, they take off, swimming away.

"I'm going to check the cave," Phorcys grumbles, pushing away from us. "Maybe there's a way through it."

He disappears into the cavern.

"Do you think he's coming back?" Caspian asks, watching the orange-tailed merman swim away.

"If there's no exit, he is," Merrick smirks, earning a snort from the prince. "I don't think he's going anywhere. He's trying to earn his way into our good graces so he doesn't get kicked out."

"For as rough as he is, I think he'd be lost without a collection," I add. I don't know much about him, but I know he had risen in the ranks of the sirens enough for Tarni and Nir to trust him. I think he needs to be around others to thrive. If his solo mission after we left him for dead is any indication, the plans he tries to execute on his own don't necessarily work so well.

"He's going to be an interesting addition," Merrick remarks as if it doesn't matter. It does, and we both know it.

"Edmund, what's your father going to do to you once you return?" My tail twitches as I ask the question, unsure I want the answer.

"I'm not sure. I'll probably be in pretty big trouble. I can always say you sirened me though." He smirks. "Honestly, he'll probably send me away like he had planned on doing. Once he's done here, *then* I'll be punished for this. I don't even know how to let you know when it's safe."

"Use a conch shell," I remind him. "They're bound to wash up from time to time or have the sailors bring them in. All you have to do is say our names into them and then your message, and throw them into the sea."

"If you have sailors you can trust, you can have them drop them out farther into the sea for us," Merrick adds.

"We'll have guards who will find them and bring them to us," Caspian concludes. "It might take a bit, but it will make it to us."

"Use the terms *mer queen* and *mer king* too in case things can't reach us for some reason." *In case we're dead.*

"There's nothing in there," Phorcys interrupts, exiting the cave. "It's just like every other cave we've been in—decidedly lacking in human skulls."

"What?" Edmund chokes.

"You don't need to worry about that." I wave my hand at the prince.

"Your friends are coming," Phorcys points out to the horizon. "I saw them through the water while I was under."

A smile creeps across my face—our collection made good time. Merrick slips under the water to watch for them as I sun myself on the rock. The sun rises over the horizon, casting the area in gold.

The water waves against my tail as Merrick swims away. I'm sure he's going to greet the collection and guide them to our location, but I miss his presence next to me.

When he returns, Llyr, Natale, Dylana, and Keone are at his side along with Relo and some of the others. They join us on the surface so that Edmund isn't left out of the conversation.

"We swam ahead," Keone explains. "The others are just a few minutes behind."

"This is interesting," LLyr eyes the location. He turns to face me perched on the underwater rock. "Having fun, Celena?"

"*Resting* is more like it." I stretch my hand out to him, and he swims over to kiss it as if I were the queen and he was showing respect. He looks up, smiling, but side eyes Dylana behind him. I fan my fins out, swishing it against his tail to let him know she's watching.

"Guys." The voice behind me frightens me, and I leap

off the rock, whipping around in the water, trident ready. Llyr is beside me, ready to strike. From inside the cave, the voice sounds again.

"I want to help." It sounds familiar, but it isn't until Murdoch peers around the cave wall that I realize Phorcys just lied to us.

I whip around to face him, leaving Llyr and the others to face Murdoch and what I assume has to also be Roni and Cassidia. Phorcys stares me down but doesn't raise his weapon. He glares at me as I snarl back at him, demanding to know what is going on.

"Celena, please!" Murdoch shouts over to me. "He was protecting Tarni."

How is she still alive? Apparently, it's as hard to kill her as it was to kill Nir.

"Why are you here, Murdoch?" Merrick growls at him.

"This is as far as we made it—Tarni's not well. We hid here and have been trying to care for her—she's getting better." He sounds hopeful as he speaks. "But she can't leave yet."

"Why did you bother to come out?" I shout, still staring down Phorcys. He snarls at me but doesn't say anything.

"I want to help you. I messed up, and I know that. I want to try to make it right."

"Do you honestly think you'll be allowed back in the

collection after everything you've done, Murdoch?" Llyr taunts him.

"I don't need to get back into the collection. I just want to...apologize."

"Here's your knife back, Caspian." There's a pause as I assume Caspian retrieves the weapon the sirens stole in the palace in Scylla.

I actually feel bad for Murdoch. He turned his back on his collection, the mermaid he cares for might not make it—I'm surprised she's lasted this long—and he realizes just how much he gave up to start a war no one won.

"They're not coming with us," Merrick says. I assume he's talking about Cassidia and Roni, but I'm not turning around to look.

"Roni and Cassidia will stay with Tarni," Murdoch informs us.

"We should take them," Phorcys mutters. "We might need them."

I shake my head quietly, telling him to stay quiet, but the siren doesn't listen.

"Cassidia comes with us—we may need her help."

I turn in time to see Roni's face twist in anger as she floats next to Murdoch and Cassidia.

"You are *not* leaving me behind," she growls. She looks ready to strangle Murdoch next to her, but her glare is deadly as she swings around to aim her accusatory eyes at Phorcys.

"You need to protect Tarni, and we may need Cassidia's skill set," Phorcys addresses her, leaving the word *sireny* unsaid in front of the prince.

"We most certainly will *not*," I snap at him. I turn to Edmund, ready to tattle. "She will *not* be sirening anyone."

The prince narrows his eyes at the blue-tailed mermaid, leveling a gaze that would make anyone but her squirm. She glances at him before flicking her gaze away casually to me.

Apparently, the decision comes down to me.

I don't trust her not to follow behind us and disrupt our plan—I'd rather have her where we can see her.

"She can come, but she doesn't leave our sides."

Her lips twitch, but she swims out of the cave. Murdoch follows in her wake. Roni fumes, still inside the shadows of the cave. For a moment, she looks as if she might lash out, but suddenly she jerks her shoulder back, flinching. She looks over her shoulder, retreating into the cave.

None of us have checked on Tarni yet. I have to make sure she's actually still alive, and in the condition they're claiming her to be in. If she miraculously recovered—or if she's dead and this is some kind of trick—I have to know.

Merrick's hum is low as I swim past him—a warning to be careful. Cassidia and Phorcys don't bother trying to follow me as I trail Roni inside the cave.

The glow is brighter inside, but not by much. Tarni lays on the sand below, Roni at her side. Tarni grimaces at me while her protector snarls.

"Get out, *mermaid.*"

Tarni's eyes flutter shut, weak enough that she doesn't care that I'm in her presence. Her friend strokes her hair, reminding me of when I took care of Coralie after these two attacked her. The thought makes me rage inside.

Turning, I leave the cave.

"Time to move," I announce. In a mumble, I add, "We need to get as far from those two as possible."

I almost feel bad for Murdoch as he flinches. He wants to believe the best in the mermaid he cares for, but he also knows the truth about her—she is a murderess, and she doesn't care whom she hurts to get what she wants. I still don't believe she could possibly love Murdoch the way he thinks she does.

"I don't have a weapon," Murdoch points out.

I'm sure the collection will have extra weapons with them, but none of us carried extra tridents or spears. I reach into my *iluse* to untangle a knife I've been hiding.

Murdoch's eyes widen as I hand it to him, but he takes it gratefully. Flipping it in his hand, he tests its weight, getting comfortable with the blade.

"I want that back later," I remind him, lips pursed.

After all he's done to us, I don't mind giving him a hard time. He nods solemnly, gripping the knife tighter in his hand. I sigh, turning away from him. A few days ago, I would have been willing to cut his fingers off, but after the last few days, I just want things to be easy, which means not picking fights that aren't absolutely necessary.

"Thanks," Murdoch says when my back is turned. I nod briefly.

"They're here," Natale announces, jerking her head back toward where the collection is swimming to us under the water. We wait as they swim up to us.

CHAPTER 12

"Mother." Dylana signals the queen over.

Marilla's eyes narrow when she notices Phorcys, but she halts in the water when she realizes Murdoch is with us. He backs up in the water as she swims straight for him.

"Why are you here?" Miraculously, Marilla manages to keep her voice even.

"We were hiding in the cave—we didn't know they'd be here," Murdoch says, trying not to stumble over his words. "I just want to help, and then I'll leave."

"Who is *we*?" Marilla demands in an unnervingly calm voice.

"Tarni and Roni are here," I inform her. She glances at me.

"Where?"

"In the cave," Dylana points. "Cassidia will be joining us."

Her eyes dart to the blue siren, informing her mother of the mermaid's location.

Marilla turns in the water, my mother by her side. Sometimes it's hard to believe this is the same mermaid who feeds seahorses in her chambers in the palace in Scylla—this fierce mermaid warrior queen, who looks as though she will slice your throat and ask questions later, is also the soft, kind queen I grew up following.

With her shoulders back and crown on, she is magnificent. My mother mirrors her movements, looking just as regal as the two slip into the cave.

Murdoch looks terrified that Tarni's torn up body might float out of the cave at any time, though I doubt they'll hurt the siren. Minutes stretch out, but no one exits the cave. I glance at Dylana, silently asking if we should check on them. Her bottom lip pinches against her top lip, but before we can decide on anything, our mothers emerge from the cavern.

"We need to go," Marilla announces. "We must return the prince to Antaire."

Murdoch glances at the cave, but he knows he can't check on Tarni. Reluctantly, he's forced to believe she is okay as he turns to follow the collection.

Edmund slips into the water and allows two of the guards to guide him through the waves. I stay close by, knowing it will concern him if I don't. Merrick nods to him, lending his support.

Cassidia swims ahead of us, separated from Phorcys. Her blue tail waves majestically in the water. Her entire body moves gracefully ahead of us, and I wonder if I've ever been half as effortless as she is. Her long hair is enchanting as it flows behind her in a white wave.

She looks back over her shoulder as if she knows I'm studying the way she moves, hoping to learn from her during the swim. She makes eye contact with Phorcys as he swims next to Merrick before she turns back to watch where she's swimming.

Phorcys keeps a close eye on me around Merrick as we move, not even flinching when a pod of dolphins joins us for a time while we swim toward Antaire. The open waters below us are colorful—more colorful than when we were here before fighting a war that was never our battle to begin with. Coral litters the ground, mixed with kelp and seaweed. Fish swim in every direction, darting out of our way as we approach.

"Never thought I'd miss a rock," Edmund jokes.

"Are you okay?" I ask, looking over.

"I'm fine," he puffs. "I clearly should work on my long distance swimming skills though."

I'm sure swimming in his heavy royal clothes isn't easy. I'm thankful he wasn't wearing one of those silly capes I've seen in storybooks and in some of the drawings Aila left of Prince Jarek—*that* would only serve to kill him. Then again, perhaps we could use it to pull him along instead of letting him cling to our arms to be dragged across the seas.

I wish we could use this time to discuss what our collection will do after we return the prince, but we can't let Edmund hear out plans. I want desperately to dive under the water and swim with Marilla and my mother for a while to learn about what they have planned.

I haven't seen my father yet, so I assume he didn't come. He's likely recuperating with Morgen and the other injured mer that were too unwell to join the new fight. At least one of us will be left alive to care for Coralie when this is all over.

Ahead, I see Marin, the merman Coralie was gushing over a few weeks ago in Scylla. I vow to keep an eye on him for her. I would hate to have her heart broken if her crush were to die in war. He seems far too young to be with us, but the choice isn't mine, and I won't challenge it.

We hit a warm current, and I shiver at the change in temperature. Warmth floods through my scales, and I realize just how cold I've been this whole time. Scylla is so much warmer and I long to be back in the colorful waters of our home.

As if he can read my mind, Merrick bumps into my shoulder, smiling at me. I tip my head toward him, allowing us to have a private moment as my hair blocks us from the world around us. He breathes deeply, sighing just enough so that only I can hear it.

I'm tired—we're *both* tired. We're ready for this fight to be over. If we can go home and never leave the Scylla courtyard again, I'll be happy.

Well, unless we go visit the caves. I'll make an exception for those kinds of trips.

Merrick raises an eyebrow at the look on my face. I bite back my sarcasm and turn away from him, but not before winking flirtatiously. His hand finds its way to my back and rests just above my tail as we swim.

It's a strange sight to see the top of the ocean without any boats. After the number of ships I've seen the last week, the world feels slightly off without them bobbing dangerously on the water, rocking with the waves.

A dolphin surfaces next to me, spraying me with water as she opens her blowhole to breath. I reach out a hand, letting it slide over her skin as she chatters next to me for a moment before moving on.

Another one surfaces near Cassidia ahead, but she only glances at it before continuing on. The siren doesn't even attempt to reach out to touch it.

"She's never liked them," Phorcys mumbles. "She only sees them as tools to be used for transportation."

"One of them probably bumped her when she was a

mer child and took her personality with it," Caspian jokes quietly. Phorcys glares at him while Merrick and I smirk.

Llyr swims suspiciously close to Dylana off to the side of Cassidia, far enough away that they can talk quietly without being overheard. I wonder how long it will be before he actually tells her how much he likes her. I've been pestering him about it for over a year now, but he's far too respectful to think he could end up with a princess. Personally, I think he would make a fabulous king once Dylana takes her reign.

He looks back, catching my eye, and I bat my lashes at him to tease him. He rolls his eyes, grinning wildly when Dylana catches him. She glances back at me, and I raise an eyebrow at her suggestively. The princess casually looks back at Llyr, and I think she's finally ready to do something about the flirtatious banter they've been locked in for months.

"I see you've been helping things along," Merrick mumbles playfully. "I've been working on it too. Nice teamwork, partner."

"Congratulating yourself a little early, aren't you, Merrick?" I pretend to chastise him. "Nothing has happened yet."

"You two make me sick," Phorcys groans.

"I have to agree," Caspian chimes in. "You two are disgusting."

"Thank you, Caspian, you've been so helpful," I sing, giving him the most annoyed look I can muster up.

He returns the same face, having mastered it far better than I did over the years. I suppose he was always more fond of studying himself in bubbles than I was, so of course he had more practice. He also had *me* for a sister, so *that* might explain it as well.

I dip under the water, wetting my hair for the next portion of the swim. At some point, we're going to have to decide how to return Edmund without getting any of us killed. It seems like a monumental task—it's as difficult as moving one of those caves we just left would be. Or perhaps it's impossible.

If that's the case, if it's too dangerous, I'll volunteer to go. It's my fault we're out here. Merrick and Caspian won't like it, but I can convince Llyr to force them to stay. If I genuinely asked him to, he would do that for me.

I tap my knife in my *iluse*. Murdoch returned it once one of the collection members offered him a spear to fight with instead. I prefer my weapons where they belong—with me.

Birds cry overhead like ugly little white stingrays in the sky, though they are much nosier than stingrays. One of the things I love about sea animals is that most of them don't make as much noise as animals on land seem to make. The dolphins and whales, of course, make beautiful sounds when calling to each other under the water, but starfish are ever silent.

The sun is higher in the sky now, and it sizzles against the skin on my shoulders—I'm not used to being in the direct sunlight for so long. I shrug uncomfortably as I try to dip down far enough to cool them off under my shoulder armor.

Marilla and my mother slow in the water, waiting until we catch up. Natale notices and nods to Keone to watch Cassidia as she sinks back in the water to join us, her lips pulled back in a grim line.

"We've decided the best course of action is to take you back as a united front, Prince Edmund. The entire collection will be returning you to your father," Marilla explains. "We hope that your father might see this as a sign of goodwill because we have not harmed you. Do you think he will view this as a threat *no matter what?*"

"Or perhaps will he be frightened enough of his son being surrounded by a hundred of his enemy to think it through before he attacks?" my mother adds the question to the conversation.

"I think seeing an entire collection of mer will give him pause, especially when he sees me with you," Edmund answers. "I don't think you should just hand me over though.

"When we arrive, I should stay in the water where I'm clearly visible. I'll direct the guards to get my father from the palace, and I can explain how you all helped me to return safely.

"At that point, I think you all need to leave before I swim back to shore. If I'm out of the water, there's nothing to prevent him from coming after you, but if there's still the potential that you could hurt me, he will have to cooperate at least a little."

"That's a wise plan, your majesty," Marilla nods. Edmund might be young, but she's treating him with the respect his title owes him. "You will be all right when we leave you?"

"I'll be fine, Queen Marilla," he assures her.

Marilla delves into a conversation about how to use conch shells to communicate with us, repeating everything we've already taught him. Edmund listens carefully as if it's the first time he's hearing the instructions. I'm positive Dylana already informed her mother of our conversations, but it's worth repeating.

"For what it's worth," Edmund says, glancing at me. "I'm sorry the treaty fell apart. I believe you when you say it was only Persephone and her mother that did this to us. I believe you about the sirens, too."

Cassidia whips around to look at him, snarling at Phorcys as Keone mumbles something to her. I'm sure he's reminding her to cooperate, but his trident twitches in his hand as he speaks, clearly annoyed.

Off to the side, I hear a click. A rush of wind follows,

filling my ears as it ends with a harpoon slicing through the water in front of Cassidia. She screams—the first real emotion I've heard come from the siren—and whips around in the water, ready to siren anything that gets in her way.

Keone turns to see where the weapon came from, lurching in the water to avoid a second harpoon. They fill the air, slicing through the water when they land.

The collection drops under the water, diving deep to avoid the weapons. They quickly double back, hiding under the boat where the sailors likely won't think to throw their weapons.

"Casp!" I gasp, nodding to Dylana. My twin launches himself at our cousin and drags her under, putting his own body between her and the humans. I hate that he has to use himself as a shield for her, but we all know it's our job to protect the reigning royals.

"Go," my mother commands, attempting to push me down in the water. "Merrick, get her out of here."

Merrick hesitates for a moment, then tries to push me down in the water.

"Merrick!" I shout, struggling against him. "We can't let him stay up there."

"Your mother is watching him." He grits his teeth as he drags me down in the water. I should fight harder, but I'm trained to trust him, so I follow his lead.

"We can't just leave them up there," I protest.

"We're not, Len—we just aren't deep enough yet." Merrick forces his tail to work harder, and I join him, realizing his plan to swing back around and attack the boat from the backside.

Merrick turns us in the water, moving under the boat, though we're quite a bit higher than the rest of the collection. We dart up in the water, close enough to the underside of the boat to touch it. The vessel is far too big for us to tip, even if the entire collection was assisting us.

We stop when we reach the edge, still hovering underneath the ship where the humans can't see us. Merrick hands me his trident as he flattens himself against the underside of the boat, his chest pressed against it as he floats upside down in the water.

Slowly, he uses his hands to pull him forward, tentatively peeking out beyond the edge of the ship. When he feels that it's safe, he moves further out.

"I'm here," Llyr announces behind me. He hands me his weapon, and I balance all three in the crook of my arm, holding onto the handles with my hands to keep them from slipping and falling to the ocean floor below us.

Llyr puts his hand on Merrick's tail to let him know he's there. As Merrick moves farther out away from the boat, Llyr wraps both hands around the end of Merrick's tail just above his fins in case he needs to pull him back.

"Try not to get too jealous," Llyr mumbles at me, smirking.

"You're just holding his tail… *I* had him *wrapped around me*," I quip, making him fumble. I snort at his response. "I doubt you're going to make me jealous, Llyr, sorry to waste your last few years."

"Wow, thanks, Celena. I appreciate you leading me on and making me think I had a chance to sway you away."

"You didn't," I confirm snarkily.

A loud sound rocks the ship, and I nearly drop the tridents.

"What was that?"

Something drops in the water as I look at Llyr, unsure of how to answer. The black thing sinks heavily in the water.

"It's a cannonball," I stutter, trying to process what I just saw. "*What…how?*"

"They're shooting *cannonballs* in the water now? What's the logic in *that*?" Llyr shouts. "Those things are meant to sink ships—what good will it do shooting it at us now? It could take out, *what—one or two* mer? Isn't that a waste of ammunition?"

"It's ridiculous, but maybe they're trying to scare us away from the prince."

Just then, Merrick does a backflip. Llyr releases him so he can return to us. Merrick flips his blue hair up, moving his long bangs away from his eyes as they wave in the water.

"What are we looking at?" Llyr asks, reaching for his trident. Merrick does the same.

"They're focused on the other side. This is our chance."

"What's up there?"

"Not much," Merrick admits, shaking his head at me. "There's a boat about halfway down the side of the ship resting on ropes. There's a bunch of windows in the side of the ship."

"So what is our plan?" Llyr wrinkles his nose adorably. It's easy to see why he's always been so popular with the mermaids in the collection.

I dart out from under the boat, popping out of the water enough to get a good look at the side of the ship waging war on my mother and collection.

A small rowboat dangles from the side of the ship. It's about the size of the one Edmund stole during his escape. The ropes dangle from the top of the ship, almost reaching the water. They're loosely tied at the top.

"The boat is our plan," I reply, darting back under the ship. "You mermen are going to grab the ropes and pull. It *should* knock the ropes loose, and we can lower the boat."

"And do *what*?" Llyr's words are punctuated, eyebrows lowered at me.

"She's going up in the boat." Merrick's tone is a cross between concern and awe.

"Celena!" Llyr chides.

"I'll siren *one* of them," I respond, sighing. "We just need to get one of them to wreck the cannon. And maybe part of the boat."

"*What?*" Llyr yelps. "I mean, I get it, *really*, but…*really*? I thought better of you, Len."

I smirk as he uses Merrick's nickname for me. I have a feeling he has adopted my boyfriend's name for me when the two are talking when I'm not around. He raises an eyebrow at me, trying to cover his slip as if it were intentional.

"Fine. Go up in the boat. Blow the ship up—do whatever you have to do. Just get it done quickly and get back down here."

"You two need to get the boat down," I remind him.

We swim out from under the boat and Merrick and Llyr assess the situation. After a moment, they swim down in the water, giving themselves space to build up speed.

I hold my breath as they crash toward the surface, leaping out of the water. I follow them, prepared to siren any humans that might overhear the boys working.

They latch onto the ropes at almost the same time, using their weight to pull the ropes loose. The coils pop free, cascading down to the water, giving plenty of extra rope.

When the mermen pull on them, it jerks the rowboat, smacking it against the side of the ship, but no one seems to have noticed. It rocks from its place along the ship, higher than it was a moment ago.

Merrick and Llyr release the boat, moving the rope hand-over-hand until it rests in the water.

"Up you go," Merrick says, offering me a hand.

I grab the side of the rowboat and pull, using my tail to propel me out of the water. Llyr and Merrick grab my hips and help push me inside the tiny boat.

The feel of the rough boards under my tail isn't an experience I care to repeat. It's one thing when a mer sits on a sunken ship—the water-soaked wood isn't nearly as uncomfortable, but this is dry, and warm from the sun— an entirely miserable experience.

The two try to pull me up, and I slowly jerk away from the surface. Suddenly the boat is moving smoothly, hurdling toward the sky. As I look up, the clouds reach out to me quickly, ready to swallow me up.

Grasping the edge of the rowboat, I peek over and realize a quarter of the collection is helping to pull the ropes in the water. They hold me in place as Merrick and Llyr surface to listen for me to call to them. I wave, letting them know I'm okay.

Turning back, I listen to the noise over the edge of the

ship. Several men are nearby, but I can't tell where unless I'm a little higher. I wiggle my fingers at the mermen, and they instruct the collection to raise me higher. The movement stops a moment after I signal them to pause—thankfully I knew it would take a moment and signaled early.

The men yell at each other on the deck of the ship, shuffling about to follow orders. In the distance, I can hear two yelling about the cannon.

Taking a breath, I sing softly, trying to call one or two to my side. It takes a moment, but five men peer over the edge of the ship, looking down at me sitting in the boat.

Two of them look surprised, not fully under the influence of my song yet, but a few more notes and I have them all. One reaches for me as if I'm made of solid gold. I banish his hands with a few words.

I instruct the men to return to the cannon and change its position. Before I can finish, a cheer goes up, and I hold the men back.

"Bring him in, boys!" someone instructs.

"Look at him, Captain, he's not as nervous as the *mermaids* usually are."

"That's because he thinks we won't hurt him," a man snaps, chuckling. He raises his voice to make sure their captive hears him. "We will, of course. We have no problem putting a little fear into captives."

"Aww, he thinks this is a rescue mission," another man shouts, laughing.

"Sorry, little prince, we're not the welcoming committee. You're not going home just yet. Swing the net over!"

"Bring him in!"

It sounds like they're struggling to get Edmund in the ship—now is my only chance.

"Go," I release the men under my sireny.

It's a moment before anyone realizes that something is wrong. Once they discover the men taking over control of the cannon, shouts go up ordering them to stop. When they don't, the other sailors try to stop the men under my song, but they won't be stopped yet.

To my horror, the shouts change, adding in cries about another ship. I claw my way up the side of the boat to see. When I reach the top, I discover that they're right —a secondary ship is on the way.

Edmund calls out, avoiding using my name so as not to draw attention to me. He's hanging in a net over the opposite side of the ship, struggling to free himself as he dangles over the water.

"Go get help!" he directs me. I shake my head, telling him I won't leave. "Go get help—we need the king. I know these men, go!"

He looks desperate as he yells to me over the noise of the sailors. In my peripheral vision, I can see the men swing the cannon around, preparing to shoot a hole in their own deck.

The majority of the sailors look more worried about the oncoming ship, but I don't have time to investigate as Edmund screams for me to hurry. His eyes grow wide as he realizes the cannon is now pointed to the middle of the deck, not too far away from me.

My heart drops into my stomach as I realize that the cannonball has the potential to travel through the ship and end up in the water where it could hurt my collection.

I don't have time to have the boys lower the boat for me—I have to escape *now*.

I nod sharply, then drop back down into the rowboat, clawing my way to the side, and I throw myself over.

CHAPTER 13

THE WIND RUSHES BY ME AS I SAIL THROUGH THE AIR toward the water. I know this is going to hurt—it's hurt every other time I've plummeted from a ship. Merrick and Llyr dart out of the way, eyes wide as they see me dive toward them.

I slam into the water fingers first, slicing through the waves. Shock races through my body as I hit the surface, working its way down to my tail, each scale screaming at me for making the choice to jump out of the boat, but I don't have time.

Angling my fingers, I aim toward the collection. They release the ropes, turning to swim away. I suppose it's an easy inference to make—if I'm swimming like this, something bad must be happening, and they need to move to get ahead of it.

Merrick and Llyr are quickly on my tail as we rush away.

"We have to go to Antaire," I gasp through my pain. Given all I've been through recently, the aching sensation fades rather quickly in comparison. "We need to get the king."

"We're going without Edmund?" Merrick questions.

"I don't know who those men are, but Edmund does—he looked terrified of them. He begged me to get his father. He seems to think the king is the only one who can rescue him."

I don't have time to see where anyone is, all I know is that I need to get to Antaire and get the king to save his son.

After a few minutes, I have to slow, unable to keep up the speed. I've managed to lead us toward the front of the collection, overtaking many of the mer.

Dylana and Caspian make their way over to us, and Llyr looks like he wants to wrap his arm around the princess. I consider pushing him over to her, but if I focus on that for even a moment, I risk losing my focus altogether. I have to convince myself to speak to the king in the first place, so losing my focus could be detrimental to my entire mission.

"She's hurt, but she's alive," Caspian whispers to me, putting his arm around my waist.

"Mom?" My head darts over to him. I'm terrified.

"She'll be okay." He looks worried. "They're taking care of her."

"Who?" My face pouts without my consent.

"The collection. They're taking her back to Metten. We're on our own, Celena. Marilla is still here though—we'll have to make sure we watch her."

"You're not your mother," Dylana reminds us. "You have other things to worry about right now-it's not your job to take over protecting my mother. The collection will watch her. The guards are with her. You two are not responsible for her just because your mother isn't here."

"We're responsible for *you*," Caspian points out.

"Llyr can be responsible for me," Dylana challenges him. I'm not sure if she did it intentionally or not. Llyr subtly beams where she can't see him. "The king knows you two, and Caspian needs to protect Celena. I'll be fine."

"Oh," Natale gasps.

I drop my gaze, looking down to where her eyes are fixated on the ocean floor. We must be close to Antaire—the bodies of dead mer and sirens litter the ground.

Colorful hair waves in the water, floating up from the corpses resting on the sand. Weapons protrude from the ground and bodies at odd angles.

Iluses sparkle in the sunlight as it filters down through the ocean. *Sarasas* lift off the mermen's chests, gently moving with the current as it slips along our path.

The entire collection stops speaking in reverence for our fallen friends. Phorcys looks more remorseful over the deaths of the sirens he grew up with than Cassidia does—she barely looks like she cares about the consequences of her actions at all. Perhaps she's hiding her feelings, but maybe she simply doesn't care about the destruction below us.

Sailors and guards are mixed among the dead. Some wear uniforms while others wear tattered clothing covered in stains that I don't want to know about. One man's beard waves in the water, looking bristly as it waves like a white cloud about to swallow him.

Spears and harpoons mix with tridents. Several of our collection switch their spears for tridents from the dead —a much more effective weapon should we swim into trouble.

The fish don't seem to mind the carnage as they swim around the corpses cluttering the floor of their home. Their colors set off the mer tails below us in a horrifyingly beautiful array.

I hadn't considered the possibility that the aftermath of the battle would still be on full display when we returned to the human kingdom. I try not to look too closely, knowing that if I do, I'll discover that the sea life has had little respect for our fallen mer. I have no desire to see missing eyes and flesh that has been partially eaten. Once their skin is gone and the bodies decompose, this area will become a boneyard for the fish and small creatures to hide in, using ribcages and eye sockets as shelter.

I drag my gaze up, unwilling to look at it any longer. Merrick's throat bobs as he swallows, also tearing his eyes away from the sight.

"This is horrific," Caspian voices what we're all thinking. "We can't even do anything about it, can we?"

"Not today," Merrick acknowledges the hopelessness of trying to do everything. "We have to stay on mission, and by the time we get through all of *this*..."

"They fought valiantly," Dylana says diplomatically. "We owe them much."

A few moments later, we find ourselves outside the palace. The steps still rest in the water, the waves washing over them. The outside is devoid of life, and no ships sit in the waters.

"The pool," I conclude, knowing our only way to get anyone's attention is by going back to the very place we escaped from.

Merrick and I veer off leaving the rest to follow us. Around the side of the palace, I locate the tunnel we vacated yesterday. Nothing blocks the entrance, so I force my way in before Merrick or anyone else can stop me.

I expect to find the tunnel blocked off again, but the bars are still bent at the end—apparently, not a priority. I hesitate for only a moment, closing my eyes before rushing in. Merrick stays with me. Caspian darts into the pool, but Merrick stops Llyr, instructing him to wait on the other side of the bars in case something happens.

Caspian looks around, spinning in the pool to get a good look at it while I dart to the surface—I don't have time to be quiet or scout the area. I need to make an entrance.

"Hello!" I splash out of the water, calling to anyone that can hear me. "Please! Is anyone here?"

When no one replies, I lower myself in the water and prepare to launch myself out of the pool. Merrick yells, but it doesn't stop me from hitting the side of the ledge, turning as I land to twist my tail around to the opposite side of the wall.

"Celena!" He sounds terrified as he surfaces, a tremble in his voice.

"I have to get help, Merrick."

"Get back in the pool—we'll yell for the humans," he insists, eyes wide. Caspian appears next to him, equally as furious with me.

"I tried that, they didn't hear me." I push off the wall, falling to the floor.

"Celena, this is insane!" Merrick's voice holds an edge of warning to it, but most of his tone is pure fear for my safety.

"Celena, *please*," Caspian begs, reinforcing his friend's sentiments.

I don't listen, dragging myself across the floor. I

almost wish we had escaped from the tiny pools we had originally been in—the floor was flat. This room forces me to crawl around the tiny partial walls the humans installed that act as a maze for me. I attempt to go over several of them, landing hard on the other side.

"Len?" Merrick calls out as I grunt when I hit the ground…again. The water behind me splashes like he's struggling to see me.

"I'm fine," I call, holding my hand in the air to prove I'm still alive. I regret everything about leaving the pool, but I force myself forward.

Footsteps sound beyond the high wall—tentative at first, but they quickly pick up the pace as the tiny feet slap against the stairs. Before they reach the end, a head of dark hair pops over the wall as the owner jumps in the air. She jumps again, gasping.

The footsteps echo off the walls as Analia rushes around the corner, running at me. Her dress is clutched in her hands as she moves quickly. I notice she's barefoot as she runs.

"Celena!" she shouts, throwing herself on the ground next to me. "What are you doing out of the pool?"

"I needed to find you," I gasp—I didn't realize how exhausting dragging myself across the palace floor would be. "Your brother is in trouble."

"I know, Father has been looking for him everywhere.

He's going to be in *so* much trouble when Father finds him."

"No, Analia." I shake my head. "You don't understand. We need to get your father."

"I don't think that's a good idea—Father's very angry. If he finds Edmund before he comes home and apologizes and fixes things, it's going to be worse for him."

"There isn't time for this, Analia—I need you to go get your father."

"No, I won't get Edmund in trouble. He always protects me, now I'm going to protect him." The curly-haired princess shakes her head, folding her arms over her chest defiantly.

"Analia, I just left your brother—bad people have him. We need to get your father." I reach out, touching her elbows. "Please, Analia. Your brother sent me—he *told* me to get your father."

Something twitches in her eyes. It's like the light shifts even though nothing in the room changes. She sucks in a breath, considering my words.

"Father will punish him," she feebly protests.

"Your father can't *punish* Edmund *if he's dead*," I present her with the facts. "Just go get him, *please!*"

She bounces to her feet, taking a few steps back. She still looks unsure.

"Analia, I wouldn't be back here if it weren't impor-tant," I remind her. "Please, go get your father."

"What if he doesn't listen to you?"

"I need you to help me convince him. Don't let him come back in here without you. You have to help me fight to save your brother."

"I thought you didn't love us anymore."

Did I ever love you? It's hard to love someone while being held hostage and threatened.

I fight to keep my head from jerking back in surprise.

"Analia, I only escaped because it was dangerous for me here, not because I didn't like you. I like you very much." Her face brightens at my words. "Now, go get your father, and hurry."

She turns, running back to the steps. The second it's quiet, Merrick's commanding voice fills the room.

"Celena, you get back over here *right now*." He leaves no room for discussion, but I'm already busy crawling back toward the water.

"Ow," I accidentally say out loud when I smack my tail off of a corner of a wall.

"Len?" Merrick calls, concerned.

"Celena?" Caspian echoes.

"I'm fine," I mutter. "Almost there."

I reach out, grabbing the side of the wall and Merrick's fingers instantly cover mine from the other side. I pull myself up, and Merrick hands his trident to Caspian so he can lift me over the wall. Caspian looks annoyed that he can't help, but he shouldn't even be using his trident with that injured arm, much less drag a mermaid over a wall and into a pool.

"What is this?" the king bellows, entering the room. Analia follows closely behind him, looking nervous.

"Your son needs help." I speed my tail up a little to raise myself up in the center of the pool. The king's eyes widen as he takes in Merrick and Caspian at my side.

"*You're* new," he muses, looking at Caspian.

"And worse than the last one," Casp regards him, hoping to make the king nervous.

"Injured, I see," the king points out. Analia's eyes are wide next to him as she stares at my brother like he's the most beautiful thing she's ever seen in her life.

After a moment, her gaze bounces back and forth between Merrick and Caspian, completely ignoring me. She blushes profusely, and I catch Caspian lowering his grin. The king shifts, irate at my brother, and furious that we've summoned him.

"Edmund needs your help," I say louder, insisting he revert his gaze to me. The king eyes me.

"We were bringing Edmund back—"

"The prince," the king cuts me off, correcting me. "You will address him as *the prince*."

"*He needs your help*," I push, annoyed. "On our way back, he was taken by sailors."

"Of course he was, I sent my men to rescue him," the king sneers at me.

"They weren't your men," I disagree. "Edmund was scared of them. He begged me to come and find you. He said you're the only one that can save him from them."

The message didn't make sense to me, but I followed his instructions to retrieve his father for him and bring back reinforcements.

"Father, you don't think…" Analia sounds scared. She clutches her father's sleeve. He glances at her for a moment before returning his glare to the pool.

"No, I don't. I think they have your brother." He nods at us.

"We don't," I insist. "We were bringing him back after he escaped your men. The boat took him—they forced him out of the water by scooping him up in a fishing net, tangled in seaweed and fish."

I try to paint a horrifying picture to get their attention. I easily sway the young princess, but her father is unmoveable.

"Where is my son?"

"He's on a boat."

"Where did you hide him?" The king's insistence to accuse us of hurting his son is frustrating. "Did you kill him?"

Analia shrieks, whipping around to face me with wide eyes.

"We didn't hurt Edmund." My words come out as a

growl. "He is on a boat with men who said they were willing to hurt him."

"It *is them*, Father!" Analia wheels back to the king, tugging on him again. "The rebels have him!"

She dissolves into tears, and the king reaches to comfort her.

"Father, they're going to hurt him," she sobs. "They nearly drowned me, and now they have Edmund, *please*! Please, go save him. Don't let them take him."

"Hush, now, Analia." He tries to stop her from speaking in front of us.

"These people hurt Analia?" I ask, demanding answers.

"They were the ones that took me when you saved me," Analia cries harder. I'm not sure if she's faking the show or if it's real, but if she had the forethought to pull this on her father, I give her a lot of credit for being able to manipulate him.

If these men that have the prince are the same ones that had been bringing Analia and Edmund to Hontan when I found them, that means these are the same men that Tarni made me siren to save Coralie.

"They're ruthless, Father, please. We have to do something."

"*If* it's them, they'll ask for a ransom, and we'll get him back," the king tries to console his daughter. "But it's not —it's the mer. They have him."

This is ridiculous—he's never going to listen to me.

"If we had him, wouldn't *we* ask for a ransom?" Merrick asks before I can. "Don't you think we'd leverage a treaty to trade with you for the life of your son? If that was our goal, why would we come to you with some story like this?"

Analia locks eyes with me, and I can tell immediately that while she's worried about her brother, the tears are *completely* for her father's benefit. I can see it in her eyes before she switches over, turning on her father with the attitude only an eleven-year-old princess can muster.

"They want to help Edmund. If you don't help him right now, I'll help the mermaids save him. Do you really want me to fling myself into a pool to get away from you like Edmund did?"

The king looks horrified. His chin drops as he steps back from his daughter to get a good look at her. She crosses her arms, eyes still shining with tears.

Analia takes a daring step toward the pool—there's no way she'll ever jump in. I doubt she could hold her breath long enough to get through the tunnel anyway.

"Analia!" The king's sharp voice gives her pause.

"It's not their fault," she yells at him.

I swim back to the wall, forcing myself up on it so they can see me better. Water trickles off me as my hair sticks to the sides of my arms, dripping down onto my fingers as I lean forward on the wall.

Analia rushes to my side to lend her support. Merrick and Caspian join me, taking places at either side to show our strength and resolve. I feel braverer with them by me.

The king considers us for a moment. When he takes a gentle step toward us, I think we've won him over. He reaches his hand out to me like Edmund does. I place my hand in his, and his fingers close around mine.

I'm shocked when he pulls me forward, and I topple off the wall onto the ground. The mermen clamor behind me, demanding the king not touch me as I try to catch myself. Analia shrieks but doesn't move.

The king turns on me, grabbing me by my hair and waist. He lifts me, throwing me across the room. I collide with one of the short walls, falling over it. My scream startles everyone, and I hear a tiny war erupt behind me between the mermen and the king.

I roll over, trying to sit up. Swallowing, I attempt to force down the pain crawling through my body. Analia snaps out of it, rushing to my side.

"Are you okay?" she murmurs.

"Get back," the king roars, coming for me.

"Father, leave her alone," Analia shouts, brushing back her hair nervously.

I crawl around one of the walls, dragging my tail behind me. I'd prefer the scooting technique I used inside of the caves, but I don't have time to protect my scales.

I'm grateful the floor isn't made of bumpy rock but is rather a smooth, polished surface.

Merrick is on the wall of the pool, swinging his tail around to face us. Caspian quickly hands him his trident, but Merrick waves it off. Instead, he pulls out his knife.

"Analia, go to Merrick," I instruct as I attempt to escape her father.

Analia does as I say, not thinking it through before she moves. Merrick whispers something to her—I assume the assurance that he won't really hurt her—and then wraps his arm around her neck and chest. He raises the knife to her.

"Let Celena go," Merrick says, voice echoing in the room in a deep rumble.

"Father," Analia squeaks. She doesn't look terrified until her father turns. I wonder which parts of her conversations with me were purely for *my* benefit—she's skilled at manipulating people's emotions.

"Get your hands off the princess," the king growls.

"Get your hands off *our* princess," Merrick counters.

From my angle, I can't see the king's face, but I can tell his jaw just twitched. He faces them for another full minute before he turns back to me.

"I'll see you mutilated for this," he hisses.

I crawl over to the side of the pool. It seems to take a painfully long time. Merrick removes his arm from Analia, leaving only the knife against her throat—Analia doesn't move, knowing the moment she does, her father will attack again.

Merrick reaches down to me with his free arm, tightening his muscles. I latch on to his forearm, and he helps to pull me up onto the wall next to him. Caspian drags me into the pool before I can pause to wait for Merrick. My twin thrusts a trident into my hands, and I whip around to direct it at the king in case he dares to step toward Merrick.

"Don't move until I'm in the water," Merrick whispers to Analia. "I don't want you to get hurt."

"Release her, *mer*." The king's eyes twitch, but I detect worry in his voice. "You have your *princess* back."

"Stay still," Merrick instructs again. He leans back, falling into the water backward. He flings his arm to the side to avoid hurting the princess.

When she hears the splash, she turns.

"We have to help Edmund!" Analia spins back to her father, demanding he refocus.

"I will have them cut in half," the king growls, eyes slicing over to Caspian and me.

Caspian turns, and Analia watches him intently as he drags me under the water. I see the king latch onto his daughter's arm, pulling her from the room.

"Hurry," I say as soon as Merrick rights himself. We rush toward the bent bar.

"What just happened?" Llyr yelps. "Caspian held us off."

"I didn't want to scare him into hurting her," Caspian protests as we careen down the glowing tunnel.

"He took Celena," Merrick explains.

"Again?" Llyr looks back at me over his shoulder as we burst out into the open waters. "Are you okay?"

"He didn't slice me open...yet," I reply. "There's a very good chance he's out here waiting for us though. We're going to have to help Edmund ourselves."

"We just have to find him," Dylana adds grimly.

"*Oh*, I don't think *that's* going to be an issue," Keone calls back to us. "Looks like they've brought him home."

A man stands on the deck of the ship, one arm tangled in ropes hanging from the boom. He leans out over the water, prepared to enter into negotiations with the king.

Edmund is bound with ropes around his entire upper body. He's gagged, but his eyes roam the waters, looking for something.

The king stands on the shores above the steps, arm posed in the air as if he's ordering his men. He glares at the ship entering his royal kingdom.

"Your majesty," the man cries, sweeping his hand grandly to the side. "We need to have a conversation."

His chuckle fills the air. The king shouts back in response, threatening the man if he doesn't hand over his son.

"Happily, sire. Which piece of him would you like first? His hand? His ear?" The man reaches for Edmund's ear, and Analia's piercing shriek from near the palace makes everyone duck as if a cannon had been shot.

The ship is not the one I dove off of. It appears the men have several captives from that ship, including one of the men I sirened into shooting a cannonball into their own deck—this must be the second ship and the reason Edmund was insistent on finding his father for help.

The vessel is brown and stands tall in the water, looking menacing. The windows are outlined in dark metal, and ropes hang over the sides of the boat. Men leer at us in the water as the entire collection surfaces.

Edmund spots me just as the others reveal themselves, tridents in hand. The mer surround the boat at a safe distance, blocking it in. Edmund's eyes are huge as they focus on me.

When he looks to his father, I follow his line of sight. The king stands in awe at the mer collection willing to fight for his son's freedom.

"Father!" Edmund yells. I look back just in time to see the man holding him rip the gag from around his neck, jarring him.

"Stay calm, son!" the king shouts back. "We'll get you back."

"We need to talk about terms!" the man shouts.

A line of guards steps up behind the king, readying

arrows in their bows. Each one flames orange as the king lifts his hand.

"You will give my son back, and I won't burn your ship, *Captain.*"

"You wouldn't burn a boat with your son on it," the captain laughs. His taunt is cut short when the king drops his hand and his men release their arrows.

They fly in a glorious arc that matches the sunset that has turned the sky a fierce orange color. The arrows land on the deck of the ship well beyond where Edmund and the captain stand. A few hit men, making them shriek in pain or collapse on the deck. One falls off the ship, dead. The fire extinguishes when it hits the water, sizzling.

The captain turns back to the king, mouth open.

"You had your chance, Captain. Now you're left with only this—hand my son over, get in your rowboats, and leave before I send my mermaids after you. If you don't, you'll be lucky if my men reach you before the mer do."

"Do it," I instruct, raising my trident toward the boat. The others follow suit, looking destructive. I don't like that the king is lording us over the men, but now is not the time to argue.

The flames cover the boat, looming over the edge. It crackles as it starts to lick its way down the side of the ship. Smoke pours into the sky, dark against the sunlight glistening through the clouds bathed in gold.

CHAPTER 14

THE CAPTAIN AND EDMUND DISAPPEAR FROM SIGHT. I can't tell where they've gone, but the king is calm, so I assume he can still see Edmund.

Men jump into rowboats and lower themselves into the water. They don't have much space between us and the boat, but that doesn't seem to deter them. Before they reach the surface, they launch their attack against the mer, trying to clear us away.

"Celena, find the prince," Marilla instructs, moving in to handle the fight.

I don't hesitate, diving under the water as my collection holds back the sailors from fleeing with the prince who is our only hope to end this war. My friends follow behind me, ready to support my mission.

From the backside of the boat, I spot a tiny rowboat

moving away from the ship. Surfacing, I can see the captain holding a knife to Edmund's neck.

"Call off your sea witches, your highness," he shouts. The king deftly shakes his head.

"Let him go, and I'll consider sparing your men." He spooks as I address him.

"Not going to happen," he shouts back, knife moving closer to Edmund's throat. The prince closes his eyes for a moment, fingers flexing at his sides.

"Should we tip the boat?" Natale suggests.

"Would he slit the prince's throat when it moves?" Keone counters.

"We could surround him," Dylana offers. "We all have tridents."

"Siren him," Phorcys says in a flat voice. "Swim up to the boat and siren him."

"What if he has his ears blocked?" I counter.

"He talked to the king," Phorcys points out.

"Doesn't mean he doesn't have something there to block it."

"I'll do it," Cassidia pushes past me—I didn't realize she was here with us. I jerk on her tail, and she turns on me.

"Stay out of this, *siren*." I'm positive if Cassidia is involved, Edmund will die today.

If the prince perishes today, I'm also positive the king

will blame the mer and come after us even more ferociously—I can't let that happen.

"We surround them. He can't take on all of us at once. Once we get Edmund out of the boat, we get him as far away as possible, and try to take him to the palace steps."

I look around the group to make sure everyone understands.

"Whoever can get to him, take him straight to the king—the rest of us will help. We only need one or two of us to handle the captain." My mind instantly flashes to the captain drowning next to his rowboat. "Don't wait—just go straight to the palace steps."

Everyone nods, even Phorcys and Cassidia—though *she* doesn't look happy about it. Murdoch swims quietly beside us, still looking uncomfortable being in our presence.

We swim up from the depths, surrounding the boat as it moves. Merrick and I take the lead position at the front of the boat—we'll be the first ones the captain and Edmund see. On my signal, we lift ourselves out of the water.

The captain stops his man from rowing. The boat floats in the water, stopping with a jerk as Merrick puts his hand out to halt it. It bounces into his hand, but he doesn't flinch.

He raises the knife to Edmund's throat again, glaring at Merrick.

"I'm not the one you need to be worried about," Merrick addresses him with a smirk and hard eyes.

"Release him," I say in my most dangerous voice. I use it when I interrogate mer for Marilla—and I *always* get my answers.

The captain's sneer fades away, leaving a hard line of a mouth and slanted eyes in its place.

"Or what—you'll siren me?" he arrogantly challenges me.

"Look around you, Captain." I nod behind him. "You're not going anywhere."

He slowly turns, observing the collection holding tridents to him.

"You won't hurt me while I have him."

"You forget, Captain," I remind him, smiling. I hope he believes we're attempting to trick the king, but really plan to double cross him. "Mer and humans no longer work together. That treaty was broken a century ago. We have our own reasons for wanting the human prince."

We lock eyes as he tries to read me. I hope I look convincing.

He places a hand on the side of the ship to steady himself as Llyr knocks his trident into the boat. The boat tips back and forth three times before settling, then Caspian repeats the process from the other side, throwing the captain off again.

Edmund attempts to balance himself, but he pitches

around with the rocking of the boat, eyes locked on me as he waits for instructions. I swim forward while the captain is distracted.

"We would like the prince now," I say, getting the captain's attention. "Please."

The captain starts to raise his hand to me but can't get it past the blade I hold over his knuckle. He looks down, paling.

"Once more, we would like Prince Edmund now, please."

The captain whips his blade away from the prince, slashing at me, but I move faster. His finger falls in the water, bumping my tail as it sinks down to where the fish can find it. Blood pours from the stub on his hand as he screams, cursing at me and promising to cut me into pieces.

I reach inside the boat and lower my blade to his leg, prepared to cut him again. He flinches and drags his knife lightly across the back of my hand, misjudging my location through the tears in his eyes.

The boat rocks as Keone and Natale work to flip the boat. Phorcys joins them as Caspian and Cassidia dart out of the way. Merrick swings his trident, aiming for the captain's head but he pulls up at the last second to avoid hitting Edmund as the boat shifts position.

I grab the edge of the boat and swim under the water, helping the collection to flip the boat as the humans topple onto me. I flick my tail, moving away so that I can turn to see where everyone is in the water. Merrick pulls Edmund out from under the boat, but the other sailor quickly follows, trying to latch on to Edmund.

When I surface, several other rowboats have converged on the collection. Caspian takes on a man dressed in a dark grey shirt and darker pants as he uses an oar to attempt to injure my twin. His trident takes the man out easily, piercing through his chest.

"Len," Merrick's shout draws my attention back to him, and I discover a boat attempting to rip the prince away from him. Edmund is still tied up and can't help with his escape—his struggling makes him look like one of the creatures that accidentally crawled into a brine pool.

I pierce a sailor's wrist with my trident, twisting as he shrieks. He loses his grip on Edmund, but the sailor behind him lunges toward the prince, thrusting a spear into the water

Reeling back. I send the flat end side of my trident into the sailor's face, destroying his aim as his spear enters the water. Edmund bellows in pain.

"It's his leg," Merrick quickly states, letting me know he will survive the strike.

I pull my trident back as Merrick attempts to move Edmund out of reach. Caspian and Llyr appear next to me, tridents up.

"Untie him so he doesn't drown," Caspian instructs, handling the sailors in the boat I was fighting.

I rush to Merrick and Edmund, fishing my knife out of my *iluse*.

"Hold still, I'm going to cut the ropes."

Edmund flips over in the water so that he's floating on his back. Merrick supports him, letting the prince rest his head on his shoulder to ensure he stays above water while I'm working.

I work my fingers between the bottom coil of rope and the prince's stomach, lifting it enough to slip my knife between him and the rope upside down. I saw it back and forth until the rope snaps. Quickly, I rush to snap more of the ropes, peeling off layers as quickly as I can.

Merrick keeps an eye on the fighting so I can focus on freeing the prince. Edmund slows his breathing, trying not to move as I work.

"Almost there," I mumble as the fighting grows louder behind me. "Merrick?"

"They're okay so far. They took out a couple of sailors."

"Assuming I survive this, I'm going to drive out all the mercenaries," Edmund grumbles.

"You're father is here," I inform him.

"I saw."

"He tried to hurt Celena…again," Merrick takes the opportunity to inform him.

"What did he do?" Edmund bolts up in the water, knocking Merrick and nearly causing me to stab him—I get my finger out of the way just in time. "Sorry. What did he do?"

"We'll explain later," I grumble. "Hold still."

With the lower part of his arms free, he reaches up, trying to remove the ropes around his upper arms, hindering my ability to help him.

"Edmund!" He stills as I lecture him.

Once he's free, I instruct Merrick to return him to the king. I turn, ready to defend them from behind. Swimming backward isn't nearly as easy without latching arms with Merrick and allowing him to direct my moves. Merrick and I call to each other as we move since we're unable to feel each other's movements.

"Len, we've got a problem," Merrick shouts as we round the corner of the burning ship. Several small boats turn toward us, making their way through the water as our collection battles against them.

There are more boats than there were before—the king has sent his men in the water, but I can't tell which ones are our enemies and which are our temporary allies. More boats turn toward us when they see the prince.

"Len, time to switch," Merrick decides, summoning

me. I know he's right—I have a better chance of moving the prince while Merrick defends us.

I rush to his side, brushing against his arm as I take Edmund's from him. He darts forward, kissing me quickly.

"Careful," he whispers before taking off. I have no doubt he'd kill every human here to ensure my safety as I drag the prince to shore.

"Merrick." My voice trembles as he looks back. I whisper, "Don't do anything stupid."

He flashes the most brilliant grin at me, revealing his dimples. His eyes sparkle as he tips his head, flipping his bangs back out of his face. He purses his lips, blowing a tiny kiss to me, winking as he leaves to face the humans alone.

"Hold your breath," I tell Edmund. He gulps in air, and I submerge us under the waves, swimming until he squeezes my arm as I'm wrapped around his waist and back.

The palace steps aren't terribly far away when we surface, but we have to get by several boats before we're in the clear. The king spots us, relief washing over his face when he sees Edmund in the water. He waves, trying to get us to come to the step.

I wonder if perhaps the king has taken one too many hits to the head recently.

Edmund turns on his back to float while I swim

toward the steps, much like Merrick and I do, only the prince isn't trained to fight. He attempts to kick his good leg but quickly gives up.

When he reels back and kicks out, it surprises me. The movement bobs us under the water, but when I turn, I see a man in the ocean behind us, swimming toward us quickly. Bravery—or more likely, *stupidity*—has encouraged the man to take us on in *my* world instead of his.

Edmund kicks again, trying to keep the man at bay. I release the prince and flip under the water, pulling the man's legs. He bounces over the surface of the water until I drag him down, moving him far away.

The man claws at me when I release him, but he only has so much time to swim to the surface before he's out of air. He picks his life over his revenge and attempts to claw his way to the surface.

Edmund struggles in the water with another man— this one clearly a sailor. His beard barely moves, despite being soaking wet from the ocean water. He holds a knife in his hands, and it glints gold in the light of the fire.

Edmund punches him, holding his collar—I'm impressed.

"Celena, behind you!" Edmund shouts to me, striking the man again.

I turn just in time to see a boat sneak up on me. Rushing at it, I slam into it full speed, turning it over in the water. I swim away upside down, monitoring the surface as I rush to Edmund's aid.

Twirling in the water, I spiral down to the depths with the bearded sailor. His eyes are alive with fear, and his nails dig into my arm just below my armor, making me wince, but I refuse to let go. His hands had been around Edmund's throat as he attempted to choke him when I intervened. Edmund had almost held his own, but the man's arms were longer and stronger than the prince's, and Edmund didn't stand a chance.

Bubbles slip from his lips—so many that it's hard to see. I release him, clawing once at his face. If he wants to live, he'll have to swim quickly.

Leaving him behind in the water, I find Edmund swimming toward the steps slowly. He rotates between swimming on his stomach and on his back, checking in front of him and behind him as he moves. At least he had the foresight to do that.

"Edmund!" the king screams from the shore. Somewhere in the background, Analia screams for her brother as well. I'm not sure if Edmund can hear them—he's incredibly focused on his survival right now.

We're closer to the steps, and several of the boats have moved, but two battle directly in our path—guards and mercenaries fighting against one another.

"We have to go under," I prompt Edmund. He nods.

Below the waves, everything sparkles with an orange

tone—a mixture of the reflection of the fire from the boat and the setting sun. Bubbles shine like bursts of light every time a sailor hits the water.

Bubbles slip from Edmund's nose slowly, and I know he'll need air soon, but I can't afford to stop yet—we have to make it further.

Splashing sounds behind me, and I think part of the ship just crashed into the water loudly. A light wave confirms my suspicions as it washes over my back, moving my hair as I guide us around the battle above us.

Edmund's fingers dig into my waist as I carry him upside down, his chest against mine. He wraps himself around me tighter, fighting not to panic as he begins to choke.

Further. Don't stop.

I beat my tail, accidentally slapping his legs as I move us through the water, but I can't angle myself away from him—I need to get him air. His grip loosens, and I panic.

Darting up, I surface right where both boats can see us. I shake Edmund, and he coughs, gulping in air as he sputters.

"Breathe," I direct, not wasting time trying to soothe him. He continues to choke but tries to hold his breath again for me. Before I can drop us into the water, he chokes again.

"Hurry, Edmund," I mumble.

If I had seen any starfish below, I would be wishing on

it, but right now, all I have is the palace steps ahead of me. Water laps against them, rising and falling at different levels with every crash of the waves. Sometimes they cover the higher steps, sometimes the lower steps, but never more than halfway up.

I focus on it as a punch sounds directly over our heads. We both look up as a guard slams his fist into a sailor, knocking him back. The man staggers but pushes himself forward to clash against the guard.

"Hurry!" he shouts to us without looking.

I heed his warning to flee and take off with Edmund. Dipping under the water, he clings to me again. When we surface, we're only a few lengths away from the steps.

I picture my great-great-grandmother Aila sitting on those steps with Edmund's great-great-grandfather Jarek. Aila always said that Jarek would sit toward the bottom of the steps while she and Persephone sat partially in the water. Jarek didn't mind getting his boots wet if it meant he got to be near the mermaids and the ocean. She told us he could stare at the sea for hours and loved watching the sunset with his mermaid friends.

I imagine their evenings looked much like this— without light from a burning ship overtaking the sunset while people died all around them.

We crash into the steps, and it nearly knocks the wind out of me—it's hard to see the steps under the water without actually *being* under the water to see them. Edmund hauls himself up, being careful of his leg.

"Look out!" he shouts before he can scramble up all the way.

The prince reaches down in the water, scooping me into his arms. He hauls me onto the steps, tossing me high as a rowboat crashes against the stairs, pinning his already-injured leg between the boat and the step.

He screams in pain as I collide with the steps, high out of the water—I have no idea how he threw me so high. The king and his men rush past me. One guard kicks at the boat, forcing it back so hard that he nearly falls in the water.

The king and a guard pluck Edmund from the steps and pull him up to the ground, leaving me to sag against the steps, trying to catch my breath. My ribs throb from the impact with the steps.

"Celena, go!" Edmund begs through his pain. "Get back in the water and go!"

He moans as the men stumble, trying to move him quickly. I watch them drag him for a moment.

"Come back when it's safe, but go!"

Turning, the sun is setting over the horizon. It glints off the water magically. The fire illuminates the water and the side of the rocky palace cliff—much of the ship is submerged in the water now. It crackles loud, sizzling when fire meets wave.

The palace guards retreat once the prince is safe—they'll all be safe inside the palace if they can lock the mercenaries out. The men stumble up the hill, checking for enemies as they move, but are greeted with nothing but an empty courtyard and path to the ocean.

Bodies float in the water, bobbing lifelessly. The collection is smaller yet again, but Marilla is still alive, calling for me from the ocean. I scurry down the steps, bumping painfully into each one until I reach the water. I push off of it like Aila did so many times before they were banished from Antaire. The water swallows me up, darkening as I sink below the waves.

CHAPTER 15

THE MER COLLECTION IMMEDIATELY FOLLOWS, DROPPING down to the depths of the shallow inlet near the palace. From our vantage point, we can see the guards attempting to finish the battle in the water above us.

Boats are tipped over, floating upside down. The burning ship sinks entirely in the water as Merrick races to me. We collide, and he wraps his arms around me.

"Are you hurt?" His face is so close to mine that all I can think about are his lips on my skin. I shake my head.

"Are you?" My hands close around his upper arms, just above his elbows as he stares into my eyes.

Instead of answering me, he kisses me. We don't move at first, our lips just pressed together, but after a moment, he tips his head, separating his lips.

"We're all still here, thanks," Llyr interrupts, elbowing Merrick.

"Like you don't want to do that," I chide, shaking my head.

"Maybe I already did," he grins, glancing at Dylana. My jaw drops.

"When you work fast, you really work fast, Llyr," I joke.

"Worth it," he nods, grinning.

"Celena!" Caspian barrels into me, colliding against Merrick and me.

"Your arm?" I ask.

"Still attached," he replies, eyes sparkling.

A new body drifts down in the ocean, landing on top of a merman that died in the initial battle a few days ago —things are starting to pile up. I cringe as it hits its resting place.

"Where is Edmund?" Dylana questions, looking concerned.

"With his father in the palace," Marilla interjects. "He was wounded, but he'll be okay."

"What is *that*?" Keone asks suddenly, pointing at the surface.

"Is that the king?" I ask in horror.

A large boat sails in, overtaking all of the remaining rowboats. It's not as tall or as wide as the ship that burned a few minutes ago, but it carries enough authority —and weapons—to make any man nervous.

The king's flags sail from its mast, confirming that the

king is angry and wants to end this. He stands at the front of the ship, pointing to the men in the water.

The sides of the boat are low enough that his men can haul in victims from their guard or take hostages from the collection of mercenaries in the waters.

His guards reach out, pulling men from the sea. If they are found to be the enemy, they are slain and returned to the water to wash away with the tide. What the king doesn't notice is that the captain has somehow survived and is in the water below him.

"The captain is going after the king," I mumble.

"What?"

"The captain is going after the king!" I shout, darting away from the ocean floor as I flip my tail as hard as I can toward the surface. Merrick takes off after me, begging me to wait, but I can't.

I'm not sure what possessed the king to take to the waters, but it was a terrible idea. He had been safe inside with his children, and yet he decides to come out to fight a bunch of sailors who had already lost any control they might have had? Revenge is in his blood, it seems.

The captain swings himself up onto the boat, surprising the king. The man steps back, crashing into one of his guards. The captain takes a menacing step toward the king, knife in hand. A guard blocks him, taking the strike and he topples backward, flipping outside of the boat.

I reach the surface and jump toward the open part of the ship. My hand catches the captain's foot, and I pull back. The man pitches forward, slamming into the deck.

The captain turns on me. Somehow, he managed to keep his knife in his hand, though it looks like he bit through his lip when he fell—a tremendous amount of blood falls from his punctured lower lip. A broken tooth is missing from his mouth, and I'm positive I can see it in the background behind him.

He slams the knife at me, driving it into the wooden deck as I recoil, barely missing the attack. The captain growls at me, wincing when he realizes the damage he's done to his face.

A guard comes to my aid, wrenching the captain around as the king kicks at his head. Merrick grabs hold of me and drags me backward.

"Careful there, princess," he teases. "I'm pretty sure bad things happen when mermaids end up on boats."

Above the water, the king staggers to his feet. He moves toward the captain, but the sailor is faster. He grabs the king's leg and pulls it out from under him, making the king fall to the deck of the ship again.

The captain pulls his hand back, preparing to strike, but the guard snaps his hand from behind him. The captain recoils in pain—it looks like his wrist is shattered. My jellyfish stings must feel like nothing compared to the pain of a shattered bone.

The king scrambles back, not realizing how close he is to the opening in the ship's wall. Merrick moves to warn him before I do, but neither of us surface in time and the king crashes backward into the water.

The flash in the water is so quick that I'm not entirely convinced that I see it until I drop under the waves. Cassidia has somehow found her way around us and is rushing toward the king. Phorcys darts past us, racing after the blue siren. Her icy blue tail looks serene and gentle compared to Phorcys' fiery orange one, but *she's* the one we need to worry about.

The mermaid siren catches the king and drags him down to the depths, twisting as she swims to disorient the king. Phorcys shouts to her, but she's on a mission and doesn't hear his cries as he pleads with her not to do this—he knows the mer wrath will be swift.

"She's going to kill him," I shout. Given the number of times I've had to swim at full speed this evening alone, I think once I return to wherever the mer settle, I'll take up permanent residence on a lounging couch and never move again. Perhaps I can train a dolphin to fetch things for me.

Cassidia slows near the ocean floor, a mere length from the dead bodies resting on the sand. The king struggles, kicking at her tail, but she holds fast. Her white hair flows out behind her, and once again, I'm in awe of everything about her. It amazes me that Nir was the royal and she wasn't.

Phorcys reaches them and attempts to rip Cassidia's hand away from the human. She glares at him, saying something we can't hear from this distance. Phorcys argues, trying again to loosen her grasp.

The king's dark clothing helps him to blend in with the darkening water. The sun has disappeared from the sky, and while we still have light to see by, it won't be long before we don't.

Phorcys attempts to wrap his arms around Cassidia and pull her away, but she crashes her head back, slamming into his face with her skull. The merman looks up, catching my eye and it renews his commitment to stop her. He pulls at her angrily as she puts up a fight.

Bubbles escape the king's mouth as he cries out—Cassidia buries a broken shell piece into his side. His hair is long enough to float in the water, but not quite long enough to cover his eyes as he stares at the mermaid in front of him. Blood blossoms in the water, dispersing quickly—the fish don't seem to notice as they swim around the scene.

My hands are on Cassidia's wrist before she realizes I have joined them, far too distracted by the king and Phorcys. I slice into her with my trident, slamming into her arm just below her shoulder. It was a risk attacking her near the king, but it was the only thing I could do to stop her.

Merrick reaches the king and pulls him toward the surface, leaving Phorcys and me to handle Cassidia. She glares at me.

"You've ruined everything," she says calmly. "You killed Nir, you killed Tarni, you let the human prince and king go. You even destroyed the siren collection—they're all dead because of you.

"Look around, *Celena*—all this is because of you." She points to the bodies on the ocean floor in the dwindling light. "You killed all of them. *Why*? Because you wanted to prove some point your great-great-grandmother was trying to make a century ago?

"She failed *then,* and you failed *now*. Congratulations, you've sealed the fate of three kingdoms, and destroyed the entire sea nation."

"Aila didn't fail—she protected the collection." I ready my trident, knowing an attack is imminent.

"She turned her back on her own blood. If we had all worked together, the humans would be gone, and the sea would be a peaceful place."

"Instead you turn it into a war? Nir's father was an idiot to think he could take on the humans like this— we've avoided them for a century—we could have gone on avoiding them forever, and everyone would still be alive," I challenge her.

She twitches in the water—my only signal that something bad is about to happen.

Cassidia dives at Phorcys as he hovers in the water behind her. She wrenches away his trident and rushes at me. I wait for her to approach me, using the force of her movement to set her off balance. I move at the last second, and she crashes forward, tilting at an angle she wasn't expecting.

Phorcys is close behind her, but only has a knife to defend himself with now. The struggle is written on his face—protect a siren he's likely known his entire life—a trusted advisor to his former king and prince, and an ally of his princess—or help the mermaid who holds his future in her hands.

The merman grits his teeth and moves slowly—*intentionally*—in the water behind her as she starts forward toward me. He has the look of a predator closing in on his unwitting prey. Cassidia's piercing blue gaze is fixed on me with deadly precision as she swims toward me slowly.

"Nir—*and* his father—were protecting the ocean, *unlike your* queen," she addresses me in a cold voice.

"My queen protected the collection. Yours *sacrificed* your mer." My fingers close tighter around my trident. Cassidia's blood is still caught near the points at the end from my last attack.

"It was a sacrifice we were willing to make for the

sake of the seas, wasn't it, Phorcys?" She expects the merman to be on her side. She doesn't realize his alliances have changed.

"There are a lot of things I'm willing to do," he growls as if he's supporting her, but he keeps his deadly eyes trained on his former collection mate.

I will spend the rest of my life leery of Phorcys—his allegiance changes like the tides.

Cassidia moves to strike, and I hold my hand up in warning. She quirks her head slightly, narrowing her eyes.

"I wouldn't do that if I were you."

"Leave her be, Cassidia."

Fear flashes over Cassidia's pretty features, leaving her nearly unrecognizable for a moment as she discovers she is alone in this fight.

"Nir would want us to finish this." Cassidia raises her voice. "So would Tarni."

"They're both dead, Cassidia. We're all that's left."

"Roni is still here. They have Tiko and the others—"

"Tiko's not getting out." Her face twitches slightly at his words, and I wonder if she has some kind of connection to the siren with the periwinkle tail being held at Scylla— or Metten...I have no idea where the prisoners are.

"You and I could take them on together." She turns slowly to face him, risking her back to me. I don't move.

"This is about survival, Cassidia—I'll take my punishment with *them*. I won't work against them." He slams his trident into the sand so that it's pointing up toward the water. He reveals a knife in his hands, making it an even fight.

Cassidia's shoulders straighten, and she flips the broken shell in her hand. I expect her to charge at Phorcys. Instead, she flips in the water toward me for the final time—she wants to take me down with her. I dart back, but she has the advantage.

Phorcys reaches her just as her knife drags along the bottom of my tail just above my fins. My purple scales separate under the jagged shell, several pop off, falling to the ocean floor. I cry out in pain.

Caspian collides with my back, pulling me away as Phorcys drags his knife across Cassidia's hip. She screams, thrusting her hand at Phorcys to injure him. She collides with his shoulder, infuriating him as the broken shell opens his skin.

The collection closes in, unsure if they should get involved.

"Phorcys!" I yell. I may despise the mermaid he's about to destroy, but I don't want her to die—she should suffer for her actions for the rest of her life. Unlike Persephone, I'll see to it that she won't die early.

Llyr rushes into action, trying to break up the brawl,

but Phorcys is a force, and no one can stop him as he drags his knife through the mermaid again.

Cassidia twists in his arms, but Phorcys has her pinned against him as he holds his knife to her. He makes eye contact with me, and his eyes soften for just a moment before he nods to the surface, indicating that I should help Merrick with the king.

The two drop in the water, twisting as they fight against each other. He's right—it's more important to protect the human king.

"Don't interfere," I warn the collection. "This is a siren matter—the *last* siren matter."

Swimming is excruciating with my new injury, but Caspian guides me to the surface as Llyr oversees the fight below. We race to the top of the water, slowly exiting to determine where we need to go.

The captain's body floats on its back in the water a few lengths away from Merrick. He swims slowly with the king—they're both injured. Several other bodies bob in the water too, and I wonder if Merrick just took on all those men to protect the king.

"Father!" Analia screams. She elbows a guard and races to the steps, crashing into a wave as it crests on the stairs leading into the ocean. It nearly knocks her off balance and sends her tumbling in the ocean, but the guard she hit catches up, reaching out to save her by her elbow.

She jerks, feet nearly slipping out from under her but he holds her in place. She pins him with an adoring, awe-filled gaze before turning back to her father and Merrick.

"Father!" she screams again, sounding like she's been sobbing.

The king tries turning around in the water to face his daughter, but Merrick holds him tightly, making it difficult for him to flip off his back. Merrick says something sharp and the king stops struggling.

The guard pulls the princess back up the steps, out of the way of the other men who rush down to help pull the king from the water. They wait anxiously.

"Is your brother all right?"

"Edmund's inside," she calls back, voice quieter.

"Is he safe?" the king calls as he and Merrick approach the steps.

"Yes, Papa."

The men trample the water with their heavy boots, not slipping like Analia did. They reach out, pulling the king from the ocean. He only makes it a few steps before he collapses into a sitting position, hand on his chest, and gasps.

Angry tears in his shirt reveal open wounds on his sides. One of his boots is missing. The king has marks on his face, which will bloom into angry purple tones tomorrow. He looks worse than his son's crushed leg.

Analia sobs when she observes his injuries and begs

the men to take him back to the palace. They lift the king, sharing his weight, and move toward the opalescent dwelling as he lolls limply in their arms.

Merrick doesn't look nearly as injured as the king, but it's clear he's been through a battle on his own. I touch his arm, making him jump. He tears his focus away from the king and quickly scoops me into his arms.

"Phorcys is about to kill Cassidia."

"What?" he demands, eyes wide.

"Celena!" Analia calls when she notices me with Merrick. I turn to face her, but Merrick refuses to release me. "Edmund said to tell you to stay. They're setting his leg, but he needs to speak with you right away."

I nod, unsure if it's wise to stay.

"It might take a few hours, Celena, please don't leave," she begs. "Whatever he needs, it's important."

The princess lifts her dress and runs up the path to the castle. Once she's inside, Merrick, Caspian, and I dive back under the waves to see which siren won—if by some miracle it was Cassidia, I doubt the collection let her last long.

Phorcys floats in the water, shoulders bent over low. They sag with each heavy breath he takes. Cassidia lies on the ocean floor, arms stretched above her head, hair tossed over them. Slowly, Phorcys puts his knife away and sinks to the floor next to the blue-tailed siren.

He rolls her over and cradles her in his arms. His face

is hard, but the tiniest flicker of regret pulses out of him —at least that's what it looks like to me. Phorcys reaches down to brush the hair out of her face as she dies.

Her entire body is covered in open wounds—Phorcys showed little mercy during their battle. She blinks, slowly slipping away. I suppose we'll never find out how she learned to siren so well.

The collection watches nervously, ready to take on the merman siren if they need to. They move, making a way for us as we swim slowly over to Phorcys and Cassidia.

Perhaps it's a good thing we have to stay and wait for Edmund to speak with us.

Marilla intercepts us, eyebrow raised as she waits for a report.

"The king has been hurt—they took him inside. Edmund sent his sister to beg us to wait for him."

Marilla sighs, knowing we don't have much of a choice. Perhaps this evening will convince the king that all we want is to live in peace, far, far away from the humans.

I turn back to Phorcys just as he sets Cassidia down. He takes the shell out of her hand. Swimming up in the water, he moves toward Marilla.

The collection seizes their weapons in their hands and prepares to stop him. Phorcys ignores them and opens his hand palm up, displaying the shell to the queen.

"I'm prepared to follow you," he addresses her, "and to take whatever punishment you deem fit for my actions during the war."

Marilla stares at him for a moment before moving—her version of hesitation disguised as something meant to make the mer before her wait in fear. She reaches out and takes the blood-covered broken shell.

"I'll consider your punishment. You will have a trial, and we will proceed with sentencing when we return."

Phorcys nods like a good soldier. He drops his hand to his side, and Marilla continues to stare him down. She drops her chin just enough to be a simple nod, indicating that the collection should move.

Everyone turns their backs on Phorcys, casting one last look at the blue siren. He follows behind them, stony-faced.

I slip under Merrick's arm as we follow behind Phorcys and the collection.

We swim away, but Marilla only lets us go so far before she commands our attention.

"We are staying—we will not swim in the dark tonight. We're far enough away that we won't be hurt, and deep enough that no man can reach us, but we'll take turns keeping watch anyway," the queen directs the collection. I'm glad I'm not in charge at this point.

We settle onto the sand, curling up close together. I nestle against Merrick, and Caspian protectively rests on my other side, the backs of our hands touching so that we know the other one is safe. Dylana finds us, and we lay so that our heads are near each other. Llyr positions himself next to Dylana, mirroring my positioning with Merrick.

I know Marilla has our best soldiers on watch duty, so sleep comes easily.

CHAPTER 16

THE OCEAN SPARKLES WITH COLOR WHEN I WAKE. A school of brilliant red fish swims a few lengths over me. I curl into Merrick as he begins to stir next to me, taking a deep breath. His lungs fill, moving me so gracefully that I smile, finger slowly moving down his chest.

He blinks awake and grins at me.

"Good morning."

I reach up and move his blue bangs out of the way, clearing his vision. He reaches for my hand trailing down his skin and brings it to his lips, kissing it gently. My scales race with a spark of energy.

A starfish rests against his tail, and Merrick flicks it gently, letting the ripple motion inform the starfish that it's time to move. Merrick's fingers drum lightly on my hip.

The sun cascades through the water, glimmering

against every piece of debris that floats in the ocean. I imagine much of that is from the boat that burned last night. Tipping my head straight out from my neck, I see it in the distance, submerged in the ocean.

"How sore are you?" Merrick gives me a cocky half smile, wincing as he stretches his tail to see how bad the pain is. He flinches more than he did when he waved off the starfish a moment ago.

I sit up, instantly regretting it as my back screams in pain.

"Oh," I groan. "I regret everything."

I lift my hand to my head, pushing back my pink hair.

"Here, let me." Merrick places his hands on my shoulders and turns me to face away from him. I stare at my sleeping twin as Merrick gently untangles my hair with his fingers.

"Good morning," Dylana says, sitting up. Somehow her hair has managed to stay perfect.

"Celena?" a merman's voice says. "For you."

I reach out, taking a conch shell from the merman. His tail is a dark red color mixed with purple tones on the sides—it's stunning. He nods before swimming away.

"I take it we're being summoned?" Merrick muses, continuing to work on my hair. I lean back into his hands, closing my eyes as he works his fingers through my locks. A sigh escapes my lips and Caspian stirs.

Lifting the conch shell to my ear, I close my eyes and

focus on the words. Edmund's voice bounces around inside the shell.

"Celena, it's Edmund. We need to speak. Bring the queen with you. My father's still recovering, so I'm in charge, and we need to finalize the treaty while we still can. Please hurry."

"Time to go," I say with a sigh. "Dylana, we have to go to the palace. Get your mother."

We swim back to the palace at the front of the collection. We move slowly—slower than usual. I think we all need a break—it's been two weeks since we left Scylla, and even longer than that since the fighting started.

When we reach the palace, the collection stays back, rising up out of the water en mass as our small group approaches the steps where Edmund is waiting. He attempts to stand, but the guards on either side of him have to help.

Edmund hobbles down the stairs, looking as if he's walking on knives with every step. He finally drops down to sit slightly higher than the waves and looks helplessly at me.

I swim up to the steps and rest my hand on the bottom one. Marilla and Dylana join me.

"I'm sure you don't want to, but you're welcome to join me," Edmund says, waving his hand at the steps. He winces with the motion.

The prince's leg is braced with something. It's

bandaged, but it looks like some of it is falling down from his walk out of the palace.

I pull myself out of the water, sitting on a low step. Wrapping my hands around my tail, I pull it to my chest. Dylana and Marilla stay in the water, letting me be their ambassador.

"I don't have the power to put this treaty into effect until my father approves it," Edmund admits. "But we can finalize everything right now, and when he signs on, it will be enforced."

"Everything we discussed before is still acceptable?" Marilla asks.

"I've had my people write everything up for us. If you can sign it, I can bring it to my father. I have copies for you to read the terms before you agree."

Edmund raises his hand, and two men bring down two large pieces of paper. The signing of the treaty is more of a formality, but it's important in the human culture, so we patronize him. Marilla holds a conch shell in which she will record the treaty, and all parties will agree before the conch is sealed.

Dylana and Marilla each take a copy of the paper, reading it over. They mumble the words quietly at the same time to ensure it's the same on both pages. Marilla speaks into the shell as she reads.

The prince leans forward as they're reading to softly speak to me.

"You don't look like you fared well last night." He glances at my cuts.

"The blue siren sliced me open—don't worry, she's dead."

"Well, I suppose that should give my father some ease."

"Your leg?" I inquire. Just looking at it makes my fins hurt.

"It's going to take a long time for it to heal, but the doctor says I should walk again." He sighs. "I'm better off than my father though."

"What did they say about him?"

A wave crashes on the steps, nearly washing me back into the ocean. My hand darts out for the step but is caught instead by Edmund's hand. He holds me in place as the wave washes back out to sea.

"It's pretty bad, Celena," he whispers. His eyes say what he does not—his father might not survive.

"I'm sure he'll be fine." I squeeze his hand before I let go. The next wave doesn't try to pull me away.

"Until then, I'm in charge. I'll be acting on his behalf and handling the kingdom until he's moving around again." Edmund's voice is stronger, knowing the guards standing a few steps up are listening. "Of course, he'll advise me, but I'll do all the footwork for him while he rests."

"On only one leg?" I tease.

"I'll find a way." He grins back at me. He motions to my tail. "*You* manage with only one."

"How is Analia handling all of this?"

"She hasn't left my father's side." His face drops. "I'm worried."

"We agree to these terms," Marilla says, interrupting our conversation. She swims toward the steps to hand the document back. "I am prepared to sign these. Dylana will be signing them too, just in case it takes time to convince your father."

If Marilla is suggesting she might not be around when the treaty is finally enacted, she must be assuming the king will say no, and we'll be forced to wait until Edmund takes over years from now. If that's the case, we need to get as far away from here as possible.

I glance out at Merrick. He's just far enough away to give us space, but still close enough to hear when we're speaking loudly. I see his tail twitch through the water— he must realize Marilla's hint too.

"I think that's wise," Edmund replies, a hint of sadness in his voice. He doesn't believe that his father will sign it, even after everything he witnessed. My heart sinks like the burning ship did last night.

Marilla and Dylana are presented with pens similar to the utensils we use under the sea to write with, and they scrawl their names on the papers. With a flourish,

Edmund signs the copies as well, leaving room for his father. They all take turns speaking into the conch shell.

"We look forward to a fruitful treaty with you and your kingdom, Prince Edmund." Marilla nods to him. Stretching out, she hands him a different conch shell. "This is for your father when he is ready. I hope he receives this well and considers our proposal."

"Thank you, Queen Marilla. I will pass this along to him. I hope that we can conclude this quickly, for all of our sakes. Please know that from this day forward, I personally will be acting in concordance with the stipulations of this treaty and will encourage my men to do the same."

"As will we, your majesty." Marilla nods once more before offering him her royal goodbye and swims away, taking the collection with her. Dylana follows quickly behind me after giving me a look.

"*This* seems more like what Jarek and Aila would have experienced," Edmund snickers. "I suppose this is goodbye."

"I suppose it is." I turn to look out at the sea as the collection sinks under the waves.

"I'll try to keep you updated," he offers quietly. "I might encourage Analia to send you shells too—I'd like her to see you as a friend."

"What? I'm not a pet anymore?" I joke.

"You were never a pet, Celena." His voice grows serious.

"I know, Edmund. I appreciate you listening to me on all of this."

"I appreciate you making this treaty happen." His smile is sad even though his eyes sparkle. "A century later and it ends the way it began. Goodbye, Celena. I look forward to your conch messages."

"Goodbye, Edmund. I look forward to yours as well."

"Maybe I'll send some to Merrick too so he'll stop hating me," he calls teasingly as I slip into the ocean.

"He doesn't *hate* you...much." I grin as I turn to wave one last time, dipping below the surface.

"So it's done," Dylana grins. "It's all over. We just have to wait for the king to give his permission—"

"Or for him to die—" Caspian cuts her off.

"Let's hope it doesn't come to that," Marilla calls over to us.

"Either way, it will happen soon—it can't take too long, can it?" I ask, musing out loud.

"We must be patient, Celena." Marilla glances at me. "For now, we will go home to Scylla. The humans couldn't find us there for a century, and I don't think they'll find us there now. But we must leave Metten immediately, just in case."

The more I think about it, the more I'll miss Metten. I wish we had had more time to explore it while we were there before. At least we'll be able to stop to get the rest of the collection that is waiting there before we swim home.

"Perhaps some of us should hold back, just to ensure no one comes after us," Merrick suggests, reading my mind. "We could wait an extra day before following along from Metten. I don't mind waiting—I also don't mind traveling a little slower at this point."

He glances around meaningfully at the others, looking for support. They squint their eyes as he nods covertly at them.

"That's a wise idea." Dylana is the first to speak.

"I'll stay back to make sure everyone is safe," Llyr adds.

"*Everyone*...or my daughter?" Marilla's voice is short as he glances at her guard from the corner of her eye. Llyr stops swimming, eyes wide. Marilla snorts. "Hmm. *See that you do.*"

With lips still pursed, she swims away, giving her daughter permission to date Llyr. He grins wildly at her, and the princess looks like she wants to rush to him, but she restrains herself.

"Adorable," Caspian teases, rolling his eyes. "I'm obviously coming to chaperone you four. Now we can't trust *any* of you."

The water appears clearer today, though the light sparkles through the ocean all the same. A sea turtle crosses our path, unconcerned of our presence. Caspian opens his hand palm up and pushes it up in the water, creating a small wave that bounces the turtle up when it hits the bottom of its shell. He smirks as the turtle bobs in the water, but the creature doesn't care.

We say goodbye to the collection from Ambra as they turn off to make their way home. It's sad seeing them go, but I have a feeling it won't be too long before we see them again. Now that the open waters are slightly safer, I have a feeling we'll be doing a lot more traveling in the future. I'd enjoy visiting Ambra if I ever get the chance.

An hour later, we reach the outskirts of Metten. The coral is stunning as we swim over it. It towers high above the shadow of the city, blocking ships from sailing over it.

The wreckage of the boat that tried to abduct Edmund sits at the bottom of the sea. I plan to explore it later, checking to see what damage I did when I instructed them to shoot a cannonball into their own deck.

"Mother!" Caspian shouts when we swim into the heart of the Metten palace. She's recuperating on a lounging couch, tail draped gracefully over the curved rock.

"Are you both safe?" She sits up as soon as she hears his voice.

"We're fine." Caspian hugs her, moving back for me to do the same.

"We're staying in Metten overnight, but we'll follow behind in the morning." She starts to protest, but Caspian raises an eyebrow and silences her.

"Just don't get caught," she warns, knowing we're planning to leave the palace walls once night falls.

She examines my tail, then turns to Caspian to assess the injuries on his arm. Miraculously, in all of this, Caspian's injuries were mainly directed to his arms—his scales all remain perfectly in place.

Marilla only gives us a few minutes before she arrives to speak to my mother. We leave the grotto, giving them space to talk.

"So, I assume we're exploring tonight?" Caspian says softly as we set out in search of our friends.

A few seahorses float in the water, tails wrapped around bits of seaweed. An octopus slinks around the corner ahead of us, and we follow its lead.

Caspian and I find Merrick, Dylana, Llyr, and Phorcys waiting in one of the grottos. They all look up as we enter. I'm surprised they let the siren join them.

I sigh and take a seat next to Phorcys.

"How are you doing after yesterday?" I ask to gauge his level of remorse over killing his friend.

"Cassidia was never meant to survive this war. She said it all along." That's new information to me.

"How much do you hate all of us?" I refuse to look at him as he side-eyes me.

"I don't."

"We killed your king, your prince, and your princess, and you don't hate us?" I cross my arms, turning to him.

"I don't like you, but if I wanted revenge for any of that, I already had plenty of chances. I know where I float with all of this."

"You want a life when this is all done," Dylana adds, nodding with understanding.

"How bad will my punishment be?" He turns to address the princess.

"We'll see in the next few weeks," Dylana replies. "I honestly don't know how your trial will go at this point, but you'll be prepared before you swim into anything."

The mermen scowl at him, and Natale shoots him an icy glare. Phorcys eyes her for a minute, and I almost think I see the beginning of a smirk on his lips—his instinct is to flirt with her. Maybe he's more like the boys than any of us realize. It will be interesting to see his walls broken down in the coming months.

The former siren reaches up, brushing his glorious hair back, and shrugs. When Dylana motions for him to leave us, he swims out without questioning her directions. Pausing at the door, he throws a smirk in my direction.

"The shark barrier. Tie him out at the shark barrier," Merrick mumbles, making Llyr laugh loudly.

"So, what is this secret reason we're spending the night here?" Dylana brushes her hair back, smirking at me over the boys' antics.

"Merrick has something he wants to show us." I grin, refusing to give any details.

"You're really not going to tell us?" Dylana complains. I shake my head, trying not to smile. "But I'm the princess."

"I'm a princess too, so I hear."

"What if I command you to tell me?" Dylana reaches her hand out to pet a tiny stingray as it glides by.

"Don't ruin the surprise, cousin."

"We're *all* spies here," Natale jumps in. "*One of us* has to be able to figure this out."

"I'm fine with leaving it as a surprise," Keone counters. Natale gives him a murderous look, but he pulls her into his arms and grins at her. She struggles for a moment but settles when he weaves his finger in her hair and pulls her to his lips for a kiss.

"Casp, I'm pretty sure you're going to want to run that little mission of yours now," Llyr says, shrugging. The two make eye contact and have an entire conversation without us before Caspian nods once and swims out of the room.

"Where is *he* going?" I point to my brother as he swims away.

"You had your secrets, Celena, and now he has his. You'll find out later." Llyr grins at me. "But speaking of secrets, I guess *we* don't have to be anymore."

He reaches out to Dylana, and she swims over to him, a gentle smile on her lips. She takes his hand and settles against his chest as she floats down to the palace floor to sit by him. Her pleased sigh makes me incredibly happy.

"It's about time you two finally did something about this," I pretend to chide them. "I didn't like not being able to tell either of you."

"It does explain a lot of your little comments though, cousin," Dylana smirks. "At least it's finally out there."

"And the queen gave you permission," Merrick adds. "I suppose it's time to start bowing?"

"Mer don't bow," Llyr says in a tight voice. He's not used to the idea that he could end up as king one day yet.

"Oh, right, too much time with the humans, sorry," Merrick goads him.

"Did they bow to you, Celena?" Dylana asks, amused.

"No, but they called me *princess* a lot." I bat my eyelashes at her.

"What about you, Merrick? Did they call you *prince*?"

Keone asks as he strokes Natale's arm. She grimaces as we notice, but settles back against his chest anyway.

"No, I'm just the hired muscle." Merrick laughs at the question.

"Mmm, well you *do* have muscles," I say, crawling over to him. I position an arm across his chest and place it on the ground next to his hip so I can lean over him.

His eyes grow wide before his lips do. He leers at me, eyes darting from my eyes to my lips to my hair and back to my lips.

"Aw, you're cute. *Now stop,*" Llyr jokes. He laughs at himself, shaking his head at us.

I sigh and pull back. I'm not too worried—once the collection leaves, we'll have more time for alone time.

We banter for a few minutes across the grotto, each of us leaning against a wall. A few jellyfish float overhead, but their glow won't be evident until this evening.

After a while, Caspian swims back in slowly, his hand stretched out behind him. Attached to his hand is another hand, followed by an arm, and an entire body as he pulls in a mermaid.

She beams in his wake, eyes locked on his every move. I startle and sit up, taking my hand off Merrick's chest. I glance at him to see if he's as surprised as I am—he isn't.

I glare at him for not telling me about this, but I can't really blame him. He's Caspian's friend too, and we have barely had any quiet time to speak alone together since our first kiss—I can't expect him to tell me everything from the very beginning. He'll pay for blindsiding me later though.

"You all know Aeria," Caspian announces. "I ran into her out in the hallways and invited her to hang out with us and go back with us tomorrow."

Her brown hair picks up a copper tone as she moves and I suddenly realize why she seems so familiar—I saw her right before the battle with the sirens began, just outside of Antaire. I should have recognized her mauve hair first, but the shock of seeing her with Casp made my head go empty for a moment.

"I think that's a great idea," Llyr calls, obviously aware of their relationship in advance too.

"*Caspian,*" I call.

"You had your secrets, and I had mine, sister." He bats his lashes innocently at me. Caspian pulls Aeria close. She dotes on him. How did I miss this?

"It's because you were too busy swooning over me," Merrick whispers in my ear, knowing what I was thinking. His nose tickles my ear as he brushes my hair back. "You'll get used to it."

We spend the rest of the afternoon talking until the collection leaves.

CHAPTER 17

Marilla's speech is rousing before the collection leaves, but once they're gone, the courtyard is quiet. We still have time before Merrick takes us to Scur Cavern, and each couple quietly makes their way off for a few moments of quiet.

I take Merrick's hand and lead him out of the palace. He gives me a curious look once we're outside of the looming palace doors, hovering over the useless steps, but his expression changes when he understands where I'm directing us to go.

He switches positions with me and guides me down through the courtyard, past the large dwellings that sparkle in the sunlight. His hand is warm in mine, reminding me of Scylla's warmer waters.

I study him as we swim, memorizing the pattern in his tail that I already know so well. He grins when he catches me staring and pulls me up to swim shoulder-to-shoulder with him, making a flirtatious comment.

Switching my hands out, I place my inside hand on his shoulder, moving it slowly down his back, surprising him. He turns to me, and I giggle, disarming his snappy comment.

I'm grateful we left our shoulder armor at the palace. The water feels refreshing against my skin, and I finally feel as though the fighting is over.

Before long, we swim out of the palace proper and into the dwellings that sit further out from the palace. The dwellings aren't as big or as shiny as the ones next to the royals, but they're beautiful all the same.

We quietly sneak around the homes, weaving our way in and out of the homes the ancestors of our collection used to live in a century ago. I let Merrick lead me—he knows exactly where he is going.

"I'm sorry we didn't get to do this before," I murmur, taking in the sights.

"That's why we're doing it now." Merrick grins softly at me. "There it is."

I follow his finger toward a light colored dwelling. Somehow it seems perfectly like him and his father, even though his great-great-grandfather was rather different than them from what I hear.

Pausing, I refuse to swim into his family home before

he does. He shakes his head and slips inside, turning to wait for me before he takes a good look.

The room is large, with the hallways leading to other small rooms. Many of the family items were removed before the collection fled to Scylla a century ago, but much like with the abandoned siren dwelling, it's easy to see evidence of what used to be there.

I swim over and sit on the lounging couch. Merrick follows behind me, leaning heavily on the bump between us. His blue bangs dip over his eye, and I reach up to brush them back.

"Welcome home," I murmur.

"I miss *our* home," he says honestly. "I'm ready to be home with you, Celena."

I look away, embarrassed. I'm still not used to his attention.

He takes my hand in his.

"You're okay with all this, right? I know you haven't had much time to process all this."

"I'm *very* okay with being with you, Merrick. *More* than okay."

He sighs in relief, leaning closer to me.

"I'm glad to hear that. I've been waiting a very long time to be with you, Len." His fingers close over mine harder, and he refuses to look away from me. I'm trapped in his gaze. "Once we get back to Scylla, I'd like to take you on a date."

"Tonight isn't a date?" I smirk.

"Not when six other people will be with us." He makes a face.

"But that doesn't mean we won't kiss tonight, does it?" I ask.

There's *no way* I'm going back into Scur Caverns and *not* kiss this merman. If I have to force every last mer out of the ocean, I *will* kiss Merrick in that magical cave tonight.

"Oh, we can kiss." He laughs. "We can kiss in the cavern, we can kiss on the way to the cavern, and we can kiss right now."

My grin pins my ears back, it's so wide.

"Oh, you want to kiss *now*?" I question as I float out of my seat, pulling him with me.

"I want to *kiss you now*," he says as he nods. Merrick wraps his arms around my waist.

I lean into him, and his hands caress my hips. I run my fingers up his arms, pushing just below his shoulders to brace myself.

His tongue finds mine as we kiss, and I shiver. Merrick pulls back, biting his lip. I can't stop staring.

"You know," he whispers. "I *really do* enjoy being partnered with you."

I raise an eyebrow a second before he darts forward and covers my lips with his. I tip my head up to allow him to reach me easier. He breaths against me and we tip our heads in unison, kissing as if we've been doing it for years—but then, we've always known how the other would move.

His hands tangle in my hair, and I wrap myself around his waist, holding him to me as he guides my movements. One hand gently glides to my chin and Merrick holds my face to him as he slows our kiss. We settle into a slow rhythm, our kisses deep and full of unspoken words.

My fingers glide up his back, making him gasp, but he doesn't take his lips from mine. I sigh deeply against him, but it only encourages him more, and his mouth moves quickly, inviting me to do the same.

I laugh, enjoying myself—and Merrick does too—until we have to separate or risk smashing our heads together in our fits of laughter. We double over, but Merrick holds his hand out to me.

"It will always be like this between us, Len—it's the way we've always been with each other."

"We've been kissing like this all this time and I somehow missed it?" I joke, letting him guide me back to the lounging couch.

"We'll always understand each other," he clarifies. "And we'll *always* enjoy each other's company."

"You just want me for my superior kissing skills." I dare him to challenge me.

"I can't deny you're very good at that, Len." He licks

his lips slowly. "Unfortunately, I'm going to have to prove that I'm better at it than you."

"Is that a challenge?" I ask, knowing where he's going.

"It is." He grins. "Just try to prove me wrong."

I take the bait and swim over to him, sitting on his lap as I curl my tail under his to support myself.

"Fine, I will."

Slowly, I reach up and put my hands in his gorgeous blue hair. Locking eyes, I move my fingers achingly slow. I drag one hand down to his chin, intentionally brushing against the soft spot in front of his ear, down his cheek, and to the tip of his chin where I tilt his face up to mine.

"I will prove it every day," I inform him.

"I hope you do," he mumbles. His eyes snap fiercely as I lean in.

"Where are we going?" Natale sounds annoyed.

"It's just up here," Merrick replies, clutching my hand in his. I try not to give anything away as we swim up to Scur Cavern.

"A cave? Really?" Natale snips. "Haven't we seen enough of those in the last two weeks?"

"This one is a little different," Merrick says in a voice that is way too flirtatious—it's a good thing he's looking at me as he says it.

Everything is black at first, just like it was the last time Merrick and I were here nearly a month ago.

Dylana and Aeria gasp as the cave suddenly lights up, even more grand than the last time. Colors swirl around us.

"Like the storms," Caspian murmurs. Maybe he heard about the caves even though I hadn't.

"It's stunning," Dylana whispers reverently.

"Apparently, the royals used to like to frequent this place," I tell her.

"Kailania had it right, I suppose." She sounds in awe. When I look over, her jaw is still hanging open, but she's grinning like it's the most beautiful thing she's ever seen. "Any chance we can keep this to ourselves?"

Everyone glances surreptitiously over at Aeria. When she notices, she confronts us.

"Hey, Casp and I didn't say anything to you lot *until today*, so I'm pretty sure *I* can keep a secret." She softens her words with a playful smile.

My eyes grow wide as I realize this has been going on for a while. My twin shoots me an apologetic look—he and I *will* be talking before we go back to Scylla.

The cave shifts colors, turning a deep purple. Everything sparkles brilliantly, and this time, there's no sea creatures to distract us.

Kissing in front of our friends is strange, but each couple risks it for a few moments under the stormy skies inside the cave. The colors dance on the other sides of my eyelids as Merrick crushes me against him.

When we pull away, the others do as well, and we spend the evening talking, getting to know Caspian's new girlfriend, and admiring the lights.

The swim back to the palace is slow. We take our time, knowing once we return, we'll have to take turns sleeping and keeping watch.

Aeria trails behind Caspian, and he glances back, still holding her hand from a distance. I want to dislike her, but I can't. I'm happy Caspian has found someone—even if he waited until now to tell me about her.

Coralie, on the other hand, will have something to say about all this. Caspian is going to be in a whirlpool of trouble for hiding this from her.

The palace shimmers in the pale moonlight. Shells gleam on the ocean floor, reflecting the light. Everything about Metten is perfect…except for the lack of mer.

"This was an incredible kingdom once," Merrick comments as we enter the palace proper.

"Scylla is an incredible kingdom *now*. Metten holds our past, but our future is in Scylla."

"Perhaps," Merrick mumbles. "We'll see what the future holds."

"Don't get all sappy on us now, Merrick," Caspian teases. "Unless you're planning on rebuilding this place, Scylla is where we'll spend our days."

"Once the humans decide their course, our own lives may look very different, Casp."

"I plan to stay in Scylla no matter what," Dylana announces. "I wouldn't necessarily be opposed to sending you two here to rebuild, but I also don't want to lose my best two spies."

"Excuse me?" Natale yelps. Keone distracts her with a kiss.

"I don't want to leave you either, Dylana." I reach my hand out for hers. "We'll see what happens. Until then, you've got all of us at your disposal."

"Yes, now that you all let your secrets out." She chuckles. "I admit, *you* threw me, Natale."

"Me too," I smirk.

"I believe that was the point," Caspian adds. The way he looks at Aeria is even worse than the eyes Merrick and I make at each other—Llyr points out as much.

The palace looms in front of us, and we swim up the steps into the large doorway.

"Caspian and I will take first watch," Merrick announces, surprising me. "We need to talk anyway."

Knowing I don't want to be around when those two talk, I agree to take the second watch with Llyr. I have a feeling it's a safer idea than trying to get to know the mermaid my brother has been wrapped around all evening while we're supposed to be watching for enemy attacks in the middle of the night.

Natale volunteers to keep watch with Aeria, leaving Keone and Dylana to take the last shift. Everyone but Merrick and Caspian file into the palace to rest.

Dylana and I spend the evening in our great-great-grandmother's rooms. It's a unique experience sleeping in the exact room where Aila slept when she was my age. A roaseca colony floats near the ceiling, making the room glow comfortingly.

I sleep soundly until Caspian wakes me up to take my shift.

CHAPTER 18

"CELENA!" CORALIE CRASHES INTO ME, WRAPPING HER arms around me. We haven't even made it to the palace before our families rush around us.

The collection bustles about like normal, repairing the damage the sirens caused when they attacked. The mer children play by their parents' sides, no longer afraid. Rows of tables are set up, and I wonder if we're planning some kind of announcement followed by a celebration.

Coralie looks like she's about to hit me with a million question, so to stop her, I say the first thing that comes to mind.

"Starfish, Caspian has a girlfriend."

Our brother whips around to me, shocked that I would do that to him. I grin, shrugging one shoulder.

"You should have told me," I remind him.

He closes his jaw and grunts as Coralie rushes to him,

her blonde hair trailing behind her. I'll sit with her later and brush her locks, regaling her with stories from everything that happened since we left each other back in Antaire.

I frown as I see the cut Tarni gave her run from her shoulder to halfway down her back. It's a good thing the siren is no longer around for me to take my anger out on. Coralie is too sweet for what Tarni put her through—I still need to ask her if Tarni forced her to siren the humans. As far as I can tell, Murdoch never did, and I hope the same for my little starfish.

Merrick's family surrounds him. I'm grateful they're all safe. His sisters cling to him, and he wraps his arms around them in a hug. His mother glances over at me, followed by his father. They smile—he must have told them.

His mother has been waiting for this day for a long time apparently based on her expression. She bites her lip but only nods to me—we'll have to talk later. Merrick's sisters try rushing to me, but he holds them back. His father ends up pinning them to his sides so Merrick and I can escape.

Caspian extricates himself from our little sister and quickly catches up with us as we dart after Dylana. Llyr hugs his father, assuring him that he's fine before joining us. Keone and Natale follow, after greeting what is left of their families.

The palace radiates an opal glow in the sun, and somehow it's even more beautiful than Metten. We enter through the front doors and find Morgen waiting for us.

Dylana rushes to her brother, throwing her arms around him.

"I'm fine, Dylana," he murmurs, brushing her hair off her back so he can untangle his arm. "I was told *not to threaten Llyr.*"

He glances at Dylana's beau and taps a sword on his belt. It shines in a gold tone that matches his crown. Llyr holds up his hands like he's surrendering.

"I'll take you on if I need to, my friend." He grins at Morgen before swinging his gaze over to the princess.

"I get a week before I have to decide," Morgen announces. "We'll see if you last that long, *guard.*"

We all know that Llyr isn't going anywhere, so Morgen will have to harass him while he still has a higher status than he does.

Our parents follow us in, prepared for a meeting with Marilla. The cousins follow, their children in tow.

Coralie quietly swims into the palace as if she's trying not to be noticed. I covertly track her to make her think she has her privacy—that's when I discover that puffer fish, Marin, reach out and take her hand.

"Caspian!" I whisper harshly.

He turns, tracking my gaze. His fists ball up at his sides as he sets his jaw.

"I'm going to feed him to the sharks," he growls quietly. Merrick and Llyr agree and nod their heads.

"You're not going to touch him," Natale growls. "I worked far too hard to make that happen, and if you destroy it, cousin, I'm going to tell Aeria stories about you from when we were mer children."

We look at her, surprised.

"Well, it wasn't *all* fake," she snips, swimming into the meeting without looking back. It's nice to hear that she wasn't *just* using Coralie for information all this time.

I still don't like the mer boy though.

As the foyer clears out, I notice several guards bringing Roni through the hallway. Marilla had sent several mer to bring Roni back to the palace, and help take care of Tarni's body.

She glares at me, catching my sight. Phorcys eyes me from her side.

"Should I ask?"

"They're taking me to see Tiko." She sounds unsure of herself.

"He's here from what I've been told," I reply casually. "I'll swim with you."

I follow them down to the cells, Merrick at my side. Tiko's face lights up and then falls when he sees them, worried that they've been caught too.

Phorcys quietly explains what happened and Tiko's face falls even further as he realizes that Roni and

Phorcys are temporarily free while he is not. He nearly crumbles when he learns of Cassidia, and I can see Roni deflate over his reaction.

Being a siren is apparently very complicated.

Merrick and I leave as Phorcys explains the trials to Tiko. It's strange to see one of them locked up while the other two are not. If I had it *my* way, Roni would be in the worst prison imaginable for what she did when she pushed Coralie into the brine pool, but I have to wait for her trial to see her twist like that—the collection will not be kind to her when I testify about hurting Cor.

"You handled that well." Merrick looks at me as we swim back to the meeting that's already in progress.

"I'll push her in a brine pool later," I mumble, brushing my hair back angrily.

Merrick catches my raised hand in his, giving me a look. He half smiles at me and I crumble. Rolling my eyes, I let out a sigh mixed with laughter.

Marilla is already dolling out assignments when we swim in. She looks up at me and waves me in as she continues. Dylana regally floats next to her mother, hands folded in front of her as she makes eyes with Llyr obnoxiously—so much for keeping that a secret. The cousins glance at him and smirk now that they're no longer trying to keep it quiet. Most nod in approval, while others stare.

"We don't know how long it will be until the humans

start enforcing the treaty, but we will live it as law starting now," Marilla addresses us. "We must be careful to avoid the humans until we know it is safe, however. Please do not mistake this for anything other than what it is—a promise that *someday* we will not be hunted anymore. Until then, we must stay strong and stay vigilant.

"Live with the faith that promises will be kept, but protect yourselves in every way that you can until it is proven that they will do as they say."

"Thank you, everyone, for what you did for the collection," Dylana adds. "We know that many of you lost someone over the last few weeks—their sacrifice will not be forgotten."

The king looks on proudly at his wife and daughter from the side of the room. Morgen nods from his side, grinning.

"The trials will begin the day after tomorrow. Every siren and mer connected to this tragedy will answer for their crimes, judged by their peers and the collection. We *will* see justice for this," Marilla assures us. "Until then, watch them closely, but do not harm them—the trials will decide their retribution."

The small collection of cousins nods. Marilla will be repeating all of this information shortly when she swims outside of the palace to address the entire collection.

The stingrays swim into the room, begging to be fed,

and Dylana can't help but crack a smile. She reaches out to pet them, and Llyr quietly moves to find the food Dylana keeps in the palace so that she can feed the winged creatures every day.

Colorful fish swim into the room as the queen, my mother, and the others move into the foyer and head toward the door to talk to the collection. The fish swirl around the room, mixing with the stingrays in a vivid display.

Merrick knocks into my hips and nods to the fish that look just like the ones that swirled around us during our first kiss.

I turn to him and wrap my arms around him.

He kisses me first, but I kiss him back.

"We survived," he reminds me quietly, then repeats it louder for the benefit of our friends still in the room. "We survived."

Everyone grins, commenting on our mission's success.

The tides have finally shifted in the Siren Wars…just like my hair when Merrick brushes it back to kiss me.

EPILOGUE

I LOOK UP AS THE DOOR OPENS. DROPPING THE MATERIALS I'm using to create secret places on my new *iluse*, I find two mermen swimming into my dwelling.

Merrick hands me a conch, tucking a piece of folded paper into the pouch on his belt as a replacement.

"Have you been carrying this around all day?"

"Well, I couldn't exactly get back here to give it to you until now." He grins, releasing the shell into my hand. "Your brother and I have been pretty busy. I figured you'd want it though."

"Thanks for bringing it over, Merrick. I'm sure you must be exhausted."

Caspian sprawls out on a lounging couch.

"That would be an understatement, sis." He sighs, stretching out his tail.

Merrick kisses me, then swims over to the kitchen to

set down a large bag filled with food I should probably store before listening to the message from the prince.

The last two years have been filled with messages back and forth between the prince and me. Merrick has learned not to be jealous of them over the months, and *usually* waits for me to tell him about the messages after I listen to them.

"What does he want this time?" Natale asks, not looking up from her *iluse.*

Coralie's eyes are fixed on me from a few lengths away. Marin brushes his hand over hers quietly—he's grown on me.

"Probably just another update," Merrick answers for me. "Those two just like to talk."

"Who's talking?" Dylana asks as she drags her fiancée inside from the open waters outside the dwelling. Llyr holds her hand, studying me.

"Ah, we've heard from Edmund," he replies, eyeing the conch as he answers for me. "What does he say?"

"I haven't listened yet," I retort, "and *I don't think I will* while all of you are here, chattering away."

"Oh, come on," Coralie rolls her eyes as she sets the netting down she was attaching to her *iluse.* "Just listen."

"No, thanks." I grin triumphantly—they can't force me to do anything, and they can't listen themselves because *my name* is being whispered by the shell—no one else can unlock the message.

I spend the next few minutes grilling my boyfriend and brother about their mission, still frustrated that I had to teach some of the mermaids about how to hide weapons in their coverings earlier today. Most of them left hours ago, but my small collection has a mission to handle, and we can't afford to stop until we're finished.

Two hours later, with the mermen's help, we finish our projects and hide them. The fringe groups of sirens that have reestablished themselves over the last year and a half won't know what hit them. It's a shame they didn't stay hidden like they did for those first few months, but we know their plans now, and it won't be long before we stop them.

My fingers brush over the *iluse* I'm wearing, checking to make sure Merrick's scale is still hidden away where I keep it close to my heart—I'm not usually so sentimental, but I couldn't bring myself to do anything else with it once Dylana gave it back after we returned to Scylla.

The group chats for a little bit, relaxing before we start to swim in different directions outside of the dwelling we are using to hide our covert work. We couple off as if we've been doing it our whole lives.

I pull the conch up to my ear and listen as the shell unlocks its message. Tears spring to my eyes as I shout for everyone to wait—they quickly swim back, concern on their faces.

When the message ends, it fizzles away like seafoam.

"Celena, what is it?" Dylana's eyes are dark.

"The king is dead," I whisper.

No one speaks.

"The king is dead, and Edmund has taken the throne." I look up at Dylana. "It's taken two years, but our treaty is finally in effect."

We all slowly beam at each other.

"It's over. The fighting is done—we're safe." Dylana voices our thoughts.

"We have to tell your mother," Llyr holds his hand up, shaking Dylana's as he holds it.

"We need to go to Antaire," I announce. "Everything else can wait. We need to go make a formal alliance with the humans. He wants us to join him immediately—they'll meet us in the water halfway if they can tell when we'll arrive."

I don't like putting off our mission to Ambra any longer than we need to, but Larina and Quillo will just have to manage a few more days without us. The sirens can't cause too much trouble between now and the time we get back—hopefully.

"We need to make preparations and decide on a team to send," Dylana replies, already organizing the trip. "And on the way back, I know a good cave we can stop at."

Everyone smirks, glancing at their partners. I nod to Coralie, telling her that she and Marin can join us this time.

"To the palace," I say. My collection follows behind me, thrilled to finally be returning to Antaire by way of Metten to free the seas for the humans and mer once more.

I can't wait.

The story continues in Forbidden Waters (Book 4 of The Siren Wars Saga)

Acknowledgements

Oh, my fabulous, lovely friends, thank you for coming on this journey with me. I have *loved* getting to tell Celena's story and I couldn't be more happy with how it all played out.

I'm also excited for you to meet the next mermaid in The Siren Wars Saga—but don't worry, we'll be seeing more of Celena and Merrick soon!

Right now, it looks like the next installment of The Siren Wars Saga will be out in 2019, so don't go too far! Until then, I have a ton of other books to keep you occupied!

If you adored Celena and Merrick's story, drop me an email or direct message on social media and let me know you enjoyed the story—I love chatting with people!

Special thanks to Jess and Elle, my ever-present help in times of need. I appreciate you two more than you know!

To Yentl, thanks for all the mermaid drawings, lovely. I made sure the stingrays were taken care of just for you!

PS I didn't write this in the book, but Dylana and I have agreed to name one after you!

Thanks to Charlotte for keeping me sane while I was doing my mad writing dash throughout this series. I always love our chats!

And mostly, thank you to you, oh lovely reader. I appreciate you more than words can say.

Get ready...I'm about to dive into the next story in The Siren Wars Saga and info will be coming soon. PS... the covers for the next section are magical!

Turn the page to read the first chapter of the fourth book in The Siren Wars Saga...and don't worry, we'll be seeing Celena and Merrick in Forbidden Waters.

Stay inspired!

-K.M. Robinson

FORBIDDEN WATERS-CHAPTER 1

We can't always trust what we know to be fact. Even the most obvious truth can sometimes be a lie.

I've learned not to put my faith in what I know or even in my eyes have seen in the years since the war ended. Too much has shaken the reality of my world since then and nothing is the same. Even so, there are three things I *can* depend on—my sister, my friends, and my collection.

"What do you mean, *she's not coming?*" Shock waves over me like the pulsing water ripples over my tail...or maybe that really *is* the water moving over my scales as my sister flicks her tail and swims, expecting me to follow her. I tuck my knife away in my *iluse* and follow quickly behind her, the colorful coral flashing by as we move.

"The king of Antaire is dead, Iclyn—they have to go to formalize the treaty with the prince."

"You mean the *king*," I correct, brushing back a strand of hair that's caught on my shoulder. "If the king is dead, that makes Edmund the king now."

"Do you constantly need to correct me, Iclyn?"

No, but it adds a little significance to my life every now and then.

"Sorry," I mumble, knowing better than to upset her. "What are we going to do? We were counting on their support."

"We'll figure it out. Quilo is on his way—he's gathering the collection."

I assume she means our tiny collection and not all of Ambra. That's a conversation we do *not* need to be having right now.

Since we left the waters outside of Antaire two years ago, my sister has managed to get herself elected the honorary Celena of Ambra. I'm not sure how it happened, but she and her boyfriend, Quilo, positioned themselves as leaders and the collection backed them.

"We need to inform the queen," my sister mutters as we dive around a stingray.

Isla's palace isn't too far, but in an effort to beat Quilo and the others, we race at a dolphin's pace. The pearlescent building swells ahead of us as we crest the small mountains surrounding it. It glitters in the mid-morning light as Larina's hand floats back toward the conch shell resting in the pouch on her hip, it's outline pressed tightly against the fabric—Celena or Dylana must have sent the message of their change of plans.

"Do we know when they'll be here?" I ask quietly, brushing back my hair again. It baffles me how my tresses can continually float in front of me, even when I diving through the ocean at full speed, effectively pinning my hair back behind me. Larina's hair, however, is perfectly obedient—maybe that's why Queen Isla has taken to her so much—she's perfect.

"Babe!" Quilo calls as we dart around the back of the palace, seeking out the back entrance.

"So much for beating him," Larina mumbles. She glances at me as if it's my fault we didn't arrive earlier.

Quilo flashes me a smile before focusing in on my sister, grinning wildly as he wraps his arm around her hip and pulls her close to his chest. My sister giggles, brushing back her hair as he murmurs something in her ear—they're adorable and sickening at the same time. If I didn't think of Quilo as a brother, I'd have to force him out of our lives at this point.

The guards motion us into the palace. The water seems a bit icier inside the palace as we enter, but then, the palace always feels cooler than the open waters outside.

Isla motions to the lounging couches as we enter her

receiving room. The group settles onto the bumps in the couches, and I lean over toward Kenda to rest my head on my arms for just a moment as I bat my eyelashes at my best friend. She rolls her eyes and pushes my elbow with hers, forcing me to sit back up as I risk a look at the merman she was just flirting with. Her copper tail flicks in playful annoyance.

"There was a skirmish today," Kenda whispers, leaning toward me. She attempts to cover her face with her hair so the collection doesn't notice that we're talking. "The sirens are becoming more bold, Iclyn. I think we're in real trouble here."

I envy Kenda. Larina and Isla trust her enough to allow her to go on missions while I'm tucked away inside the relative safety of Ambra. I do my fair share of missions, but I've only had two dangerous missions since we returned from Antaire and I'm dying to be let out of the barriers.

Isla raises her hands as she speaks, the crystal forming a cape between her shoulders and her wrists glittering in the sunlight as it pours down through the water into the palace through the hole in the ceiling. She looks at each of us, explaining what we already know—the sirens are trying to destroy all of the work we've done outside of the reef barriers.

"Your Majesty!" A long merman bursts into the room,

trident in hand. "They moved up their timeline—the sirens are moving *now.*"

Isla looks over in shock as Larina floats out of her seat by Quilo. He grabs her hand, holding her in place. She reminds me of a seahorse tipping forward as its tail is wrapped around a piece of seaweed.

"Armor!" The queen's shout slams into us all, knocking everyone into motion. The guards rush out of the room, attempting to find shoulder armor for all of us to wear. We follow behind them, knowing it's quicker if we just do it ourselves.

Larina shoves a chest plate at me as I grasp at a metal covering for my shoulders that is clearly too wide for me. Kenda and I switch—her shoulders are wider than mine —and I shrug into the cool metal. The silver gleams against my hair and tail, making me look even more Keldorian than I usually do. I consider switching to gold to avoid the comments later, but there's no time.

The pearls against my abdomen shift uncomfortably under the chest plate but removing them would just take extra time that we don't have. Mer hover around in the water like a confused school of fish, darting around each other hurriedly even though we know exactly what to do.

We ignore the sea life as it floats around us, not even flinching as we stream out of the palace and down the steps toward the main path that leads to the open waters outside of the city proper. Without a word, we all swim toward the sirens' goal—the storage dwelling.

When the sirens first started to attack, they raided our armory, sneaking into the city unnoticed. We had heard of a few fights between wandering sirens that found each other after the war with the humans, but until they took our weapons, none of the sea kingdoms knew just how strong the straggling sirens really were. Now they plague the seas, still small in number, but with a vendetta against the mer for disbanding them after Nir's death.

Our spies gathered word that their next target is a building we use to store food and supplies. We've placed guards there, but have kept them back far enough that we can hopefully catch the sirens as they move in. In truth, the building is more useful as a place to spy on us—the sirens would have the high ground and be able to see everything we do, and because we protected it so well, it would be hard for us to take control back without losing too many of our collection in the process...unless our strategy works, of course.

Lulling them into a false sense of security seems to be the best plan of action. Once the sirens have made their breach, we can take them by surprise, trapping them inside of the dwelling, but we have to be in position before they arrive.

Strangely enough, I hadn't seen any sign of them before Larina dragged me away from my post to the palace. I play everything over in my head, second-guessing everything I saw, but I don't recall seeing any signs of the sirens outside of the storage dwelling.

Kenda barely manages to keep up with me as I swim toward the front of the collection. I'm tiny compared to most of the mer, but I can out swim most of them too—something I've been working on for years to compensate for my smaller stature. My friend struggles to breathe as I reach the front.

Larina glares at me, motioning me back with a wave of her hand. I know she only means to keep me safe, but it's frustrating being constantly shoved to the side while the others are allowed more freedom. Quilo tosses an apologetic look at me. Beyond him, one of my merman friends raises an eyebrow but doesn't say anything. His long hair trails behind him as he swims, looking as angry and magnificent as the scars on his torso do.

We position ourselves along the underside of the dwelling entrance, prepared to slam a hidden door in place to lock the sirens in. Each of us has a job to do to block the holes in the dwelling walls to prevent their escape. When the time comes, Kenda and I will work together with several of the mermen to seal hole off on the south side of the dwelling, giving us a long way to travel around the cave to reach it.

An hour passes without any sight of the sirens.

"I thought they were close," Kenda whispers to the merman next to us.

"They were supposed to be," he whispers back, eyes dark.

Larina drags herself over the sand, trying to remain hidden as she moves toward me. She looks ridiculous, but I won't tell her that. She claws at the sand until she reaches me.

"Isla wants you to go check things out. Take this group with you, and we'll reorganize in case they show up."

It amazes me that I'm not allowed to do anything interesting until the queen needs me for my speed.

I nod to my sister before turning to make sure everyone heard. One at a time, we slip away from the dwelling into the open waters, staying low to the sand until we reach the seaweed.

Winding my way through, I make my way to the kelp forest in the distance—it will be the best vantage point for spying. Debris floats in the water, catching the noon sunlight directly overhead. My shadow is hidden on the ocean floor, mixed with the rapidly moving pieces of kelp waving around me as I swim into the haze kelp forests often provide.

"Careful," the orange-tailed merman says gruffly. He may act like he doesn't care, but I think he does.

We move in different directions, Kenda staying close

by. My fingers itch to abandon my trident in favor of my knife, but I know the trident may end up being my saving grace should we encounter any sirens in the kelp forest or beyond.

Reports said the sirens were over the ridge and rapidly approaching, but they should have arrived at the same time we did, if not before. It's possible that they stopped along the way, but we won't know until we can locate them.

My armor shifts on my body as I tip myself forward to swim faster. I need to make it to the tunnel without being caught.

The sirens wouldn't dare enter a tunnel where they could easily be trapped, and hopefully they will assume we'd think of that too and avoid it—which means it's a perfect place for me to take advantage of while spying.

"Iclyn, don't!" Kenda warns as I dart out of the kelp and dive toward the tunnel under the cover of a large sea turtle swimming by. I drop my hand behind me and wave at her to assure her that I know what I'm doing.

The turtle pulls away a few lengths away from the tunnel entrance, leaving me exposed. I dart inside, turning around once I'm in the shadows to make sure Kenda stayed in place at the edge of the kelp forest. Her copper tail glimmers alongside the kelp, making her the most radiant mermaid I've ever seen—not even Larina is as striking as Kenda when my friend is in the golden sunlight surrounded by similar colors...one more reason to envy her.

I run my fingers over my *iluse* to make sure my knife and shells are still in place should I need them. Turning, I swim into the darkness of the blue cave.

The walls are accented with bioluminescent plankton, radiating blue against the blue walls Ambra is known for. The glow gives me just enough light to see by.

A school of red fish glides toward me, pulling to the side just an arm's length in front of me. Shells litter the tunnel floor, covering the sand to the point of almost making the tiny brown grains invisible under a path of broken shell pieces.

I duck against the wall as a jellyfish floats by, careful to avoid its long tentacles. I'd rather face a shark than a jellyfish. I've only been stung once when I was a mer girl, but it was enough to give me nightmares about it to this day. I shudder as I think about it.

Ahead, I can see the opening of the tunnel, specs of debris floating in front of it as a piece of seaweed waves across the opening just enough for me to notice it. When it lifts an entire arm length toward the surface without the rest of it growing longer or short, everything in my body prickles—something is wrong.

I collide with a net as I dart backward—I hadn't noticed it as I swam past it, which means they hid it well. Grappling with it, I try to untangle myself, but it's the least of my worries as several dark figures appear in the tunnel entrance.

For a moment, I flash back to the time I was tangled in a human net, being dragged to the surface in retaliation for a war we had nothing to do with. I escaped that, and I intend to escape this.

Ripping my hair away from the net painfully, I aim my trident at the sirens approaching.

You're smaller and can escape faster than they can, I remind myself.

"There, there, little mer girl," a merman siren croons. "We won't hurt you…much."

"We just need to make an example out of you for the others," a second siren chimes in, his voice deeper than the first merman.

"It's just a few scales…and maybe a fin or two," a mermaid chimes in, trying to scare me. If I've learned anything in the last two years, it's to not show any fear in the face of danger if I'm all alone. One of the main things Celena teaches is how to appear brave even if we're not. Our sister kingdom, Scylla, has been adamant that all of the kingdoms are acting as one when it comes to fighting off the growing siren collection, and as the kingdom closest to them, we've received most of their support.

"Yes, I'm sure you won't miss them at all," I reply, grinning.

"Hmm, you think you can win against all of *us?*" the mermaid mocks.

"You're right. If you have one more friend out there, it will be a fair fight." I lunge at her, thrusting my trident toward her scales. I graze her hip, and she shrieks.

The mermen look at her, and I use the opportunity to attack again, this time slamming my trident into the merman in the middle. He cries out in pain as the edge of my trident pierces the edge of his scales and rips straight through to the other side. It's barely a flesh wound, but I manage to knock him off balance enough to race out of the tunnel beyond them.

The uninjured merman takes off after me, growling obscenities at me. I look around, hoping to make it to kelp bed on the far side of the tunnel where I might be able to lose him.

An entire small army of sirens stares back at me, eyes wide when they see I'm not being held captive. For as long as it takes me to hold in my gasp, I wish that Larina had prevented me from coming on this mission, but she'd never say no to the queen.

A small collection from the sirens moves toward me, ready to assist their friend in my capture. If they get their hands on me, they'll try to use me against Isla and the collection—I can't let that happen.

I dive toward the kelp bed, out swimming the mermaid on my tail. He yells for the others to spread out to look for me. A cry answers back from within the kelp forest and I realize I'm not alone.

The sand is gritty around my chest plate as I drag myself along the ocean floor as my sister had done not too long ago before I left on this mission. I'm sure I look equally as silly, but I don't know where the sirens are hiding in the kelp. I can't swim over it because the sirens waiting outside will see me. I don't want to risk swimming face first into one of them, so my best option is crawling under them.

"Come out, little mermaid," the siren chasing me calls. "It's better if you cooperate. Come out now, and we'll only take a few scales. Make us find you, and we'll send you back to your queen in pieces."

It's like he's forgotten that I've fought in a war against the humans. I know my sister has been overprotective since I almost died, but I'm not that far out of the loop that I don't know how to go with the flow when it comes to threats.

The sirens won't kill me—they need a hostage. The worst they can do is split my tail, and even my friends from Scylla who endure their tails being cut have learned to survive it. I just need to keep these sea monsters away from my collection.

"I see you, mermaid." The siren's voice is calm and quiet, hovering right behind me.

My body tenses, tightening my muscles against my

shoulder armor. The water rushes around me as he descends on me, wrapping his bulging arms around me. I desperately wish any of my mermen friends were around to help free me.

I struggle against him, but he pulls me to his chest, his brown tail twitching around mine. My trident drops out of my hand, bumping into the bottom of my tail as it falls —for a moment, I wish I had legs so I had a chance to catch my weapon.

His arms are covered in seaweed—I assume a protective measure meant to camouflage himself—and it scratches against my skin.

Another merman appears in front of me, slipping around the long pieces of kelp as he watches me struggle. When he sees us, he moves back into the kelp out of sight, but not before I get a good look at his bold, red tail.

Like his friend, he also has seaweed wrapped around his body, but unlike the other siren, his looks stylized. The greenery is wrapped around his wrists like bracelets. A *sarasa* is proudly displayed across his chest, while fuller pieces of seaweed sit on his shoulder and fall off his hip on one side. His dark hair swayed in the water as he pulled back from us to hide.

I fight, willing myself to survive the angry siren. I wonder if they had been this bad before the war or if this anger was a recent development. I'm honestly very glad the sirens focused their rage on Scylla for all those years instead of Ambra. I suppose after a century, it's only fair that Ambra take a turn being the target, but I wouldn't object to passing off the burden to Dariah or Keldori soon.

The siren pulls out a knife and slices my belt off from around my waist. I'm willing to let go of the objects I collected this morning if it means I can escape, but I worked hard to create that belt, and temporary furry makes me forget to think things through before I act.

I bite down on the siren's arm, making him cry out and reel back just enough that I can reach my knife in my *iluse*. Pulling it out, I plunge it behind me into the siren. Without looking back, I whip the knife out of his flesh and push forward into the kelp ahead of me.

I swim directly at the red-tailed merman, unable to find a way around him before the injured siren can regroup and attack. In the background, I hear him screaming orders to the others, and a cheer rises up behind me.

"Touch me and I'll kill you," I shout, trying to frighten the red-tailed merman who's hiding somewhere in the kelp.

"Not if they kill you first," he hisses in my ear as his hand wraps around my body, pulling me to a halt. His other hand goes to my mouth to keep me quiet. "I'll help you."

He flicks his tail to push us forward, painfully

colliding with mine as he drags me away from them. I try to get away, but he won't relinquish his grip. I grunt around his hand, trying to ask what he's doing. As if reading my mind, he hisses in my ear.

"You injured Halmar pretty bad back there—they won't hesitate to kill you now, even though we need you as a hostage. I don't care if we hold you captive, but I'm not going to let them kill you. They're as blood hungry as sharks these days, and you're an easy target, Little Blue."

I cringe as he references my coloring.

We dart out of the kelp. He aims us straight for a pile of nets on the ocean floor—I tense as I realize he's about to tie me up.

"Don't fight me, mermaid," he hisses, tightening his grip on me.

I throw my elbow back into his chest. He bucks but doesn't release me. The merman slams me into the ground, forcing my face into the sand. I cough, trying not to swallow the grains.

The red-tailed siren throws a net on top of me, but before I can object again, he moves the entire pile on of me, weighing me down heavily.

"Stay put, I'll be back to free you when it's safe. Don't give yourself away. If you get caught, I'll cut you in half myself— self-preservation, you know, Blue." He starts to leave but leans down one more time. "There are two choices here: you let me calm them down and use you as a hostage, or you move even the slightest bit, and they'll catch you and kill you. Your choice."

I can barely see him swimming away through the layers of netting, his red tail flashing in the crystal blue waters as he rushes back toward his siren collection.

Apparently, I'm about to be a hostage.

Forbidden Waters (Book 4 of The Siren Wars Saga) will be available from Crescent Sea Publishing in 2019

ORIGINS OF THE SIREN WARS

A CENTURY AGO, THE HUMAN-MER TREATY WAS established to protect the mer from the humans while they guided ships through storm-plagued waters. Now, Aila and her cousin, Persephone, act as representatives for their grandfather, King Gaspar, to the human world.

The mermaids share a close bond with the Prince Jarek, but when Aila catches Persephone trying to siren him into the waters, she must work to protect her friend from her cousin without hurting the human-mer relationship—something Persephone's mother won't tolerate.

War is brewing and Aila and Persephone are caught in the middle of a battle they never saw coming—one that will last for another century.

Get your copy at
originsinfo.kmrobinsonbooks.com

BONUS SCENES

Want to read a bonus scene from The Siren Wars? We're giving out an exclusive bonus scene over on the K.M. Robinson Facebook page!

Get it by sending the page a direct message at facebook.com/kmrobinsonbooks

We're also giving away Siren Wars freebies in the newsletter. Join for free books, excerpts, and more! newsletter.kmrobinsonbooks.com

We're constantly giving out additional bonus scenes for preorder swag, giveaways, and more, so watch the social media pages carefully for the next scene giveaway.

WORLD PORTALS

Ready to learn exclusive facts about The Siren Wars and other K.M. Robinson Series?

World Portals are now available on
www.kmrobinsonbooks.com

Learn behind the scenes facts, watch videos, play games, check out our book filters, find out where to get bonus scenes, view fan art, and get access to other secrets we've hidden away inside the World Portals on the website.

You can also see the map that we weren't able to add to this version of the story due to file size limits.

The World Portals are constantly changing and information is being taken away and added all the time, so check back frequently for new content!

BONUS FACEBOOK FILTERS

Want to get your hands on some incredible Facebook filters for Siren Wars? Now you have the ability to get filters for the story, characters, etc right inside your phone.

You can use these on your photos, profile pictures, videos, and live broadcasts. All you have to do is like my author page and they will automatically show up in your filters!

I've even taken these clips and put them on Instagram Stories by saving them to my phone and uploading them to Instagram.

Visit www.facebook.com/kmrobinsonbooks to grab these filters for your photos, videos, and broadcasts! Bonus points for tagging me @kmrobinsonbooks so I can see how you're supporting The Siren Wars.

ABOUT THE AUTHOR

K.M. Robinson is a storyteller who creates new worlds both in her writing and in her fine arts conceptual photography. She is a marketing, branding and social media strategy educator who is recognized at first sight by her very long hair. She is a creative who focuses on photography, videography, couture dress making, and writing to express the stories she needs to tell. She almost always has a camera within reach. Visit her at her website: www.kmrobinsonbooks.com

The Siren Wars Saga

Book One: The Siren Wars

Book Two: Darker Depths (Coming June 2018)

Book Three: Beyond The Shores (Coming July 2018)

Origins of the Siren Wars: Prequel Novella (Coming June 2018)

The Jaded Duology

Book One: Jaded

Book Two: Risen

The Complete Series Boxset/Omnibus with exclusive epilogue (Summer 2018)

The Golden Trilogy

Book One: Golden

Forged: A Golden Novella

Book Two: Locked

Book Three: Edge

The Complete Series Boxset/Omnibus with exclusive bonus novella, Tempered

The Legends Chronicles

Along Came A Spider: A Prequel Novelette

And They'll Come Home: A Prequel Novelette

The Revolution of Jack Frost (Coming November 2018)

Virtually Sleeping Beauty: A Novella Retelling

The Goose Girl and The Artificial: A Novella Retelling

The Sinking: A Novella Retelling (Coming June 2018)

JADED: BOOK ONE OF THE JADED DUOLOGY

Her father failed in his mission to take control from the Commander, a defeat that has cost Jade her life. She will die as punishment. Now she belongs to the Commander's son—as his wife. Knowing his intent is to quietly kill her in revenge, Jade's every move is calculated to survive—until she learns her death ensures the safety of her father and her entire town.

Roan doesn't want to kill Jade, but once his family isolates her from her father and community, his only choice is to go through with the plan. Jade doesn't make it easy as she tries to sway him into falling for her. Each misstep makes him question his cause. Each moment makes every decision harder, but the Commander won't allow him to fail.

One chooses life. One chooses death. In the midst of the chaos, only one will succeed.

Now available!
Learn more about The Jaded Duology at
jadedinfo.kmrobinsonbooks.com

GOLDEN: BOOK ONE OF THE GOLDEN TRILOGY

Goldilocks was never naive. She was sent on a mission and Dov Baer is her new target.

When the girl with the golden hair betrays everyone, not even she has hope of surviving.

The stories say that Goldilocks was a naïve girl who wandered into a house one day. Those stories were wrong. She was never naïve. It was all a perfectly executed plan to get her into the Baers' group to destroy them.

Trained by her cousin, Lowell, and handler, Shadoe, Auluria's mission is to destroy the Baers by getting close to the youngest brother, Dov, his brother and sister-in-law and the leaders of the Baers' group.

When she realizes Dov isn't as evil as her cousin led her to believe, she must figure out how to play both sides or her deception will cause everyone in her world to burn.

If her allegiances are discovered, either side could destroy her...if the Society doesn't get her first.

Available now!
Learn more about The Golden Trilogy at
goldeninfo.kmrobinsonbooks.com

ALONG CAME A SPIDER: THE FIRST PREQUEL NOVELETTE TO THE LEGENDS CHRONICLES

Little Hacker Muffet
sat on her tuffet
destroying her cords and Way.
Along came a hacker named Spider,
who sat down beside her
and frightened his opponent away.

WHEN FET, ONE OF THE MOST SKILLED HACKERS IN THE Legends, discovers her best friend and leader of her group has been abducted and held for ransom, she must escape unnoticed and find Peep before it's too late.

When Spider, a new recruit training to join her hacker ring, slips out with her and claims to have a plan to save her friend, Fet is forced to bring him along. As she discovers he's not who he claims to be, she faces grave danger and learns just how deadly a spider bite can be.

Now available!
Learn more about The Legends Chronicles at
acasinfo.kmrobinsonbooks.com

VIRTUALLY SLEEPING BEAUTY

SHE MAY BE DOING BATTLE IN THE VIRTUAL WORLD, BUT IN the real world, they can't wake her up…

All Rora wants is to help people as class president, give her time to local charities, and quietly earn her way to the top level of the virtual reality system that the entire country uses without anyone noticing she's the second best player in the game.

All Royce wants to do is level up as a knight inside the gaming system, slay dragons, and eventually play his way to controlling the palace as he takes the crown away from the reigning queen.

When his Aunt Perry calls him, hysterically screaming that her goddaughter, Rora, has been inside for more than the four hours the game allows, Royce rushes over to help.

Entering the game, Royce soon discovers that Rora is trapped inside the system after an encounter with an evil magician who can change forms inside the game and control the virtual world. If he and his friend can't help her beat the game, she might not be able to wake up in the real world at all.

When virtual knights and princesses meet to slay dragons and defeat evil rulers, there's nothing stopping them from suffering real-world consequences too.

To wake her up, he must enter the game and help her beat it.

Now available!
Learn more about Virtually Sleeping Beauty at
vsbinfo.kmrobinsonbooks.com

9 781948 668057